WERECATS EMERGENT

BOOK 1 OF THE FOREST EXILES SAGA

MARK J. ENGELS

FAZED ANGLE MEDIA

Contents

CHAPTER ONE

GREEN BAY, WISCONSIN. SEVERAL YEARS AGO.

PAWLY TROTTED DOWN THE hallway while the bathroom door closed behind her. She stopped short after rounding the corner, finding the booth she'd been sharing with her brother and their friends empty. Along with the rest of the restaurant.

Tommy had some nerve. First, he had insisted she chug the first decent *affogato* they had served her after three times trying, just so they could go. And now he had coaxed their friends into ditching her. All because she wanted to pee before they left?

I know where you sleep, *brother dear...*

"I'm locking up the front door, miss," came their waiter's voice from behind her.

She turned and watched their waiter shuffle past, a bus tray in his hands. Dirty dishes clinked together as he set the tray down on their table. "I let your friends out the back. Here, let me show you."

A moment later Pawly stepped across the threshold into the alleyway behind the restaurant. She slid her hoodie off her shoulders and tied its arms together around her waist.

"Good luck to you all on the ice tomorrow," their waiter said from behind the massive steel door. "Come see us again during next year's tournament."

The door's hinges creaked until the thing slammed shut with a hollow *ka-thunk*. Darkness enveloped Pawly save for a small strip of stars twinkling high overhead between buildings and a flickering lamp opposite the alley from her.

Lana leaned up against a service door beneath it, twiddling at the dark curls above her ear with one finger. "Told them you wouldn't be long, but they wouldn't listen." Pawly's friend and teammate flipped her cell phone closed and nodded toward the street. "They're over there."

Pawly glanced over to the sidewalk where Tommy stood beside Lana's cousin, Dominik, and clicked her tongue. "It was your idea we come here for our post-game hang out in the first place," she said, stomping over to them. Then she drew back and slugged her brother in the shoulder as hard as she could. "What's your damn hurry, anyway?"

"Hey, that *hurt!*" Tommy shook his wavy, red hair from his eyes and rubbed at his shoulder. "But worth it. Check it out." He pointed at an orange splotch creeping across the moon's face.

Pawly sighed and pinched the bridge of her nose. "I thought the eclipse was *tomorrow* night."

"While you were in the bathroom, our waiter said it was actually tonight."

A Halloween eclipse. Of course. That explained the people dressed in crazy robes they had glimpsed on their way to the Resch Center earlier, laying out stones in a circle between two storefronts. Surely some sort of Wiccan high holiday or something.

She *tsk*ed and gave the moon a dismissive wave. "Our coaches told us all to keep our minds on our games tomorrow. Not stand around with eyes on the skies. Or heads in the clouds."

"'Our games *tomorrow*.' Not today," Tommy replied crossing his arms over his lanky chest. "Bad enough I've had to suffer through a hundred tellings already of your last-second slap shot story."

"Coach told us to review our offensive plays, you know," Lana said and sauntered up behind them.

Pawly slapped the taller girl on the shoulder. "That's right, Lana. And everybody loves a comeback story like ours."

Tommy sneered and tugged at the corner of his rectangular-framed glasses. "Says the captain of the team who barely scraped their way out of the loser's bracket because *she* wanted to show off."

Pawly blew a raspberry at him. Who was he to criticize her college placement strategy? She'd had everyone in the stands eating out of her palm by the time she sewed up her hat trick, putting her team ahead by a goal with a mere four seconds remaining in the third period. Surely there were big school scouts out there among them.

"Think we can still catch the eclipse, Stick Magnet?" Dominik asked with a nod toward Tommy. "Might be cutting it close."

Lana waved her arm toward the throngs lining the street. "Your campground's along this road, right outside of town. But many of the streets around here are closed off for the masquerade block party. Longer we wait, the easier it'll be for your folks' friends to get their RV out of here."

Pawly glanced down at her watch. Not quite ten before nine. "Mom told us to meet her and Dad at nine p.m. sharp."

Tommy laced his fingers together behind his head. "Mr. Biggs is a Navy man. He knows I might well be on NROTC sea duty halfway around the world by the time the next total comes around. He won't let us miss this one."

Dominik glanced up at the sky between towering walls of bricked-over windows and ran a hand through his dark, spiky hair. "Let's hedge our bets, dude. If we split up, we can likely get your telescope set up in time. But only if we go like, you know, right *now*."

Pawly shook her head after Dominik and Tommy turned her way. *Dorks.*

"Knock it off with the puppy eyes, both of you." She poked Tommy in the chest with one finger. "All right, I'll go run interference with Mom. But it's gonna cost you."

Tommy peered over the top of his glasses at her. "How much, exactly?"

"As I recall, it's my week to do dishes after we get back to Norfolk," Pawly replied, jamming her hands into the pockets of her jeans. "But not anymore, right?"

His freckles nearly disappeared as he flushed. "A whole *week*? SATs are coming up, you know. We gotta knuckle under and study. Can't much help you do that every night after dinner if I'm up to my elbows in dish soap."

"Hey, I'm behind practicing for my *cho dan* test, remember?" Pawly narrowed her eyes. "Besides, heaven forbid Mom get the idea you went and blew off our check-in."

Tommy studied the concrete at his feet and flexed his fingers. "Fine. Deal."

The edges of Pawly's mouth drew up into a satisfied smirk. "Didn't *think* you'd want to wax the *dojang* floor with a cotton ball after we got home."

"Come with me, Pawly," Lana said, flashing Tommy a sly smile. "I can show you a short cut to The Packing House."

"Thanks, Lana. But isn't that out of your way?"

"Not at all. Dominik's folks and mine are together at a pizza joint right down the street from there."

"Think you guys could ask Mr. Biggs to swing past our grandma's house afterward?"

"I don't see why not, Nik. Come to think of it, it's on the way to the campground." Tommy jabbed his thumb at Pawly. "But don't ask me what *she'll* try to extort from you in return."

Pawly batted her eyelashes and tugged at her fat pigtails. "Oh, I would never dream of charging *friends*," she replied in a syrupy voice. "I only do business with family."

Tommy shot his sister a sideways glance and pushed his glasses back atop his nose. "So that's what you call it, huh? Mind you don't forget your violin case in your locker, then."

P AWLY STUMBLED TO A stop and cupped her hands to the sides of her mouth. "Lana, wait!"

The other girl trotted in a circle and strode up beside her. "What... what is it?" she said between heavy breaths, hands resting on her knees.

Pawly shivered and glanced down at her freckled forearms. The hairs there all stood straight up despite the unseasonably mild night air. She rubbed at her biceps, recalling a similar all-over creepy feeling from a few years back. Right before the hospital called telling her mother a car had skidded through a stop light. Straight into Tommy's bike.

"I...I have to go back."

Lana straightened and put her hands on her hips. "What for?"

Pawly chewed at her lip.

It's a twins thing, Lana. You wouldn't understand.

Pawly nodded to the mouth of the alleyway. "The Packing House is that way, right?"

"Yeah. Through the parking lot and across the street. Can't miss it."

"Go on ahead to the pizza place and find your folks. If Dominik doesn't show in fifteen minutes, come looking for us. All of you."

Lana cocked an eyebrow. "What's going on?" She gasped. "You don't think the boys are hurt or in trouble or something like—"

"I don't know!" Pawly buried her face in her hands and shook her head. "I just...just have a...feeling, you know?" She dropped her hands to her sides and met Lana's gaze.

Don't ask me to explain, Lana. I'm not sure I even could.

The taller girl wrung her hands and hunched forward. "Stop it, you're...you're creeping me out. Look, maybe if we went together, then we could...wait, what's this?"

Pawly held out a business card in front of her, motioning her friend to take it. "The contact number here for my mom's *dojang* is her cell phone. Have your folks call mine should you come for us."

Lana squinted at the card and pursed her lips. "Who's 'Alex?'"

"My mom. Her name is 'Aleška.' It's Polish." Pawly turned and sprinted up the alley the way they had come before Lana could say any more.

Moments later, Dominik's voice trailed off from around an alleyway corner.

"Behind you, Stick Mag—*oof!*"

Pawly rounded the corner in time to see Tommy spiral headfirst into a pile of broken pallets. Her brother's teammate stood with his back to the brick wall across the alley from her, arms pinned by a pair of men dressed in black.

"Shut up, I said!" roared a third black-clad man before driving a softball-sized fist into Dominik's stomach. With a moan, his chin slumped to his chest.

All the muscles in Pawly's face stretched taut. It hurt to even breathe. Every follicle in her skin tingled. Bright red poured in from the edges of her vision until only the eyes of Dominik's attacker remained, leering at her from behind a ski mask. She had no idea who these guys were. But she knew for certain they were all about to hurt.

"Coward!" she screamed in a raspy voice she barely recognized as hers.

She dashed to his flank to coax him into lunging for her. After planting her foot, she launched herself sideways. She braced her fists and drove her elbow up into a pressure point below the thug's ribcage. His breath rushed out with a satisfying *whoosh* before planting his face on the pockmarked concrete.

Pawly bounded atop a trash can and pushed off toward the two men holding Dominik. One dropped her friend's wrist and ducked. She rolled sideways over her shoulder. Upon impact with the wall, she slammed her heels down hard on the other man's face before he could do likewise. Then she looped one arm around Dominik's shoulder and drilled her elbow into the crouching man's temple.

Momentum carried the three of them tumbling across the alleyway. They crashed into a recycling bin, sending discarded plastic bottles flying everywhere.

Pawly sprang to her feet after working herself loose from Dominik, prepared to defend them. But their remaining opponent just lay there, unmoving. She let out a long sigh and the red haze retreated, enabling her to see clearly once more.

While the tingling in her skin subsided, Pawly rolled Dominik onto his back. "Nik! Nik, can you hear me?" she shrieked as she patted at the sides of his face.

"You bitch!" came a voice from behind before Dominik could answer.

Pawly lurched to the side, landing on her elbows and one knee. Adrenaline and muscle memory took over as she pulled her other knee to her chest and thrust her leg out behind her with all her might.

Her attacker responded with a pained shriek when her heel slammed into the man's groin. After the thug collapsed to the pavement, a groan from the pile of pallets drew her attention. Pawly turned to see Tommy bat splinters of wood away from his face with one arm and sit up.

"Where's Lana?"

"Sent her to find her folks, don't worry. Are you okay?"

"I'll live," her brother replied with a nod.

Pawly stepped over to where Dominik's attacker lay whimpering, both knees drawn to his chin. "So will this asshole, I suppose." She reached down and yanked at the top of the man's ski mask. "Whoever he is."

Wood debris crashed and clattered about as Tommy sprang to his feet. "Holy shit, Pawly. That's Neil Symers!"

She made a face and glared down at the man. "And he is...?"

"The Bobcats' left wing."

"The *Bobcats*?"

Pawly swore and knelt beside the man she had clubbed in the head with her elbow a moment before. "How about this guy?" she asked after exposing his face for Tommy to see.

"Derek Witherspoon. Their center and team captain."

"And him?"

"Jace Rzycki. Starting goalie."

She let out a disgusted sigh and stood. "These pricks couldn't wait until *tomorrow* for your team to kick their—?"

The haze percolated back into Pawly's field of vision like a pot of water beginning to boil. *If the whole fucking squad is after us, then Lana might be...*

"Shit, guys. These two know who we are!"

Pawly turned and saw three more young men rush out from behind a dumpster, their hoods removed. Her skin pricked all over her body while she fixed her narrowed eyes on them. Blood oozed from where her nails dug into her palms as a primal scream ripped from her throat.

Then everything went red.

S HE WAS RUNNING, MUSCLES in her legs and arms working their rhythmic pattern. Though Pawly sensed her eyes were wide open from the wind rushing past her face, she couldn't see anything except hazy red silhouettes all around her. Her chest tightened and her heart raced. An instant later her vision returned, as if someone had flicked on a light switch. She gasped, able to make out the raised lettering on each brick lining the alleyway walls as she ran past. From pavement to roofline, every single one of them.

Ahead she saw four or five boys running, who she took to be Bobcats. Each wore a black sweatshirt with the exact same stitch pattern connecting the sleeves to the back. A growl rumbled forth from deep within her chest after they rounded a corner, but it was not of her doing. Every part of her seemed to act of its own accord, as if by instinct, with Pawly's consciousness unable to do anything about it. She was just along for the ride.

Pawly figured she should be panicking about now, but found herself consumed by a different sensation altogether. The tingling in her skin from earlier penetrated all the way through to her bones, invigorating her, refreshing her, comforting her. As if her body was reassuring her conscious mind that it knew exactly what it was doing.

The boys skidded to a halt short of the chain link spanning the alley. They turned as one toward Pawly, faces twisted like the Edvard Munch painting featured last week in Sister Agnes' art history class. Their cries became ever more desperate as Pawly crept closer to them. One even knelt before her, clenching his hands together as he wailed.

She stopped before the kneeling boy and yanked him to his feet by a fistful of his shirt. Though he had to weigh much more than her, he felt no heavier than the body pillow laid across her bed at home. Ignoring his panicked gibberish, Pawly fixed her eyes upon her reflection in the boy's mirrored shades. Her throat clenched, squeezing out something between a grunt and a squeak.

No, wait, that *can't be...*

A monster stared back at her. Gray fur covered its eyes and forehead like a mask. Snowy white surrounded the thing's mouth and chin. Long, thin wisps of hair stuck straight out from either side of its nose.

Anger welled up within her. Had the bastards dressed her up like their fucking team *mascot* while she'd been out? She jerked the boy's face close until pain erupted across her face. With a yowl, she dropped the boy and covered her bruised nose with both hands. And noticed the black, fleshy pads covering her palms for the first time.

Pawly drew one hand to her face. She cringed after her fingers brushed the side of what felt like a snout, jutting forth from where her nose had been a moment before. She held out her hand, palm facing her, and flexed her fingers. Long, black claws emerged one by one from each fingertip.

Her lips drew tight alongside the sides of her muzzle. She felt the night air upon her gums and realized she was grinning. And that her body was within her control once more.

Pawly narrowed her eyes and brandished her claws beside the boy's face. "Not so tough *now*, are you?" she tried to say, but all that came out was a ragged snarl. It must've sounded fierce all the same, since the boy launched into a new round of hysterics. After dropping him, the punk collapsed to the concrete and clutched his knees to his chest.

She drew a breath and nearly gagged. A pungent odor flooded her nostrils, coming from a puddle growing around the seat of the boy's pants.

Something landed beside her. Pawly drew back by instinct and glimpsed the faint residual of a female form occupying that space only a split-second before. Stars appeared an instant later after something whacked the back of her head but good. She spun around to face her attacker, her body asserting control over itself once more. "M-Mom?" Pawly's mind commanded her mouth to say, but it could only manage a pained whimper.

What is she doing here? Oh, God, don't let me hurt her. Wait, does she even recognize me?

"Pawly! Can you hear me?" came her mother's voice, clear and strong as she brushed her blond bangs away from her eyes.

"Yes, Mom, I can! What the hell is happening?"

Her mother's brow knit. Obviously, she didn't speak Tasmanian Devil either.

Mr. Biggs' dark features emerged from the shadows a moment later. He called out to the punks and waved an arm toward the alleyway behind him, as if he were helping them try to...

Pawly whirled about and slashed at the boy trying to tiptoe past her. He shrieked and dropped to the pavement, clutching at the gash on his arm. Pawly joined him after a blow landed behind her right ear, twice as hard as the last one. She howled and threw both arms over her head.

The exhilarating scent of fresh blood stirred up by the boys' flight from the alley set the gray hair covering Pawly's arms and legs tingling. Pain forgotten, she pounced and slammed Mr. Biggs into a brick wall as he passed with all the force her body could muster. Pawly then took off down the alley after the boys, her mother hollering something after her she couldn't quite make out. She turned her head enough to glimpse Mom following her. And closing fast.

Pawly pressed forward, the scent of blood ahead and a loud yowl from behind egging her on. Her instincts took over, unwilling to permit any interloper deny her *her* quarry. The red fog crept toward the center of her vision with every step, every leap. With a moan, Pawly at last surrendered herself to the electrifying sensations washing over her.

Chapter Two

London's Heathrow Airport. Same day.

GOOD FORTUNE ALWAYS MADE Ritzi grateful and nervous at the same time. Pragmatism, along with lived experience, taught whenever one had good fortune, bad fortune would surely follow.

But sometimes it worked in reverse, as seemed to be the case this evening. He and his mother had left Warsaw on their return to Chicago five hours late, after LOT's crews traced out a malfunction with the plane's hydraulic system. Then something spooked their pilots enough to set the plane down at Heathrow. Better that than risking an "incident" six miles above the North Atlantic, to be sure.

Minutes dragged into hours. Finally, word came mechanics had cleared their plane for flight. Their gate crew would begin re-boarding soon, so Ritzi excused himself to visit the restroom one last time. Intercontinental flights had become part and parcel of his biological research career years before; Ritzi was keen to minimize in-flight bowel movements. Along with opportunities to bang his knees against yet another lavatory door.

A bright blue box of Jaffa Cakes caught his eye as he made his way back to the gate area. The shopkeeper was glad to delay his closing down just long enough to sell Ritzi an armful. Sharing a box with his mother over coffee would help him relax and get some sleep. Because she would certainly insist they leave Chicago right away to make the twins' team party in Green Bay.

Ritzi trotted back to the waiting area. There he spied his mother with her head cocked toward the speaker above their heads. He pieced together enough from the tinny, garbled voice to proclaim, "Sounds like they're only pre-boarding now. Still time if you want to call Alex and Barry and let them know we're on our way again."

"No," came her curt reply.

He stared at her and blinked. "Excuse me?"

"No, I shall not call." She stretched out her feet and turned her attention to the paperback she cradled in her lap. "Nor you. Twins' championship games come tomorrow. Everyone has brains full of thinking already."

Ritzi took a seat beside her and crossed his arms. "Is that why you forbade me to call them when we landed?"

"Correct," she said, not looking up. "For we had no idea when we might depart."

He looked up at a group of attendants transferring an elderly couple to a pair of waiting aisle chairs. "Our leaving looks pretty imminent now, *Eomeonim*. Shouldn't we give them the good news?"

"Why? Events may confound once again. Better no news than bad news. Wheels down at O'Hare, then we call."

She had a point. Once back in Chicago, the Blue Line would get them home to Jefferson Park quickly enough to where his car was waiting. Then they'd be able to say with certainty when their family could expect them. And not a moment before. Fickle airlines, anyway.

"Do you want me to call Papa, then?"

She shook her head side to side, her focus still steadfast on her book. "I did. When we first landed. Rang and went to voicemail. Left him a message."

"It was getting late already when we left. And Szczecin is a five hour-ride from Warsaw, you know. Maybe he begged the Wojcieszaks for their couch and will drive back to his place in the morning?"

His mother looked up at him with a shrug.

Ritzi drew his cell from his blazer's inside pocket and flipped it open. He wandered over to the window and dialed his father's land line. He left a message with their updated itinerary on his answering machine. Although it might be tomorrow before his father would hear it, Ritzi felt more at ease in doing so. His father was fond of getting together with his old grad school buddies, eclipsed only by his fondness for sharing *siwucha* with them whenever he did. And lots of it. By this time of night, Ritzi knew odds were good that his father would be either half lit or sound asleep.

He flipped his phone closed and reached to replace it in the jacket of his blazer when it rang. Ritzi flipped it back open and smiled, recognizing Barry's number on the phone's display. "*Tak słucham, Pan Bernardyn!*"

"You'd better fucking well listen," boomed his brother-in-law in Polish, responding to Ritzi's greeting. "Because our whole fucking world just exploded. And you're the son-of-a-bitch left holding the match."

His wide eyes narrowed as he cupped his hand around his phone's mouthpiece. "What are you talking about? Are Alex and the twins all right?" he said in a harsh whisper over the din coming through the connection. "And where *are* you? I hear a lot of road noise or something."

"We could ask the same of you. Thought we'd get your voice-mail," shouted Barry's father from the background before Barry could reply. "You and Sunny should be high above the Atlantic Ocean right now."

"She and I are at Heathrow, Dory. Our plane had to make an emergency landing for some mechanical thing." He glanced back at his mother, still sitting beside their gate with her book in her lap. "We're just about to re-board. Now tell me what's going on."

"A rival hockey team jumped Pawly and Tommy tonight," Barry said. "They were fighting them off...and...and she *turned*."

Ritzi scratched at his temple. "'Turned?' I'm not sure I—"

"Oh Christ, Ritzi! She went fucking *feral*, okay? Claws, fur, whole nine yards. Same as you and Alex."

Ritzi's mouth fell open, the panicked realization his niece and nephew might be no more human than he or his sister clawing away at his consciousness. With a low growl he willed the red shadows back to the periphery of his vision.

"Hey! You there?"

He blinked and shook his head. "Oh, sorry. Yes, Barry, I'm still here."

"That's not the worst of it. She drew blood. *Human* blood."

Ritzi staggered forward and gripped the seat back from the row of chairs in front of him. His breath came in desperate gasps as he catalogued years of testing, decades of research, every assurance he had given his sister and her husband—his best friend long before becoming his brother-in-law. Telling them their kids would *never*...

He smacked his lips, feeling like he'd swallowed a cotton ball. "Where are you?"

"We're all *en route* to Pilot Island. Though God only knows what we're gonna do once we get there. Or how long we'll be."

Ritzi glanced down at his watch. "We should be seven and a half hours into O'Hare once we push back. I'll catch a flight to Green Bay from there then call Dory. He can cross over with the boat to fetch me as I'm cabbing it to Northport."

He heard mumbling in the background before Barry's voice came back on the line. "No, Dad says Northport is a fucking zoo with all the lookie-loos going to Washington Island. He'll meet you at Gills Rock. Which is where we're headed now."

Ritzi gulped. "Is...is Pawly *with* you?"

Barry let out a long sigh. "Yes, fortunately. She's right here in the RV. Lucky fucking break it's Halloween, though. Alex managed to chase Pawly down and subdue her without attracting attention. Or using her darts."

Ritzi crossed himself. Not having examined Pawly after her transformation, he couldn't be sure whether the paralyzing agent tipping said darts would have even worked. Or whether it would have stopped his niece's heart. "And is she...secure?"

"Alex and Sheila're trussing her up with the cord they ripped out of the window blinds. Sheila figures if she can lash Pawly's wrists and ankles to the bedframe, she won't be able to claw her way through her bindings."

"Wait, who's Sheila?"

"Service buddy's fiancée. A nurse at a Navy hospital in Portsmouth."

Ritzi gasped. "She *knows*? No one outside the clan or the CIA can know, Barry! Does her fiancée know too? This is completely unaccepta—"

"Was kinda hard to avoid given the circumstances, you know! So sorry to monkey fuck all your precious calculations, *Doctor*. For as much good as they've done us."

Ritzi bit his lip and glanced across the waiting area. His mother's brow creased upon meeting his gaze. Then, she turned and nodded toward their fellow passengers lining up at the jet bridge door. "Look, Barry, I...I gotta go. *Eomeonim* and I will be in the air soon. I'll call after we touch down at O'Hare." He hung up and strode over to where his duffel's strap lay on the seat beside his mother.

"Someone is hurt," she said, glimpsing his trembling hand. "Tell me who."

He cursed under his breath. "I'll explain after we get seated. We can't afford any more delays," Ritzi said, then stomped off toward the jet bridge.

She caught up to him while Ritzi stood fumbling around in every pocket of his pants and sport jacket trying to find his boarding pass. He smiled sheepishly as his mother handed him his and offered the sour-faced gate agent hers. Together they trundled down the jet bridge. At least they had Priority Boarding, securing dibs on the overhead bins.

A moment later he and his mother were in their seats. He let her sit beside the window so he could lean away from the aisle to whisper in her ear. "Give me a moment," Ritzi said and pulled the tray table down from the back of the seat in front of her. He smoothed out his boarding pass face-down on the tray table before producing a pen from his blazer pocket. His *Chosŏngŭl* was a bit shaky, but hearing her gasp suggested to Ritzi she got the gist of it.

Pawly a cat-human. Know now. Like Alex. Like me. She has changed. Family running. To island. We follow. Now.

His mother clambered over him and almost knocked over the person traversing the aisle beside his seat. "Sorry. Excuse please, please excuse," she said as she yanked her tote bag free from the overhead bin. "I must make phone calls. So your father will know. Together, we plan."

"But *Eomeonim*, I—"

"I will fly later," she said, elbowing her way through the crowded aisle toward the cabin door. "Check your messages when you land," Ritzi heard after losing sight of her.

Door County, Wisconsin. Hours later.

R ITZI GRIPPED THE GRAB rail to steady himself and stared out across the foam-topped rollers surrounding their boat. To his right, at the helm, sat Dory. Twin Detroits screamed in harmony as the family's launch raced toward Pilot Island.

Centuries ago, Frenchmen like Nicolet and Radisson had named this passage *Porte des Morts*. "Door of the Dead," from which present-day Door County and the Lake Michigan peninsula it sat on took their names. In the cold water below their feet lay dozens of shipwrecks, though Ritzi hardly worried about them. Their craft was a decommissioned Coast Guard motor lifeboat Dory had bought at auction years before, every bit as shipshape and seaworthy now as the day it had left the service. And Dory was an accomplished seaman, a senior Coast Guard enlisted man before going to work for the CIA. He aimed their bow straight toward the old lightkeeper's cottage, fashioned into the family vacation home after Dory's father retired from the Coast Guard.

The elder man hadn't said a word since they cleared Table Bluff. Ritzi attributed his silence more to worries about his grandchildren than the choppy water all around. On any other day, regardless of the weather, Dory would have been regaling him and anyone else aboard with his latest plan to make his pride and joy just a little faster, just a little more maneuverable, just a little more comfortable.

"Let me guess—'rend not the pelt while it remains on the bear,'" Dory blurted out at length, not bothering to look up. "That's what Niko told you over the phone, right?"

Ritzi winced. That was exactly what his father had told him as he stood at his gate at O'Hare, waiting to board his flight to Green Bay. Dory's friendship with his adoptive parents predated their taking him and Alex in decades before. The elder man well knew Papa's oft-quoted repertoire of proverbs from the old country. Including that particular one, long having been one of Papa's favorites. Coming out of Dory's mouth now, however, it sounded more like an indictment.

"I know my son, Ritzi," he went on as he rubbed at his close-cropped hair. "I'm confident Barry thinks you and Niko were doing just that, telling everyone just how certain you were the twins would never inherit their mother's Affliction."

Ritzi stared down at the deck plates below his feet. He had silently grappled with a similar notion the entire flight across the Atlantic.

"Like mother, like daughter, I guess."

Ritzi looked up at Dory and blinked. "I'm sorry, what now?"

"Is Pawly going to crave hunting humans now, too?" the elder man asked while he rubbed at the corner of one eye with the heel of his palm. "Because she tasted human blood during her first morph."

Ritzi turned away and stared off past their port bow. "She'll be predisposed, yes."

The salt-and-pepper stubble covering Dory's chin stood straight out as he sucked in his lips. "Do you think the rabbit hutch will help? Along with other treatments like the ones Niko had given Alex?"

"A reasonable hypothesis for us to work from. No evidence to suggest otherwise."

"Stands to reason keeping Tommy away from humans if he morphs will help his Affliction be more manageable, right?" He nodded toward Ritzi. "Just like yours."

Surely not a matter of if *Tommy morphs, Dory. A matter of* when.

"It might be less pronounced, yes," Ritzi replied. "Before Papa and *Eomeonim* took in Alex and me, Grandfather used to tell us kids how those sorts among our ancestors managed to sate their urges working as thieves or spies. For them, it was all about the thrill and not the kill. Others...well, they became enforcers and assassins under their biological mandate." He shivered, recalling the most stoic of his elders choking up as they spluttered on about some of the latter, those who had sought to deny their Affliction its due. Recounting of the dying's tortured screams as their bodies rotted away from the inside out until finally, mercifully, oblivion granted each their sweet release.

Dory cocked an eyebrow. "Overachievers among the former surely did likewise."

"I don't recall any of them being dissuaded by...wait, what are you getting at?"

"Wouldn't a certain *jopok* be glad to have Pawly and Tommy both as—?"

"Out of the question," Ritzi answered with a wave of his hand. "You of all people ought to know that, Dory. Wasn't it *your* idea we cut ties with the Koreans just as soon as Papa had perfected Alex's treatments? To placate your bosses at the CIA, as I recall."

Dory shrugged. "Be that as it may, working with the *kkangpae* as an enforcer *did* sate her bloodlust. Kept her body from self-destructing in the meantime, right?"

"Yes, but Papa knew it was only a matter of time before she was found out, or...or worse." Because, Ritzi knew, every sortie might well have been her last.

"Niko spent years customizing Alex's treatments to her specific body chemistry. Are we going to need that kind of time to work up something similar for Pawly?"

And Tommy, don't forget.

"We need not reinvent the wheel, no. But I will need a fair bit of time regardless to pilot a formulary and test it on the twins."

Dory pinched the bridge of his nose. "Just what would you have us do with Pawly until then? Chain her hand and foot to a wall in our basement?"

"I recall your discussing your agency's counter-insurgency task force back when we were still trying to figure out how to best help Alex," Ritzi replied, crossing his arms. "Maybe that could keep them out of public view and allow their urges to fully manifest."

Rather than risk mortal injury trying to quell them.

"Barry wouldn't hear of it, at least not right away. Though the twins are nearly adults now, he still thinks of them as kids. Not soldiers." Dory tugged at his face and sighed. "And my director would shit kittens if I dropped a choice morsel like this in his lap. Even if he warmed up to the idea, it'd still take a while to put something together."

Ritzi stared down at the deck plates in front of his feet for some while, rubbing his chin. "I don't like the idea of any of us working with the *jopok* again. Especially with all the Noh family factions jockeying for position in light of Sung Jin's failing health. They're getting reckless. Desperate."

"The twins would be in Chicago at least. Not in some forsaken corner of Iraq or Afghanistan. Which Barry and Alex might find at least marginally easier to stomach."

Ritzi met Dory's gaze and narrowed his eyes. "I still don't trust them. *Somebody* ratted Papa out to the DEA. Somebody made him out to them to be some kind of drug kingpin. Their seizing all records of pharmaceuticals he developed and administered to Alex and I just so we could stay alive got him deported."

"Now look, we've never been able to establish a conclusive connection between the Nohs and—"

"I have eyes, don't I, Dory? You and I both know they must be involved somehow. Surely in retaliation for Papa leaving them high and dry, without a chemist."

"*His* father was a Polish Army doctor assigned to the North Korean oversight group right after the armistice with the South was signed, remember? And the rest of you went with him and got acquainted with the Nohs." The elder man turned away and squinted through the gray mist, toward the spar lights marking the end of the island's single dock. "'The devil you know,' I guess..."

Ritzi chewed at the inside of his cheek to keep from screaming. His family could end up indebted to the Nohs again; he couldn't afford to be wrong. Like he had been wrong about the twins' Affliction since before their birth. But time and options had run out for them. Dory had long been their answer man, their go-to guy, their man with a plan. Now here he was, grabbing at straws, no better than the rest of them. Surely difficult discussions and damned-if-you-do decisions awaited their entire family. Grateful to spot the island's rocky shore at last, Ritzi sidestepped the helm and made his way forward.

Without a word, Dory cranked the rudder to starboard and they glided up to the dock. Ritzi looped the bow line around a mooring bollard and drew it taut with practiced ease. He hopped down from his perch only after Dory killed the engines.

"Pawly was still out cold when I left," Dory said as he stood and zipped up his bomber jacket. "Alex should be in the house keeping watch over her."

Ritzi's eyebrows shot up. "All by herself?"

"Sunny told Alex on the phone that once she took her kill, she needed to put it in the freezer right away. Tommy took one look at the dead rabbit and ran off. Alex said my tough-guy son hobbled out into the woods after him, but I doubt he got far."

Ritzi nodded, grateful for his sister carrying out their mother's instructions. But he worried for his nephew, knowing the lad would certainly find himself overwhelmed by all this. No one had told either of the twins anything, after all. Because *he* had led everyone to believe the twins would never have a need to know.

Dory finished tending their stern line and rubbed his hands together. "I'd have hauled both their asses back by the scruff of their necks, but *somebody* had to come get you. Now go on, I'll catch up."

Ritzi hoisted his day pack atop his shoulder and hopped over the gunwale. A moment later he strode along the rocky beach toward the lighthouse, silently bemoaning how he and his sister had become Pilot Island's apex predators years ago. And wishing for an angry bear to choose that very moment burst forth from the trees and devour him.

THE COTTAGE'S STORM DOOR slammed shut behind Ritzi. He stood stock still, staring speechless at a pair of iron pipes bolted in the shape of an *X* across the oaken portico between the great room and kitchen. Pawly hung there, chin to her chest, face obscured by a tangled mop of strawberry blond hair. Oversized metal hose clamps secured her wrists and ankles, visible through the fur covering her skin.

Alex stood nearby with her eyes fixed upon her daughter's unconscious form, as though the rest of the world had ceased to exist. He maintained a respectful distance until she turned and met Ritzi's gaze, affording him a good look at the dark trails in the gray fur covering her cheeks. Her ear tufts twitched as she rubbed at the sleeves of her jacket, lips moving but no words coming out.

Ritzi stepped over and drew his sister into his arms. "I'm so sorry," he said before chastising himself for the quaver in his voice.

"Not half as sorry as I am. For trusting you in the first place."

He sighed and shot Barry an imploring look. His brother-in-law sat upon the wooden futon covered in well-worn red vinyl beside the kitchen fireplace. The dim glow of dying coals glinted off a metal plate secured with gauze and bandages over Barry's ruined left eye.

This marked the first time Ritzi had seen his best friend upright since Barry left for Korea on deployment. Injuries from his latest (and certainly last) clandestine operation there had left him bedridden for weeks aboard a Navy hospital ship. At first, no one had expected Barry to even survive, let alone walk again. Ritzi thrilled at having him home.

But this was not at all the sort of reunion Ritzi had envisioned. The two of them had sparred under his mother's tutelage throughout their childhoods. Barry's most enthusiastic beat down felt like a playful poke in the ribs compared to the murderous glare he cast Ritzi's way now.

Even before Barry had worn a SEAL's trident, everyone knew of his steadfast resolve and his hot temper. "Lucky for you I wore myself out chasing Tommy," Barry said at length. As if to suggest he would sooner jump to his feet and thrash Ritzi as look at him.

Ritzi pursed his lips and turned his attention back to Pawly. Tatters of his niece's prized Washington Capitals hockey sweater, autographed by her latest heartthrob, Alexander Ovechkin, hung from her wiry frame. Slender ears stuck out from either side of her head, covered in gray fur, save for tufts of black at the tips. The toes of her shoes were gone, exposing the fur around her paw pads. Certainly, her hind claws had torn them to shreds while she raged.

"The boy couldn't have gotten far," Ritzi said after turning to look out the window. "I'll go sniff him out after we tend Pawly." He stepped up to the log rack beside the futon and pulled two chunks of birch from off the top. Their paper-thin bark curled and burned in an instant after he tossed them both into the fire. He grabbed the bellows from atop the mantle and crouched down beside the grate. "Has she been stable?" he asked while he stoked the coals.

Alex nodded. "Yes. *Eomeonim* called shortly after your plane took off from London. I used the Epipen thingy just like she said to."

Ritzi stood back from the rekindled fire and stared up at the wall clock. "I've forgotten how many time zones I've flown across," he said, cradling his forehead with one hand. "What time was it here when you injected her?"

"About midnight."

He drew numbers in the air with his finger to counter the effects of sleep deprivation and jet lag on his calculations. "The xylazine will wear off soon. Please bring me the rabbit."

Alex nodded and stepped over to the kitchen freezer. Ritzi pulled the poker its place beside the hearth and slid the thing into the red-hot coals beneath the grate. A moment later Alex returned, an oversized Ziploc bag in her hands.

"We may not *need* to do this, you know," Ritzi said and clasped his hands atop Alex's shoulders. "But if Pawly responds aggressively..."

She winced and rubbed at her right thigh. Ritzi could almost feel her scar tingling beneath her pant leg. "Is there no other way?"

"I'm sure *Eomeonim* went through this with you about our kind already. If she or I or Papa thought there *was...*"

Alex turned her eyes toward the floor.

Ritzi lamented the cruel irony, returning from his World Health Organization recognition banquet in Geneva when Barry first called. *We've commercialized production of synthetic tissues for war victims in Africa. But we're no closer in coming to terms with our Affliction than when we first began.*

"If it would make you feel better, sis, I can—"

"No." Alex held the bag out at arm's length to Ritzi. "If anyone's going to do it, it's going to be me."

Barry gave his wife a hesitating nod.

"Very well, then," Ritzi replied and positioned himself directly in front of Pawly, facing her. "Whenever you're ready."

Alex pulled the poker from the fire and examined it, careful not to set her whiskers alight. She sucked in her breath while her ears drew back along the sides of her head. After stepping up to Ritzi's left, she dropped into a fighting stance with the poker's cherry red tip held out before her just below waist height. "Do it."

Ritzi pulled forth the rabbit carcass and jammed it up under Pawly's nose. She let out a low growl right before her eyes flashed open. Equal parts feral rage and primal desire filled them to overflowing. Her disheveled blond pigtails played across her face as her head tossed this way and that. She gnashed her teeth and yanked at her bindings, instinct commanding her to break free. Commanding her to kill.

He dropped the rabbit and lunged to one side. "Now!"

With a loud cry, Alex stepped in and plunged the poker deep into Pawly's right thigh. The stench of seared flesh filled the air all around them.

Along with the girl's screams.

Chapter Three

The following day.

P AWLY RUBBED THE SAND from her eyes and blinked toward the high ceiling. Keeping her head on the pillow, she turned to her left and right. She recognized the upstairs dormitory of her family's cabin once her eyes came into focus, illuminated by the bright sunlight streaming through the windows beside her bed.

Which she knew faced *west*.

She groaned long and loud while pangs rumbled through her stomach. Tommy was due on the ice by one-thirty that afternoon and her by three. The cabin was a little more than two hours away from Green Bay *if* the water wasn't too choppy. It had to be well past noon by now.

Her stomach turned sour. She had practiced hard and played harder to help her team make it to the championship round. And now she was likely going to miss her final game, if she hadn't already. What the hell were her parents *thinking*? Coach Leeson would surely kick her out of the league for skipping out on her and her team mates. Though just as well. Like any of them would even so much as speak to her again.

She rubbed at her forehead. Feeling something slick and slimy on her hands, Pawly spread her fingers and stared up at the gray hairs plastered to her skin. Like when she had tried to hose out Muffin's hutch during her shed early last summer.

Then she remembered. Remembered *everything*.

Pawly sat up and threw off her sheets, sending clumps of gray and black fur flying in all directions. Several landed on the floor and skittered away like dust bunnies during spring cleaning. She swung her legs over the side of the bed and tried to stand. A stabbing pain in her right thigh took her breath away an instant before she crumpled to the floor.

"Oh, you're awake."

Legs flailing and pain forgotten, Pawly scooted across the floor away from the *thing* stepping toward the foot of her bed. White hair hung from its jowls, bringing to mind a portrait of President Chester A. Arthur from her American History textbook. Silver-gray fur covered the rest of its body where Pawly would have expected to see skin.

And it was a woman, dressed in the clothes Pawly remembered her mother wearing the night before.

Pawly clamped a hand over her mouth and drew in a long, sharp breath through her nose. "B-but I thought it was..." she mumbled with a wave of her trembling hand a moment later. "I thought those crazy stories were all, you know...make-believe."

"That's what your Uncle Ritzi and I wanted you and your brother to think, dear," came a gravelly voice Pawly couldn't help but recognize as her mother's. "And everyone else, for that matter. We could hide in plain sight that much easier with you two telling tales all over town how we morphed into cats," she went on, whiskers twitching.

Fucking whiskers *twitching*.

"Most parents delight in seeing their children follow in their foot-steps." Her mother's mouth crooked into a sad smile as she knelt down. Rough, fleshy pads situated below her fingertips brushed against Pawly's cheek, replacing her mother's comforting caress with a sensation of utter wrongness. "Last night brought me not the least bit of joy."

Pawly's mother dabbed at the corner of one eye and stood. "Now let's get you downstairs so you can have...have some..."

Her eyes rolled up into her head as she collapsed.

"Mom!" Pawly screamed and scooted over beside her. For all she knew, whatever had made her mother sprout fur had also made her heart stop.

Calm down, Pawly. Think! Do just like Mr. Drueker taught us in PE class.

She cupped her hands around her mouth and shouted for help toward the iron grate in the center of the dormitory floor. Then she drew her ear close to her mother's nose and listened for her breathing. Whiskers tickling her ear as her mother exhaled gave Pawly a start. While she felt around in the fur covering her mother's wrist for a pulse, someone thumped their way up the kitchen stairs.

After finding her mother's strong though rapid heartbeat, Pawly marveled at the lustrous sheen of her fur. It looked coarse and wiry but was surprisingly soft to the touch. Just like hers had been. Just like...*hers.*

Pawly's father squatted beside her a moment later. He met her gaze with his one good eye while he rubbed at the rough red hair covering his cheek. "Breathing? Pulse?"

She nodded. "Both seem okay, but I—"

"Good," he said and scooped her mother up into his arms. Once Pawly had seen him twirl her mother above his head like she was a baton. Though now, still recovering from his combat injuries, his movements were slow and shaky. But he seemed otherwise to be taking everything in stride. Like having a catwoman for a wife was *normal* or something.

Wait, did everyone else know *all along that...that I might...?*

"Last night was rough on all of us, lil' fighter. Your mother especially," her father said, indicating her mother's limp form in his arms. "After seeing you were okay, it must've all caught up with her."

Pawly heaved herself up atop her bed. "Is...is Mom going to be all right?"

Her father grunted and shuffled his way to the stairwell. "I suppose so. *Ritzi* told us to expect this." He spat out her uncle's name like something of a swear word, despite the two men having been best friends since long before she and Tommy were born. "Can you stand?" he asked, eyeing her as he trudged down the stairwell one step at a time.

Pawly tensed while she steeled herself. "I...I think so."

Her father nodded toward the Navy-issue wool blanket folded atop the sea chest by the foot of her bed. "Cover yourself up and come along. Best if you moved around a little anyway," he replied just before Pawly lost sight of him. "Because soon enough you'll need to use the bathroom."

Grunting and groaning, Pawly stood and wrapped the blanket around her before hobbling off after her father. She made her way across the room and down the stairs, biting her lip to keep from crying out every time she put weight on her wounded leg.

A fire crackled away in the old stone fireplace beside the great room portico. Pawly hobbled over to one of the stout wooden chairs arranged around the kitchen table and sat down. Her father laid her mother out on the cracked red vinyl covering the shabby futon in the corner. "Are you hungry?" he asked as he shuffled across the kitchen toward Pawly.

She drew a hand to her belly after her stomach grumbled in reply.

With a chuckle, her father plunked down in the chair next to her. "We took a pound of sliced ham and a loaf of bread out of the freezer when we got here and put them in the fridge. Should have a jar of mustard in the cupboard somewhere, too. Let me catch my breath and I'll make us up some—"

The sound of the breezeway door slamming open against its stop cut him off. Grandpa Dory entered the kitchen and stopped as his gaze met Pawly's. Had his sideburns turned gray overnight? She drew the blanket's hems together below her jaw with one hand while he turned and shouted toward the breezeway, "You can come in now, son. She's up."

Tommy shuffled into the kitchen a moment later. His hair was a mess; his clothes dirty and covered with cockleburs. Pawly's twin brother gazed up at her with red, puffy eyes. Fear, revulsion, and pity all flashed across his face before he whirled around and dashed out the open door. He stumbled back into the kitchen an instant later with a muffled *oof!*

"He means for you to *stay* in until we're through," a man barked in a low, guttural voice. "Now go. Sit down."

Tommy slunk over to the chair beside Pawly without making eye contact. She looked back up and gasped at the sight of a man stepping across the threshold, gray fur with dark spots covering his head and forearms and bare feet. Dressed in a pair of faded jeans and a well-worn Loyola University Ramblers ice hockey sweater—her Uncle Ritzi's favorite. One she knew he kept together with several sets of old clothes at their cottage for working out in the woods.

Pawly's gaze darted back and forth, between the beast man lumbering through the doorway and her mother's fur-covered form lying unconscious on the futon. Same gray fur, same tufted ears, same flat nose at the tip of a cat-like muzzle. The man drew a hand over the white fur covering his jowls and grunted before taking a seat at the table across from her.

Her grandfather pulled the kitchen door shut and glanced around the room at everyone in turn. "Welcome back," he said, glancing toward Pawly before setting his gaze on the beast man. "And thank you, Ritzi, for tracking down Tommy." Then he turned back to Pawly and her brother. "Now look, you two, I know this all comes as the biggest shock of your lives," he went on, slinging a black plastic case atop of the kitchen table and flipping its latches open. "Ours, too, frankly. But *this* is our reality now and we must deal with it. No more running off, hear me? There's no running away from this."

Tommy responded with a silent nod and went back to studying the table top.

Grandpa D looked at Pawly and her father both in turn. "And I don't want the pair of you overdoing it either, understand?" He nodded toward the futon. "Is Alex sleeping?"

"Near as I can tell, Dad. She passed out upstairs once she saw Pawly was all right. I brought them both down here because I knew you'd want to debrief us."

Uncle Ritzi's tufted ears drew back along either side of his head. "Your doctors said you needed to take it easy, Barry. Anyway, wouldn't Alex be more comfortable in a real bed? You could have dropped her coming down the stairs."

"I wanted to tend her down here until all of you came back," her father replied, an edge in his voice. "And your sister's hardly that heavy. Besides, I'm finding out the hard way doctors don't know nearly as much as they *think* they do."

A growl escaped Uncle Ritzi's throat. "Don't you think you and I have been *through* this too many times al—?"

"Knock it off. Both of you."

The two men glanced back and forth at Grandpa D and each other, but said nothing more.

Grandpa D produced a satellite phone and battery pack from the open case's foam padding. "I want to get Sunny and Niko on with us before it gets too much later," he said, inserting the battery pack into the phone and powering it up. He keyed in a number and set it on the table in front of him, activating its speaker. Everyone heard it ring once, twice, three times before Grandpa Niko's voice boomed "*Dobry wieczór, Pan Teodor.* Sunny is with us on the line, too."

"*Dobry wieczór, Pan Nikodeme,*" Grandpa D replied. "And *ahn yeong ha seyo* to you, *Seon-yeong-ssi.* Do hope we're not interrupting anything."

"No worry. Niko-darling and I finish hot phone sex fifteen minute ago."

Tommy snickered and covered his mouth with one hand. Pawly couldn't help but crack a smile, her grandmother's snide remark helping ease the heaviness that threatened to crush them all. Their father's amused smirk suggested he thought likewise. Their uncle's expression remained neutral, just as expected whenever picturing one's own parents consumed within the throes of passion.

A trio of beeps sounded from Grandpa D's phone. "All right, all right, the crypto link is secure. Now let's get down to business. Sunny, are you expecting Nat and Annie to join us?"

"No. They called an hour ago on layover at Narita. In the air to O'Hare by now."

Pawly bit her lip. For the last eighteen months, her Uncle Nat and Aunt Annie had talked of little but their upcoming mountain expedition to China and the Korean Peninsula. Their tiger population research was surely now hampered, having to cut their trip short on *her* account.

"It would have been nice to have them on the line now," Grandpa D said, "but we can catch them up later. Ritzi, Niko, this is your show. Tell Pawly and Tommy what the rest of us need them to know."

Their uncle's whiskers twitched as he sighed. "There is a lot you'll need to learn which we can't possibly lay out for you all at once."

The twins' father shuffled in his seat and crossed his arms. "Mostly because *we* are still trying to figure it out."

Their uncle paused a moment before continuing. "As I was about to say, research into kleptomaniacs suggests their behavior may be influenced by levels of serotonin and dopamine. And by imbalances in the brain's opioid system." He indicated their mother's sleeping form with a nod. "The urges she and I experience as a result of our Affliction require us to sate them in different ways." He waved his hand toward the twins. "It'll likely be much the same way for you two."

Tommy exchanged a confused glance with Pawly. "Is that why I haven't...you know—"

"Ritzi and I fully expect that you will morph in time, lad," Grandpa N said, cutting him off. "But if we're careful, your urges won't manifest themselves on the same level we think Pawly's will."

Pawly tried to swallow, but her mouth was too dry. "What...what do you mean?"

"For big cats, like other predators, taking down prey releases dopamine into their brains," came *Halmonim*'s voice. "Massive quantities. Prompting them to enjoy the pursuit. And to repeat it."

"The bigger the prey, the bigger the high, too," their Uncle Ritzi added. "Even if your 'prey' is merely metaphorical, like some complex scientific problem you're trying to solve. You'll surely crave the high, surely come to find it addictive. More than any drug ever conceived. As your mother and I know all too well." He placed a hand—or a *paw*, rather—across his chest before continuing. "Because *my* first morph occurred under controlled, closely monitored conditions, my intellectual pursuits go a long way toward sating my urges." He glanced over at Tommy. "Which is what we hope for you, young man."

"But that would have never worked for your mom," the twins' father said, breaking his silence. "So, the Korean mafia hired her as an enforcer for some while. Long before you two were even born," he went on, waving his hand toward Pawly and Tommy. "Make no mistake, those *jopok* and their *kkangpae* were some bad dudes. All about kneecapping shop owners behind on their 'association fees,' then threatening their families with the same if they didn't keep quiet. But we all knew if Alex didn't sate her bloodlust, her need to *kill*, her body would...would've..."

He stuck his trembling fist into his mouth.

"Her body would have self-destructed," Uncle Ritzi said in a monotone as he stood. "I've never seen it happen, but my grandfather told me the stories about it before he was killed. It's...it's horrific."

"Why...why are our mom's urges so different, then?" Tommy asked, his voice barely more than a whisper.

Their uncle stepped toward the futon, where their mother still lay unconscious, and sighed. "Because, son, she'd tasted human blood while consumed by rage during her first morph," he replied at length.

Their father reached over and took Pawly's hand in his. "Just like you did, kiddo. Which is...which is why..."

Pawly almost gagged from the bile welling up in the back of her throat. She craned her neck toward her mother, still passed out on the futon. "Is she...is she going to...?"

Am I going to...?

"Not if we have anything to say about it," Grandpa N answered for everyone. "My adopted daughter deserved our best efforts, now so do her children. We've managed to keep your mother alive and healthy this long with your uncle's help, long after we severed our mafia ties. But now we have to rethink our approach."

"Ow!"

Tommy yelped just before Pawly felt a sharp pain near the base of her neck.

"Hey!" she cried and turned back to see Uncle Ritzi holding a tendril of her hair in one hand. An auburn one she concluded to be from Tommy's head dangled from the fingers of his other. "It will take time for us to work up suitable drugs and pilot an administration regimen. We'll likely start with what we know has helped your mother and I manage, but we'll need to analyze these samples first."

Everyone jumped after the twins' father banged his fists on the table. "So, we're just going to pimp Pawly and Tommy out to the Nohs in the meantime like it's no big deal. Is *that* what you're trying to tell me?"

Uncle Ritzi took the twins' hair samples in one hand and pulled open a cupboard door beside the kitchen sink. "We can't rule it out as an option, Barry," he said, producing a pair of clear plastic tubs and their lids. "You know as well as any of us how our Affliction's bloodlust works." He dropped one hair sample into a tub and snapped its lid closed, then did likewise for the other. "Satisfaction delayed is satisfaction denied, you know. And satisfaction denied can be..." He swallowed. "Satisfaction denied can be fatal."

Chapter Four

Days later.

Ritzi hopped atop the pier and hauled the bow line after him. He knelt down and hitched the cleat while Dory secured the stern line. "Don't bother," Ritzi said after Dory stepped over to the helm and reached for the ignition switch. "They're coming now. I can see *Eomeonim*'s car."

The silver minivan faded into the fog after his mother shut off its headlights and killed the engine. Shrill beeping pierced the still air as the van's back door rose. Nat jumped out of the passenger seat and brushed his choppy jet-black bangs from his eyes. He stared listlessly out over the water in the direction of Pilot Island until a *thud thud thud* from behind the van's rear door broke him from his trance. Nat slid the door open to reveal Annie hunched forward in her seat, glaring at him while she rubbed at her eyes. She stepped out of the van and pulled her frizzy tangle of long brown hair into a messy ponytail while Nat set their luggage and groceries out on the pavement beside him. A moment later the three of them buttoned up the van and shuffled off toward the dock, each laden with daypacks, duffel bags, and paper sacks.

Ritzi smiled as they approached and held out his arm. "Allow me," he said before taking their bags one by one and handing them to Dory. The older man stowed them in the aft compartment while Ritzi took his brother and newly minted sister-in-law into his arms and hugged them close. "Thank you for coming."

"Wild horses couldn't have kept us," Annie replied, returning his embrace.

His mother's face cracked into a lopsided grin. "Nor wild tigers. So it seems," she said and handed Ritzi her car keys. "Here. You drive home now. Use my van as you need."

Ritzi waved his hand toward Nat and Annie. "How long *are* you two back for?"

Nat climbed into the boat and held out his hand to his wife. "As long as need be. We were almost back to base camp when your call came in. Our expedition chief suspended any additional sorties until our return."

Annie sat down on the gunwale and swung her legs over. "I doubt he'll want his medic *and* his lead zoologist away for long."

"We brought back more specimens from our last trek than we expected, babe," Nat said with a shrug. "The others'll be a couple weeks at least cataloguing them all. We need not hurry back."

"Good. Annie will examine Pawly and Tommy." His mother grabbed the edge of the windscreen to steady herself and stepped over the gunwale onto one of the seats. "Taking all the time she needs."

Annie snorted. "Mum, they *did* pay for my medical school. They're not about to let me stay away for long. If it'd help, I could write out a doctor's note for Pawly's school principal before we leave," she said, a lilt in her voice.

Ritzi couldn't help but chuckle. Annie's snarky humor evoked a smile from his mother and Dory both, providing welcome respite from the panic and despair of the last forty-eight hours. He marveled at the love Annie showed Nat and the rest of their family—the family she never herself had—that she would endure all this craziness. And had proven herself eminently trustworthy with their family's secrets. For that, Ritzi was glad.

Barry's service buddy, Top, and his fiancé were another story altogether. Christopher Biggs and Sheila Turner had both seen Pawly and Alex in their ailuran forms on Halloween night. Barry had assured everyone the couple was trustworthy and reliable, being he and Top had been shipmates for years. Ritzi figured Top owed Barry at least that much, given Barry had taken a bullet for him during their last tour in Korea. Doubts nagged at Ritzi nonetheless, but they were far from the top of his list of worries.

"Don't run off without your samples, now."

Ritzi glanced up to where Dory stood holding Ritzi's daypack over the gunwale to him. "You and the others won't be back now until you take the boat in for winter layup?"

"That's the plan," Dory said with a nod after Ritzi took his pack from him. "We should have everything we need now for at least that long. Though Sunny or I will call if our plans change."

Ritzi stooped down and loosed the bow line from its cleat. "Oh, *Eomeonim*, did Janie have everything ready for you?" he shouted over his shoulder.

"Of course. Your admin is always on top of things. Why she has been trying to call you. Yes," his mother replied as Dory worked the stern line free. "Most important, she said."

Ritzi gulped, trying to swallow the lump in his throat. Janie badgered him endlessly to take time away from work to be with his family, insisting on vigorously running interference whenever he did so. If she was calling him *now*, knowing he had booked off until further notice, then something big was going down. Certainly nothing good, either.

The boat pulled away from its slip while Ritzi tossed the bow line over the boat's windscreen. With a wave to his family, he turned and strode ashore. He gave a final backward glance when he reached the edge of the parking lot. Just in time to glimpse their family launch charge past the breakwater and disappear into the fog bank, both motors at wide open throttle.

Ritzi opened the driver's door of his mother's minivan. He slid the seat back before getting in, knowing he would surely bang his knees on the steering wheel otherwise. Once settled, he drew out his cell phone and flipped it open to find he had fourteen missed calls and eight new voicemails.

He groaned after spying the bar-and-bell icon atop his phone's display screen. Cursing under his breath, he poked his way through his phone's menus to turn off Silent Mode. Then he scrolled through his calls to find every one he had missed from either his lab or Janie's personal cell.

Ritzi keyed the van's ignition and put it in gear. He drove to the street and stopped at the red light before opening his first voicemail. "So sorry to bother you during your family crisis, Doctor Opoworo," came Janie's tinny voice. "But the vice chancellor just called saying the Board of Regents is meeting this afternoon. They're moving to deny your petition of—"

He hung up his phone and mashed the accelerator an instant before the light turned green. Engine roaring, the van tore around the corner and sped off down the highway.

J UST OVER FOUR HOURS later, Ritzi stuck his wallet out the driver's side window toward the card reader. It chirped in reply an instant before a motor hummed to life and drew back the cyclone fence gate blocking his path. Ritzi gunned the engine a split second after judging his mother's minivan would fit through the opening, not caring whether or not he scratched the paint. Nor did he pause after passing through, as protocol dictated, to ensure no unauthorized vehicles followed him in. Those samples from the twins in his pack were getting hotter by the minute. They needed to get into a refrigerator, and soon.

He parked the van and made his way to the building's foyer, eyes tracing the cracks in the sidewalk as he walked. When at last he gazed up, his mind overlaid an image from his memory of the same building on another, happier day. Maroon and gold bunting draped from the lintels. The Loyola school ensemble gathered out front, belting out stirring renditions of *Ad Majorem Dei Gloriam* and Poland's national anthem. His father was the center of attention for each and every attendee of this very building's ribbon cutting.

"Sir! Excuse us, please!"

Ritzi looked up in time to dodge two men dressed in dark green coveralls, each pushing a dolly with a tall metal cabinet strapped to it. Both cabinets were from his lab, recognizable by one's scratched paint and the other's dented door.

He chuckled and watched the men roll their burdens up a metal ramp and into the back of a green-and-yellow Mayflower van. Centrifuges, spectrophotometers, electrophoresis cells surely filled the cabinets—things his creditors would eagerly repossess if they learned of a pending eviction. But only if they could *find* them.

Ever the trustworthy admin, Janie appeared to have made excellent progress already. He held out hope the Regents would come around following future appeals. And abide by the terms of his lease in the meantime. Janie, however, had insisted he hedge his bets. Just like his grandfather's tales from when Raczkiewicz and Sikorski had fled Paris for London to keep ahead of the Nazis.

He trundled through the propped-open glass door and down the foyer steps, headed to his suite. Janie stood just inside his office's open doorway, tapping her lip with a pen while she studied the clipboard in her hands. She looked up after Ritzi stepped across the threshold. "I'm...I'm sorry. About the Regents and all."

Ritzi looked her up and down. Her hoodie and jeans stood out; he couldn't recall seeing her wear anything other than a skirt and blouse to the office before. She looked past him up at the wall clock. "You came straight here from Door County? Wow, you made good time."

"Uhm, yeah." Ritzi tried to process whatever implications Janie's coming to work on a weekday dressed in such a dowdy outfit held. Were the custodians on strike? Was she swabbing toilets in between taking phone calls? "I'm surprised, frankly, that I didn't blow the motor in my mother's minivan. Let's you and I not tell her, okay?"

"Your secret is safe with me," she replied with a chuckle. "Not that I'm likely to see her again, anyway."

"What?" Ritzi's eyes went wide. "Why not?"

The phone opposite the lobby from them rang before she could answer. Janie sighed and stepped over to the partition wall beside her desk. "Good afternoon, Creative Morphogenics Incorporated," she said after reaching over the wall for her handset. "Oh, no, I'm sorry. We've temporarily suspended all operations during our reorganization. But check back at our website for updates..."

He shook his head and wandered off into the wet lab. Janie had gone over their cover story with him on the phone from the Wisconsin state line all the way into the city. Hearing her deliver it to an actual caller just now made everything chillingly real.

Movers were just strapping down the last chemical storage cabinet to a platform truck. The men gave Ritzi a quick nod as he approached before tugging their load past him toward the lobby. The two men who had brushed past him and Janie a moment before cinched their dollies' web straps around the upright freezer and refrigerator he kept samples in.

Oh, shit. The twin's samples!

Ritzi dropped his daypack to the floor. He knelt down and frantically worked its zipper until he coaxed out a small blue soft-sided cooler.

"The chairs are still in the break room if you want to eat your lunch in there," came a voice from behind.

He turned to find Janie standing behind him, hands in the pockets of her jeans. "Oh...uhm," he replied, the blue cooler lost in his hands. "This isn't food." He opened up the bag and drew out several plastic containers. "These are specimens harvested from some, ah...wildcats we'd encountered up at the cabin." *Yeah. That's it.*

Janie pursed her lips. "What did I tell you about focusing on your family while you were away? Geez, you're hopeless." She snatched the containers out of Ritzi's hands and stepped over to a large open box across the room from them. "I've got a big Styrofoam cooler in this box packed full of dry ice and all the stuff I knew would need to keep cold. Should be just enough room for these."

Ritzi glanced down at his watch. "I can see these men out if you want to go. No sense crowding into a train at rush hour if you don't have to."

Janie smiled and finished stowing the twins' tissue samples. "My ride's here already. And besides, I'm on my own time."

He blinked and stared down at her. "But then, why did you—?"

"You know me better than that, boss. I wouldn't leave you hanging, even if you'd asked me to. And besides, my agency said they'd give me a day's wages if I tendered my resignation immediately. So..."

She shrugged and turned toward the two men opposite the cavernous room from her rolling away the fridge and freezer. "That should be the last of it," she shouted. "I'm sure my...*ex*-boss here will want to pack up his office himself."

The fellow pushing the freezer rolled his dolly up beside them. "I've gotta go scope out the job we're doing tomorrow, sis," he said, nodding toward the man with the fridge. "Wennie's gonna take the truck back to the shop once we get everything strapped down. He can drop you off at your apartment on the way."

Ritzi cocked an eyebrow toward the *OLSZEWSKI MOVING & STORAGE* patch sewn onto the man's coveralls above his left breast pocket.

"My brother's outfit was the only one I could get on short notice," Janie said. "No worries about a conflict of interest, though. He's doing me a favor."

"Thank you...Janie," Ritzi said, drawing a hand to his mouth. "And thank you too...uhm..."

"Krzysztof," the man said with a nod. "And don't worry about storage fees either. You just let Janie know when you get to your new facility and we'll bring you your stuff."

Ritzi stared after the man as he guided his dolly around the corner and out of sight. "Most clients would have just as soon fired me rather than give me time to help Kris handle our father's estate after he died," Janie said, throwing her arms around his neck. "Annie and your mom covered the phones for me for a month straight and never once complained. *Reka reke myje, tak?*"

He returned her embrace and patted at her back. *Yes, Janina. "One hand washes the other," indeed.*

"You...you should go now," Ritzi said at length, his voice husky. "Don't keep your brother's man waiting."

She drew back and nodded toward the door of Ritzi's office. "I set out some boxes for you in there," she said before turning to leave. "And leave your samples and specimens to me. I'll put 'em all back in your fridge and freezer as soon as we get to our warehouse."

A moment's passing, a door slamming, and Ritzi was alone. He shuffled into his office and ran a hand across his father's old desk, situated opposite the room from his own. Blowing dust from his fingers, he stepped over to his workstation and poked its power button. Waiting for his machine to gather its wits, he picked up the stack of envelopes Janie had left in his "in" basket. Ritzi rifled through them one by one, not bothering to open any. With a mere glance at the envelopes, he knew each letter featured one form or another of FINAL NOTICE printed in big, bold letters above the salutation.

The sound of a fist pounding against the lobby door drew Ritzi's attention away from his mail. He dropped the letters onto his desk top and dashed out his office door down the hallway. Beyond the reception area, he spied a courier standing beside the lobby door, her gaze focused on the note in her hand.

"Maur...Mau-rye...Mau-rye-see...uhm, Doctor Opoworo?" she said, scratching at the hair beneath her bicycle helmet as he unlocked the door.

"Yes, I am he," Ritzi replied as he swung the door open. "But how did you get past security?" He pointed over the woman's shoulder down the hall toward the building's main lobby. "They're supposed to accept and inspect all incoming—"

"I just came from the Chancellor's office. The admin there called ahead to tell them I was coming." The woman twirled her messenger bag around to her front and produced a large manila envelope from one pocket. "And told them I was to give this directly to you as soon as possible." With that, she turned on her heel and strode back toward the entrance, mumbling into the two-way radio strapped across her chest.

Ritzi clutched the envelope to his chest and scurried back to his office. He stopped in front of the framed photo hanging on the wall behind his father's desk, taken the day he and Ritzi had cut the ribbon together in front of this very building with Loyola's then-president and vice chancellor. His father had wrangled with the oversized scissors while Ritzi held the ribbon taut, their faces barely large enough to contain their smiles.

Details of his father's experimentation on Ritzi and his sister as kids had come under scrutiny following an NIH audit months before. Loyola's incoming president had been quick to distance herself from his father's work even before anyone knew the final outcome of his deportation hearings. Regardless, Ritzi had appealed months ago to the Council of Regents to permit him to carry on the groundbreaking research his father had begun years before. Around which the university had built its entire molecular genetics commercialization program, right here in this industrial incubator.

Hands tingling, Ritzi tore open the envelope and quickly unfolded the letter. Hope turned to shock, then turned to anger with each successive read of the Regents' statement. Not only had they voted to deny his petition, their vote had been unanimous. And hence, their decision was now final. Unappealable. Irrevocable. The deciding vote cast by the Vice Chancellor himself, his father's friend of nearly thirty years. The man's swirly signature in blue ink crossed the bottom of the page from margin to margin. Right below the eviction notice.

Ritzi's world went red.

With an angry yowl, he lunged and slashed at the photo. Long black claws sliced clean through wood, gatorboard, Plexiglas. Frame pieces clattered atop his father's desk. Strips of photo paper twirled and fluttered toward the floor.

"No!" Ritzi yelled and clamped his palms over his temples. He stumbled backward until his back hit the wall. His claws pricked the skin on the top of his head while he slid slowly to the floor. He sat there, keeping care to remain motionless. Lest he scalp himself.

Ritzi screwed his eyes shut and focused on his breathing, just like his mother had taught him years before. In through the nose, out through the mouth. One breath at a time. Another and another and another still.

At length he opened his eyes. Drops of rain trickled from the sky beyond his office windows, leaving dark splotches on the neighborhood basketball court beyond the cyclone fence. He crossed himself and clasped his hands together before dashing off a silent prayer. For Pawly and Tommy. For himself. For them all.

Though their father had been successful stabilizing his and Alex's condition, everyone knew he had merely forestalled the inevitable. A killer's nature was their kind's gruesome birthright. One which, left unsated, threatened his niece and nephew's very lives. Just as it had Ritzi and his sister a generation before, whose continual abeyance had of late left him tired. So, so tired.

Darkness shrouded the room by the time the grumbling in Ritzi's stomach roused him. Dim light from his screensaver illuminated the gouges left by his claws in the drywall. A delightful pain throbbed beneath his fingertips as he held them up to his face. His claws had receded for now, but he resolved to indulge himself later tonight. Once unsheathed, his claws would ache to rip into bone and sinew.

But for now, a bowl of *pho* would have to do. He glanced down at the floor around him and found no shed fur there. Good. After rubbing at his face and neck and feeling none there either, Ritzi hoisted himself up and stared down at the clock icon on his computer's screen. His favorite *pho* shop down the street would be open for another half hour yet, so he called in his order.

Ritzi made use of the bathroom before stepping out. He scented his meal cooking from halfway down the block, raising his spirits. The shop's proprietor hailed from Hanoi, so Ritzi made sure to order the man's hometown specialty *pho chua* whenever he could. Such a pity few others did. During the summertime, the fragrant smell of fruit vinegar and roasted peanuts would waft into his office through the open window. But now, a familiar bite in the air heralded winter's swift and imminent arrival.

Yes, he would savor his hot soup. And, yes, he was going to miss this neighborhood.

Not long later Ritzi stood in front of his office door, a plastic bag in each hand. He waved his back pants pocket at the card reader. It beeped in response to the card tucked into his wallet. Taking the two bags into one hand, he pulled the door open and let it close behind him.

Plunging him into complete darkness.

Hell of a time for the lights to go out. Figures.

With cautious steps, he shuffled along the walls toward the light switch opposite the lobby from him until he banged into something with his toe. He fumbled about in front of him and identified the credenza behind Janie's workstation. The low whirring noise from the tower beneath suggested her computer was still running.

So, the power's not *off, okay. Then why is it dark in here?* Ritzi drew a hand to his mouth. *Oh...oh, wait, could it be...?*

He dropped the bags of food onto her desk and fumbled about for her mouse. Twiddling it, Ritzi hoped to bring up Janie's screensaver. Even a dark monitor should have come to life to await a user password, but he saw nothing.

A bright flash of light confirmed Ritzi's suspicions. Though his Talent had been key to his academic and commercial advances, the frequently inopportune timing of its manifestations was a puzzle still. He breathed deep and watched, eager to see whatever was coming next.

One by one more flashes followed, leaving artifacts behind in his mind's eye, resembling pinpricks of colored light. Red. Green. Blue. Purple. More and more appeared, forming themselves into the familiar shape of a double helix against a black backdrop.

He gasped and felt around for Janie's desk drawer. Finding it a moment later, he yanked it open and pulled out a stack of sticky notes. His shaking hands rummaged around in the pencil tray for something to write with. The first pen he found bent and cracked as soon as he tried writing with it. Next, he grabbed what felt to be a pencil—it snapped in half. With a roar, he tore the drawer from the desk and hurled it across the room. Various and sundry items skittered about the floor before the drawer disintegrated into splinters against the wall.

The image of the helix formed by the flashing lights continued to grow and change. It folded over on itself once, then again, the nucleotides changing partners like girls rolling between their boys' arms during a *Trojak* folk dance.

Then Ritzi saw *it*. His heart swelled; his unseeing eyes grew moist. Against the pitch black he saw the one selection set that had eluded him, eluded his father, all this time. So simple. So damn simple.

Ritzi wasn't about to let this opportunity slip away. Nails morphed into claws and down fur sprouted from his skin as he shuffled toward the wall. There, he followed the wall into the corner, then sank the claws of one hand into the drywall with a grunt. He slipped off his shoes, then stabbed his foot into the wall like he was wearing crampons. He scaled the wall until he reached the ceiling. There he transcribed a formulaic representation of each and every molecule he could see, frantically carving letters, numbers, and symbols into the wall's dark surface.

The characters shimmered in silver but then faded to a dull gray. Ritzi belted out an angry roar, bit his lip, and concentrated. The images' intensity returned, though they were not nearly as sharp as they had been. His breath came in great gasps as he clawed at the walls and floor, desperate to record the answers he had sought for so long. Before they evaded him once again.

T HE MORNING SUN CRESTED the building opposite the basketball court and streamed into Ritzi's office foyer. With a groan, Ritzi leaned his back against the wall and got to his feet. He milled around where he had finally collapsed last night, shed fur fluttering to the floor as he rubbed his face and forearms. A nauseating scent drew his attention toward the upended container on Janie's desk formerly containing the *pho* broth now dripping slowly to the floor. One empty foam box lay open beside it, not a scrap of fatty flank or tripe or tendon to be had. But the other, filled with the *pho*'s now-wilted greens and garnishes, remained untouched.

Ritzi flicked the light switch. After blinking the spots away, he noticed the shreds of threadbare carpet below his feet. And the final term of an eleventh-order genetic synthesis algorithm carved into the underlayment beneath. His eyes traced it backwards along the circular swirls covering the floor. The algorithm's equations continued up the wall, covering all three in the foyer with similar scratches from floor to ceiling.

He rubbed his fingers across the scored drywall, his eyes wide. The formulae he needed, the genetic sequences he required—they were all *here*. And here right now.

But hypotheses and calculations were one thing. The equipment, the supplies, the money required to implement them was quite another. The first two he and his father had managed to scrape together through the years. Though the last one they needed urgently, to have somewhere they could continue to work without the continual threat of eviction. Or, he realized as he looked around his laboratory's bare foyer, the current certainty of it.

He patted at his forearms to ward off a sudden chill. Then realized he was no longer wearing his blazer. A moment later Ritzi found it, wadded into a ball and tossed into one corner of the foyer. Breathing fast, he pulled his cell phone from one pocket and flipped it open. After twisting the screen to activate its camera, he swept the lens around the walls and floor until certain he had captured all the equations on video. Then he took the phone in his other hand and did the same thing, silently praying this footage would be at least marginally less shaky.

CHAPTER FIVE

NORFOLK, VIRGINIA. ONE WEEK LATER.

PAWLY HAD CHEESE ON her mind. An entire pound of gooey mozzarella, in fact, covering a mountain of grilled chicken, ranch dressing and tomatoes. All of it surrounded by a delightfully doughy crust and finished off with a lattice top. A full stomach and a touch of flair from one tasty package.

She had enjoyed authentic Chicago pizza numerous times while visiting her family there. But it never quite stacked up to the New York-style stuffed pie her father would bring home from Del Vecchio's on his way home from the base. Just another thing she would miss from her childhood home.

"Guess it's up to you to whip these two into shape, Top. Del's closes in an hour," her father said, holding the screen door open for Mr. Biggs.

"And your dad told me he ain't ordering until all this stuff is inside the U-Haul," Mr. Biggs added as her father's longtime friend and shipmate set Tommy's bedroom dresser down beside the truck's ramp.

Pawly groaned and gazed about the garage floor, covered wall to wall with the family's possessions. "Yes, sir."

Her dad and Mr. Biggs exchanged satisfied nods and hustled back into the house.

She growled and kicked the empty cardboard box beside her, sending it skidding across the van's wooden floor. "We'd've been done by now if you weren't goofing off trying to play Tetris with our stuff!"

"The van is only so long and so high, sis." Tommy emerged from behind where their living room furniture stood stacked to the ceiling. "There, that's better," he said and stepped back, chin in one hand. He knelt and peered behind their upended sofa. "Hey, hand me the hutch roof, would you? Should be just to your left."

Pawly set the floor lamps down beside a wood frame nailed to the bottom of a sheet of plywood, propped up against the inside of the van. She grabbed it with both hands and glanced over her shoulder toward the garage's far wall. There she spied the halves of her rabbit's carrier, still nested one inside the other since the last time she'd hosed it out. "Where did you put Muffin?" she asked and slid the thing to Tommy.

After stowing the hutch roof in a crevice behind the sofa, Tommy brushed past Pawly and hopped out of the truck. He trotted over to a mound of duffel bags heaped up in one corner of the garage. "I built her a pillow fort right over here. Then I set down some alfalfa pellets for her to—hey!"

Pawly dashed up behind Tommy. He plucked Muffin out of the pile of stuffing lying beside the gaping holes torn open in his blocker and catch glove. "My goalie pads!" he screamed, dangling the bunny at arm's length in front of him. "I'll fix you, you lop-eared low life."

"Give her to me!" Pawly said and held out her arm to him. "You're scaring her."

Tommy stuffed the bunny into the crook of his arm and knelt down beside their father's tool box, sitting with its lid open on the floor nearby. "Okay, right after I take the edge off those choppers of hers." He rummaged around in the tool box with his free hand for a moment before pulling out a three-square file. "Now open up and say—ow!"

Muffin leapt from Tommy's arm. Pawly shoved him aside and caught the bunny in mid-air. "She doesn't know any better, moron. Serves you right, anyway. I *told* you to wait until I set up her—"

"What the hell is going on out here?" came their father's voice an instant before his head poked out from the kitchen doorway.

"Tommy left Muffin out of her hutch and she chewed up his..."

A metallic tang wafted through the air, biting at the inside of Pawly's nose. Tommy yowled and fell to his knees on the concrete beside her, clutching his shaking hand. More scents, sour and acrid, overpowered the scent of Tommy's blood, dripping from his fingers.

"Pawly, take Muffin in the house. Lock the door behind you," her father said when he knelt down and picked up the end of a garden hose off the floor. "Don't open it until I tell you it's okay."

She glanced over at Tommy and gasped. His eyes were wide open and bloodshot. His canine teeth peeked out from beneath his upper lip as he gulped down air in ragged gasps, each exhale nearly a growl. "But, Dad, I—"

"Go, dammit!" he said, never once taking his eyes off of Tommy.

Her brother stood, leaning up against the wall for support, shaking his head side to side. His entire body trembled like the videos Pawly had seen of animals suffering through the final stages of rabies before they were put down. Drool trickled out of both corners of his mouth while he turned and focused his gaze on Muffin.

And *roared*. Then, teeth gnashing, Tommy sprang.

The bunny thumped at Pawly's forearm before launching from her hands. Red fog flashed into Pawly's vision as if someone had flipped on a light switch. She groaned as spasms of primal longing and delicious ecstasy crashed over her like an ocean wave.

P AWLY STOOD, PANTING WHILE tingling sensations coursed the length of her body. Cold air pricked at the inside of her nose when she inhaled, a stark contrast to the comforting warmth consuming the rest of her. She blinked and focused on a spot near her feet as the red haze retreated to the edges of her vision.

She dropped to her knees, sending dead dried leaves skittering in all directions. Pawly had to thrust out her forearms to avoid planting her face in the soft dirt. Side to side she shifted her weight to steady herself before sensing a damp spot between her thighs she didn't remember being there before.

Oh, I so did not just—

Pain crisscrossed her groin as her fingertips poked the crotch of her jeans. She jerked her hand to her face, shredding the front of her pants. Between mumbled curses she squinted at her trembling fingers, illuminated by the moon's light. And studied her fingernails, each now long, curved, and pointed. Claws.

Her claws.

Pawly blinked and breathed in deep to steel herself, a mistake she realized an instant too late. The surrounding scents overwhelmed her senses as if she had gulped down a whole jar of her Grandpa D's homemade horseradish. A firestorm raged in her sinuses, threatening to melt a hole into her brain. Something between a yelp and a whimper squeaked out between her parched lips, while words attached themselves one by one to the smells and flavors swirling through her mind. Oak. Cedar. Peat moss. Blood on her hands. Blood in her mouth.

This was no tinny aftertaste like when she had last had a nosebleed. This was like when she skated into Tommy's blind spot at hockey camp last summer. He had socked her square in the chops while drawing back for a slapshot. Right now, her tongue rasped about to find safe haven from the metallic taste but found none. Blood covered her gums, her teeth, her fangs.

Her fangs.

Pawly glanced around toward the ground beside her knees. To her left lay what she guessed to be a rabbit, dead or dying as heat ebbed from its still form in time with her racing heart. She reached out her hand toward the thing's rusty-colored fur.

A flash of gray streaked with black filled her field of vision before she went tumbling across the forest floor. Pawly came to rest face up on the hard ground with a rock stabbing her between the shoulder blades. Something had her wrists and ankles pinned before she could even manage to lift her head. Her eyes came into focus the instant before a furry hand clamped down hard over her mouth. "M-Mom?" she tried to say but could only manage a dull mumbling.

Her mother returned Pawly's gaze with a withering stare, clearly the hunter here. And Pawly was her *prey*.

"Listen to me!" Her mother addressed her in the same gravelly voice Pawly remembered upon waking at their cabin, following her first transformation three weeks ago. "Blink three times if you can understand what I'm saying."

She did.

"So, you're lucid this time. Good." Her icy glare melted away, replaced with a warmth Pawly couldn't help but recognize. "I'll take away my hand, but I need you to keep quiet. Understand?"

She nodded.

Her mother dropped her hand and jammed a knuckle into Pawly's mouth. The back-and-forth motion from the fur on her finger made Pawly's whiskers twitch. "Spit it out if the taste bothers you," her mother told her after turning Pawly's head to one side. She tried to but couldn't get rid of the glob of curdled blood in the back of her mouth quick enough. It oozed its way down her throat, making her gag. She finally conjured up enough spit to swallow properly, though she thought sure she would soon be giving it back. With interest. Mom straightened up but straddled Pawly still.

Gripped by fatigue, Pawly took three tries mouthing her words before she managed to sound them out. "Whu-whut's...goin' on? Where...where're we—?"

Her mother gasped and laid a hand on Pawly's forehead. "Shhh, I said keep quiet," she said, pressing down. "Good to know you can actually speak still, too. Ritzi thought you might before long." She nodded her head to her left. "The golf course is over there. We're in the woods behind the clubhouse."

Pawly's brows knit. "That's three...three blocks from our—"

"No more talking, I mean it. You need to save your strength."

Pawly stared up at the stars while a chorus of crickets chirped all around her. *Maybe Mom's right. Why don't I just lie here and rest, just...just for a little...*

"Hey, kiddo, don't drop out on me just yet." Her mother patted at the side of Pawly's face. "I'll carry you home if I have to but right now, I need to know something. Do you remember how you got here?"

She furrowed her brow and shook her head.

"A predator's scent rolls off you when you're preparing to change, Pawly. And now Tommy…" Her mother squished her eyes shut and shivered. "Muffin must have bit Tommy or scratched him or something. Next thing we know he…morphed."

She fixed Pawly with a somber look. "Muffin's fear scent must've caused the predator within you to go berserk, too. You took off after her and I took off after you. Our bloodlust can overpower you if you aren't careful. It'll make you do crazy things like that."

Pawly's forehead wrinkled up while her mother glanced back over her shoulder as if looking for something. "Don't worry. Tommy will be fine," her mother said and scratched at the ground behind with her toe claws. "Your father and Mr. Biggs managed to wrestle him into the root cellar before he even finished changing. His rage should wear out long before he can chew or claw his way through the door. Likely we'll find him curled up on the floor asleep by the time we get you home."

A sickly smell seemed to come from everywhere at once. Pawly turned her head left and right but couldn't locate its source.

"Did you notice it, too?" her mother said after sniffing at the air herself. "The scent of your own fear is strong." A tear leaked forth from the corner of her mother's eye, quickly absorbed by the fur covering her muzzle. "So, so strong. Every creature gives off scents relative to its state of mind."

Pawly's eyes went wide.

"I know, dear. We all told you and Tommy this before we left Pilot Island, remember? But I suppose everything's all still new and confusing just the same. Ritzi and I will work with you more once we get to Chicago. Promise."

Tears streamed down the sides of her mother's face, leaving dark trails between the spots on her cheeks. "Every time you and your brother would take the ice, I would hear the other mothers whispering. Their kids swore the two of you had eyes in the backs of your heads." She rolled off of Pawly and leapt to her feet. "But I should have known better. Your Eyes of the Lynx were just beginning to manifest and your uncle and I both ignored the signs."

She sniffled and rubbed at her eyes with the back of her wrists. "Just as well, I guess. Ritzi wanted me to let you take a clean kill so we'd know whether a small animal can satiate your bloodlust. Because that's how he and I have managed all these years."

"But, Mom, what...what about Muffin?"

"Our longings were why we started keeping a rabbit hutch to begin with. I vastly prefer hunting wild game, but, you know, just in case I can't get away for what your father calls my 'me time.'" Her mother chuckled and offered her a hand up. "Don't worry, any bunny you adopted as a pet was forever off limits."

After pulling Pawly to her feet, her mother threw an arm around her shoulder to coax her along. "Speaking of which, let's get you home so I can look for Muffin solo," she said as they made their way together along the trail toward the street. "I can find her for you much faster that way. Prissy thing'll end up in some coyote's belly for sure if she stays out here too—"

Mom bared her fangs and roared. Claws out, she swatted at a raven trying to put down on top of the rabbit's blood-spattered carcass. The big black bird squawked and flapped about as it tumbled across the forest floor, stirring up leaves and debris. Moonlight filtering its way through the canopy above cast an eerie glow on the fur covering the rabbit's back. "No, Pawly!" she cried and threw her arms around Pawly's head.

But her mother was too late to keep Pawly from spotting the tattered remains of a pair of pink gingham bows looped around the bunny's limp ears. An instant was all it took to sear the horrible image into her memory.

Pawly buried her face in the tuft of soft fur covering her mother's chest and began to cry.

Chapter Six

SZCZECIN, POLAND. NEXT MORNING.

RITZI TOOK A DEEP breath, savoring the aroma from the plate his father had set before him. Household etiquette in Poland required hosts care for their houseguests, and his father had laid it on thick during Ritzi's stay. As if he were a stranger in his own father's house.

"A bowl of cereal with milk would have sufficed, you know," Ritzi said, poking with his fork at the pile of scrambled eggs topped with sliced wild mushrooms. "You've been stuffing me like a Thanksgiving turkey every day since I got here."

"You're *welcome*," his father replied without looking up. After slicing through a loaf of dark bread, he handed the heel to Ritzi. "Eat up, because I don't expect we'll have time to break for lunch today." He then sat down across the table from Ritzi behind his own plate. "So, I wanted us to have a proper breakfast at least. Now let us pray."

The elder man recited a short blessing, thanking God for their food and for His continued generosity. After crossing themselves, Ritzi stuck the crusty bread into his mouth and tore off a hunk.

"Something to wash that down with, son?" Not waiting for an answer, his father picked up a squat stoneware teapot and filled the empty cup in front of Ritzi's plate.

Ritzi drew the cup to his lips and blew. "Guess we'll be non-stop go now that those protein chains are finished synthesizing," he said after taking a cautious sip.

"Right. I wanted for us to establish a reliable baseline with the samples you harvested from Alex before you return to the States." His father scooped up a spoonful of eggs onto his own slice of bread and took a big bite. "And I could use your help correlating the results to those eleventh-order algorithms of yours."

"I know, but Alex is expecting me back before long to help get Pawly ready for her—"

The beginning of Chopin's *Minute Waltz* trilled from Ritzi's cell phone, cutting him off. "Speak of the devil." He reached across the table and flipped the thing open on the table in front of him. "Greetings, sister!" he said, poking at the speaker button. "Papa and I were just talking about—"

"It's Tommy," Alex cried. "He morphed."

Oh, dear God. "When, Alex?"

"About an hour ago now."

Ritzi thumped the table top with both palms. "Where are you? Where is Tommy? Is he secure?"

"We're back in Norfolk, packing. Barry's got him locked in our root cellar."

Ritzi buried his face in his hands. "Then he should be okay until his rage passes," he said slowly, carefully, peeking through his fingers at his father.

The elder man nodded. "What about Pawly, dear?"

"I had to..." Alex breathed deep. "I had to go after her. She started raging, too."

Ritzi slumped back in his chair. "Sounds like you've had quite a night."

Alex answered him with a sardonic chuckle. "She calmed right down after she took a kill. You were right, Ritzi."

"How is everyone now? How are you?"

Alex let out a long sigh before launching into a recap of the night's events. The exhaustion in her voice moved Ritzi and their father both to keep their questions few and discussion brief. They no longer needed to dread how or when Tommy's burgeoning ailuranthropy would at last manifest, for which Alex and their father were begrudgingly grateful. But Ritzi had entertained the idea Tommy could serve as something of a control for whatever treatments Pawly might need. Treatments that he would, at some point, have to create. And in that endeavor, his score now stood at oh-and-two.

After agreeing to text after she and her family were up the next morning, Alex hung up. Their father stepped up behind Ritzi and clasped him on the shoulders. "We're close, son. Soon we'll have Alex and the twins out of harm's way once and for all. Those algorithms you transcribed back in Chicago have taken us further than we've ever been."

"I know, but I'm still worried. Alex came into her own under duress. So did Pawly, but she was much older." Ritzi stood and faced his father. "Now Tommy's gone and done the same thing. 'Malignant manifestations,' isn't that what you called them?"

"Yes, the twins' ages might complicate things. The Affliction seems to impact each of you differently, after all."

Ritzi broke a wry smile. "At least Alex and I had you and *Eomeonim* helping us. We would have certainly been shot dead long before now. Or have become someone's lab rats."

"Well, we were about a hundred years too late for the pair of you to be picked up by some travelling freak show," his father said before punching Ritzi's shoulder.

"Doesn't mean it couldn't still happen, Papa. Alex's bloodlust had gone unsated long enough after her first transformation that her body has begun to turn on her now."

His father held up one finger. "We think it *may* have. Yes, her sudden onset of narcolepsy is worrisome, but there are other explanations we need to vet first. And don't forget, your body and hers have managed to stave off the Affliction's self-destruct sequence for years already."

Ritzi tugged at his chin. He and Alex had regularly indulged themselves with rabbits from their hutch. Complemented by wild game from Pilot Island, and, as they grew older, from the Delmarva Peninsula and the foothills around Stanford. Though for Alex, of late, even that didn't seem to prevent her bloodlust's bodily demands from exacting their toll. And neither Ritzi nor his father could be sure the same fate didn't await the twins, their Affliction having manifested years after it would have normally.

"Now let's hurry up and finish eating," his father said and waved his hand at the plateful of now-barely-lukewarm eggs in front of Ritzi. "We've got work to do."

R ITZI'S FATHER SLURPED DOWN the last of his venison stew and slammed his empty plate down on the dingy lab bench beside him. "Right then, let's hit it again. I'm going to get this right even if it kills me."

"At these pressures, it just might, Papa," Ritzi replied, glancing back and forth at the gauges all around him. "Likely it would kill me, too, what with our reaction temperature trending higher by the second."

The elder man yawned and rubbed at his eyes with the heel of his palm. "I built this still with my own two hands. Welded every seam with just the right current with just the right rod heated to just the right temperature. The finest *siwucha* in all Szczecin comes from right here," he said, patting the still's main column. "If any rig is up to the task, it's this one." He turned and squinted in Ritzi's direction. "Just how much of Alex's solulyte do we have left?"

Ritzi eyed the flask simmering slowly away above the low flame of a Bunsen burner next to him. "About a hundred milliliters."

"Enough for two or three more shots. We're surely sighted in now, son. If we don't have luck with these, we'll call it a night." He stepped up to a pair of valves astride the still and laid his hands atop them. "Ready when you are."

After flipping down his face shield, Ritzi plucked the simmering flask from its lab stand. He bit at the inside of his cheek and held the flask up to the glass funnel. "I'm pouring...now."

His father stared up at the second hand of the wall clock and counted down from ten. "Engaging," he said when his count reached zero. The still hissed and shook as the elder man twisted the valves wide open. "Son, look!" he said and stepped over to examine the frothing liquid swirling through the sight glass. "It's working! At last, it's working!"

Ritzi looked over toward the glass and smiled. After countless test runs over the previous fourteen hours, the superheated water containing Alex's specimen took on the pale lavender hue his calculations had predicted.

"Keep 'er coming, son. Steady...steady..."

His father's voice grew distant as a musky, masculine scent froze Ritzi in place. He found the sudden strong aroma unsettling and eerily comforting at the same time. Branches of the big oak above the shed's roof scratched at its surface as the wind picked up, carrying the scent away with it.

A loud *bang* followed by the sound of rushing steam jarred Ritzi back to the present moment. His father darted around the still jamming every bleed cock he came to wide open. Ritzi glanced back up at the main pressure gage and gasped. Its needle was only just now dropping down out of the red zone.

His father swore as he yanked on the cord connected to the roof damper. Steam swirled all around them as he turned to face Ritzi. "The hell's into you? You know better than to dump the whole damn flask in at once!"

Ritzi remembered the flask in his hand and held it up in front of his face. It was empty. He crossed himself with his other hand, knowing an uncontrolled introduction of excess solulyte rendered any resultant reaction unstable. He and his father had been lucky their still hadn't exploded. *Damn* lucky. "Papa, I...I don't know what—"

"Save it. We'll talk in the morning while I'm watching *you* mop up this mess." His father nodded toward the collection flask opposite the room from them and pushed his way past Ritzi. "At least this time we've got something to show for our trouble."

By the time Ritzi joined him, his father was already pipetting the eggplant-colored liquid in the collection flask onto a glass slide. The elder man placed the slide onto the stage of the microscope beside him and flipped on its lamp. "Let's have a look, shall we?" he said, pushing his glasses atop his forehead.

Ritzi looked on as the man squinted into the microscope's eyepiece. "Oh," he said twice, then three times as he twirled at its knobs, making Ritzi's heart sink lower each time.

Finally, his father backed away and reached up to take off his glasses with a trembling hand. He shook them toward Ritzi, opening and closing his mouth. Terror gripped Ritzi's mind, rendering him unable to speak, too. "I'll...I'll be in my study," his father said at length before he turned and stormed out of the shed.

Of course, Papa. Where you go to drink. And to cry.

Ritzi slid out of his lab coat and stepped over to the microscope. He peered through the microscope's eyepiece and twiddled at its focus knobs, gasping as Alex's treated sample came into view. Ritzi stared with macabre fascination at one cellular structure there then another, finding them all curiously more formed than his mind's eye had pictured. Exposure to great temperature and pressure provided a glimpse into outcomes of the aging process on his kind's unique physiology. Their father had pioneered such a protocol to help determine individual drug regimens for him and his sister, whose byproducts now told a much more horrifying story: *Alex's body is breaking down.*

He slid the slide back and forth on the microscope's stage, desperate to find the smooth and normal-looking cell walls that might refute his original conclusion. Such structures from a test subject—Alex in this case—processed thusly would show a little bit of "prickling," as he and his father had come to call it. But before his eyes now were cells whose features resembled the quills of a porcupine. Sharp. Irregular. Irrevocably damaged. And certain to self-destruct.

Ritzi's breathing became shallow, his pulse raced. Red haze percolated at the edge of his vision like a pot full of water boiling. He burst from the shed, tossing off his shoes and socks and shirt as he dashed toward the tree line. His skin itched from head to toe as fur burst forth from every follicle.

When Ritzi reached the chain link fence, he drew in his breath and sprang. After coming to rest atop the thick limb of a massive beech tree, he dug the claws on one hand deep into the bark below his feet to steady himself. He sniffed at the night air and listened, whiskers twitching as he glanced down toward the yards of his father's neighbors. No dogs barking, no people talking, neither anyone nor anything appeared to have noticed him. Good.

He pulled his claws free one by one and tugged at the waistband of his trousers. Ritzi scanned the forest preserve's expanse in front of him for several moments until a hare's scent captured his attention. A primal yowl escaped Ritzi's throat as he bounded off into the darkness, seeing only red.

Chapter Seven

Chicago, Illinois. That same evening.

P AWLY STEPPED THROUGH THE locker room door and took a deep breath. The scent of the ice mixed with Zamboni exhaust and a trace of ammonia purged the stink of sweat and mildew still clinging to her clothes. The rink in their new neighborhood was small, the air inside stale and the girls' locker room still featured urinals.

But none of that mattered. Pawly couldn't help but smile, having so missed being on the ice. Missed the exhilarating feeling of air billowing through her hair as she lapped the rink during her warmup. Missed swatting about that little rubber puck to poke around a goalie's perimeter, searching for an opening.

For the first time in weeks, she felt *normal* again.

It wouldn't last, she knew. Her parents had lectured her and Tommy both on how their lives would never be the same again. Over and over again in the moving van, all the way to Chicago. How no one chose their Affliction. How it had chosen her and her brother. Despite their family's best efforts to ward it away.

That wasn't going to stop Pawly from trying to live her life again in whatever small ways she could. Her Uncle Ritzi had given to her and Tommy and their parents several long and detailed explanations regarding what things were likely to trigger their rage. Her parents had weighed the risks of blood on the ice versus the concentration she and her brother needed in order to play well, requiring them to focus their consciousness much like her mother and uncle's ancestors had. Much like she had tonight, in fact, together with some other talented girls. Maybe she could help pull together another championship team in time for the spring invitationals. Wouldn't Lana be surprised!

Skates screeched across the ice to Pawly's left. She turned to see two of her brother's fellow team hopefuls push off and hustle the puck between them as they bore down on the net. Tommy crouched in the crease, stone-still, watching. Just like the ambush predators which lynx were known to be.

Her brother's calm demeanor made Pawly grind her teeth. His change had affected him in ways he wouldn't talk about even to *her*, his closest confidant. By outward appearances he seemed to take everything in stride. Maybe he actually looked forward to changing into a *Khajiit*? Neither their uncle nor their Grandpa N knew for sure what other ways his Affliction might manifest itself. Which pissed off their dad every time anyone brought it up.

The player with the puck drew close to Tommy and swung hard toward the net. Tommy's head bobbed up and down before his opponent hatchet-chopped the ice and flipped the puck toward his teammate with the back face of his stick.

Pawly followed the black blur after the other guy whaled the puck toward the wide-open net behind Tommy. And right into his mitt.

Such a well-played feint would have thrown even an NHL starting goaltender for a loop. Tommy's reputation as "The Stick Magnet" preceded him. He had been a solid player before, and had brought his A-game along to tryouts. Certainly, he would exploit his Affliction to angle for a hockey scholarship. That way, he could spend his summers cosplaying at gamer geek conventions instead of standing watch on NROTC sea duty. Maybe he'd turn pro and make a career out of it.

A high-pitched whistle to her right gave Pawly a start. She turned to find a tan-skinned girl with long, black hair standing beside the bleachers, fingers jammed into the corners of her mouth. "Great setup, Michael. But you'd better up your game, Caesar. New goalie's on to your tricks already!" A wide grin broke across her face while she waved an arm over her head toward the players on the ice.

Another whistle sounded, this one from the boys' coach. "What she said, chowderheads." He cast the girl a knowing wink and pointed toward Tommy and the two boys circling the net. "All right, you three can come back next week. Now get showered and get scarce so I can lock up. It's getting late and we were over on our light bill last month."

The three boys whooped and high-fived one another. One shoved off toward the bench afterward while the other two pulled off their helmets and wiped their faces with their sweater sleeves. Tommy and his new bronze-faced teammate turned and waved toward Pawly and the other girl.

"Do you play?" Pawly asked.

The other girl's mane wagged back and forth as she shook her head. "Oh, no. No no, not me," she said and jerked her thumb toward the two boys. "The dark-haired guy is my step-brother, Caesar." The girl reached out to Pawly and smiled. "And my name is Salvación. Friends call me Sally."

"Pawly. Pawly Katczynski. My family and I just moved here from Virginia," she replied and gave Sally's hand a firm shake. "Coach seemed to take notice of your interest. Do you enjoy watching the games?"

"Oh, yes, I do. Don't get to see much from the concession stand, though." Sally picked up a cardboard box sitting on the bleachers next to her. "I help restock on practice nights because I'm stuck here until my mom comes to pick up Caesar and me. But now and again I take a break to catch some action." Her gaze followed Tommy as he and Caesar hopped over the threshold and disappeared into the locker room. "And, you know, take in the scenery," she said with a nod in Tommy's direction. "Like our new goalie."

Pawly snorted. "*That* dork? I've been stuck sharing a bathroom with him ever since he finally figured out how to use the potty." She chuckled and crossed her arms over her chest. "Your red-haired Romeo there is Tommy. My twin brother."

Sally's eyes went wide. "Oh, I *thought* I recognized you two from school! You're both new at St. Connie's, right? Your great uncle's barge slip is right next door to my stepdad's machinery business." She cast her gaze downward and shook her head. "Told him last month how your dad lost an eye in combat." Sally looked back up at Pawly. "Is...is he gonna be okay?"

"Yeah, he should be," Pawly replied with a wan smile.

Sally shifted her grip on the box in her arms. "My stepdad was Navy, too, but I'm glad his enlistment ran out long before he met my mom. I can't imagine what it's like to leave behind your school and neighborhood and all your friends to move halfway across the country."

"It's not that bad, really," Pawly said with a shrug. "Dad's gonna start training recruits at Great Lakes, so Tommy and I expect we'll be at St. Connie's now until we graduate. Many Navy families move a lot more than we have."

"Are you all settled in? I'm sure I could get Mom and Caesar and Caesar's dad to help me help you guys—"

"Nice of you to offer, but I think we're set. We're just getting to know the neighborhood, though. Our parents both grew up here, but Tommy and I are still learning our way around."

"Say, I've got a few hours of studying to get in this weekend but I'm otherwise free," Sally said and strode off toward the concession stand. "Why don't you come over to my house Saturday night? We can make our own pizzas and put on a scary movie and, oh!—I can dig out last year's yearbook. To give you the run down on the good-looking guys."

Though Pawly had known Sally for not even five minutes, the girl had already put her at ease. And she wouldn't at all mind their spending more time together. "Thank you. I'd...I'd like that."

"So!" Sally said over her shoulder. "Welcome to Jefferson Park, then!"

CHAPTER EIGHT

SZCZECIN, POLAND. DAYS LATER.

RITZI FLIPPED OFF THE patio light and began to count. At thirty he opened the back door of his father's rented house and stuck his head out. He sniffed at the night air, whiskers twitching as he glanced to his left and his right. The neighbors' backyards were empty, all their lights dark.

He drew in his breath and launched himself toward the now familiar beech tree limb. Once beyond the chain link fence, safe within the canopy, he turned back toward the house and listened. Nothing was moving; his father's bedroom window remained dark. Having seen the bags below his father's eyes before he marched past the kitchen and on straight up to bed, Ritzi believed his father would surely remain there until morning. He had put their take-out venison stew with dumplings away in the fridge without taking a single bite.

Forgive me, Papa. I hunger for something fresher.

He worked his claws free and pulled up the zipper on his trisuit. After turning back toward the forest preserve's expanse before him, Ritzi's senses soon registered a doe's scent. Followed by the snap of a dry twig.

Ritzi yielded to his animal instincts with practiced ease, giving them just enough reign to put him on the doe's trail. He had already eyed the fool thing before it looked up from its foraging and took off, its white tail erect. Two bounds later, Ritzi had already closed the distance between them.

He darted left and the deer darted right. The claws on his feet ripped curls of bark from the tree as he circled back. Intoxicating scents of blood and fear required him swallow lest he begin to drool. Though he hardly felt the dull ache in his leg muscles, Ritzi knew they would hurt like hell come morning. It was a discomfort he would gladly endure—a fix like this would last him weeks. Well and good, for he had no idea when he might feel comfortable enough with his work's progress to indulge himself again.

Within seconds Ritzi had caught up to the beast. He sprinted alongside as the doe ducked and weaved through the underbrush trying to shake him. His arms drew around the front and back of the thing's head. One squeeze would give him leverage enough to plunge his fangs into its neck and tear it wide open, assuring a quick and minimally painful kill.

But with a twist of its head, the damn thing ducked beneath his forearm and bounded away. Off-balance, Ritzi clipped a low-hanging branch and planted his face into the rocky ground, tumbling end over end several times before rolling to a stop. Cursing under his breath, Ritzi sprang to his feet and sniffed toward where he heard the crazed animal darting wildly through the trees toward the edge of the park.

Instead Ritzi got a snootful of a different scent altogether. But not an unfamiliar one—he recognized the same musky, masculine scent he had noticed before zoning out in his father's lab days before. Undaunted, Ritzi shook his head and dashed off after the deer. Before he could hit his stride, a grotesque, gurgling cry echoed off the trees all around him. Crossing his arms over his eyes he plunged into a patch of tangled briars, emerging afterward into a small glade surrounded by lush evergreens. In the grassy knoll beyond lay the doe, unmoving, a growing puddle of blood forming around a gaping hole in its neck ahead of the shoulder blades.

Beside the doe's head knelt a man, covered in fur and sporting a long, scraggly beard. He was otherwise naked except for a *mawashi* wrapped around his loins like a *sumo* wrestler. Blood dripped from the ruff below his chin as he fished one hand around inside the beast's chest. After a moment the man's muzzle broke into a fanged grin. With a grunt he pulled the deer's heart free from its chest then tore off a hunk with his teeth. "Come," he said between bites, holding what was left of the heart out in front of him. "Join me."

Ritzi reached out and took the heart into his shaking hand. Exhilarating sensations racked his body from chest to groin as he stuffed the still quivering organ into his mouth. He ripped off a piece and swallowed, letting the familiar and loathsome feeling of primal fulfillment consume him.

"You needing more than I, yes?"

He cast a blank look up toward his *de facto* host, still too stunned to speak.

"Have rest, then," the other man said with a wave. "I take other parts of animal. Yes."

Instinct trumped resolve. In not even two bites Ritzi devoured the rest of the heart. When he looked up again, he found the fellow poking at the fur on his wrist.

A ringing phone sound preceded a male voice answering in Russian. The man replied in kind as he preened the long hair beneath his jowls with his other hand. After a moment's conversation, he poked at his wrist again, affording Ritzi a glimpse of his watch. A childhood memory flashed through his mind, straight out of a *Get Smart* TV rerun, in which Agent 86 called in to CONTROL using a watch phone just like this one.

"My driver comes. Join me for a drink?" he said between bites, or so Ritzi thought from what he could piece together from the man's old school Belarusian.

"N...no, thank you. I needed to blow off some steam just now. But I should get back to my father soon."

Then the man knelt beside Ritzi and resumed ripping into the deer carcass. After picking the deer's ribs clean, his host sat back and smiled. "Another time, then. An honor to at last meet all the same, *Pan* Stupek," he said and extended his hand. "A doctor these days, yes?"

Ritzi's eyes shot open. It had been decades since his clan's slaughter, decades since he and his sister had abandoned their family name. And even longer since he had encountered any of the Forest Clan, having thought by now they surely had all dispersed or died out. "I...I go by 'Opoworo' now," he replied in a quavering voice before returning the man's gesture. "Doctor Maurycy Opoworo."

"'Blaznikov' you may call me, *Panie Doktorze*," the man said as he took Ritzi's hand in his and squeezed.

CHAPTER NINE

CHICAGO, ILLINOIS. THAT EVENING.

PAWLY STOOD BEFORE ONE of the photo plaques anchored to the cinder block wall opposite the ice rink's concession stand, a cold bottle of Coke in each hand. Framed by peeling paint, the picture featured a younger Caesar sporting the banner of Ruiz Equipment Sales across the front of his sweater. Sally had explained a moment before how her stepfather's used machinery outfit began sponsoring a Pee Wee league several years ago to drum up business.

Too bad, Pawly mulled as she awaited her new friend's return from the storage container in the alleyway, that the girl believed herself too curvy and too clumsy to play hockey. A bit of conditioning for her lats, some drills to develop her coordination, some cardio to build up endurance—Sally would make an awesome blueliner. Pawly resolved to work with her on that.

She stared up at the clock on the wall opposite the concession stand counter and sighed. Tommy had been fifteen minutes already in the locker room. His coach had called after them while they shuffled off to the showers that he wanted to lock up right away, so what was taking him so long? Bonding with his new teammates over locker room talk?

Any morning at their house before school and he would have been pounding on the bathroom door by now.

The alleyway door at the rear of the concessions area creaked open and banged up against its stop. "Sorry to keep you waiting, Sal," Pawly said as she turned away from the wall clock. "Who knows what's keeping that dork brother of mine. Could you please put this other soda back in the fridge when you get a sec?"

But the only reply Pawly received was from a rickety ceiling-mounted heating unit as it started up with a shriek. She made a face at the thing then set the bottles down on the counter in front of her. "Sally? You there?" she said and wiggled her arm free from her hockey bag's strap. After sliding her bag up against the front of the concession stand with one foot, Pawly leaned across the counter. "Hello? Anyone?"

Her nose went up in flames. Or, at least, it *felt* like it had. Pawly's mother had taught her and Tommy to recognize that peculiar, sweet-and-sour smell, prickling at the inside of her nostrils as if she were trying to pick her nose with a bore brush.

Fear. Primal fear. *Prey* fear.

"N-no! Don't t-touch *mmphumphmm!*"

Pawly vaulted the counter and dashed past the hot dog roller and popcorn popper. She burst through the open doorway into the alley to find the storage container's open door swinging in the wind. Beyond the container a pair of men trotted toward a black Chevy Camaro. Pawly glimpsed the hem of Sally's skirt visible below their knees. "The hell're you doing?" she called to the goons, far better dressed than average street punks.

Neither answered while one threw open their car door. Pawly glimpsed Sally's wide eyes above the patch of duct tape covering her mouth when the other man stuffed her into the back seat.

Oh, hell no.

A *ki-ahp* and Pawly was airborne. In mid-air she thrust her heel toward one of the men before he could duck behind the car door. His collarbone gave way with a satisfying *snap* before the man collapsed into the car's passenger seat.

Smells of cigarette smoke and cheap aftershave overwhelmed Pawly, almost making her gag. The wounded man's partner lunged for her. She leapt back an instant too late. The man raked her chest with both hands after trying to bear-hug her.

Imma break *those hands, asshole!*

The man sprang to his feet and charged, both fists swinging. Muscles beneath his tailored suit contracted and relaxed in time with the tiny ripples cascading across the suit's fabric. Which to her, even in human form, advertised the man's every move like a flashing neon sign.

Pawly ducked beneath the sloppy haymaker he launched toward her head. She gripped the man's side and shoulders as hard as she could and heaved. Fabric tore before he slid across the hood of their car, leaving a trail of red behind him.

Bile welled up in the back of Pawly's throat when she glanced down at the pavement. Drops of blood dotted the pavement where the man had stood a moment before. She flexed her fingers open and closed and gasped. Moonlight glistened off the blood covering them.

And her claws.

Fuck!

Pawly pulled her hand inside the sleeve of her jacket and wrapped an arm around Sally's shoulder. "Nod if you can understand me!" she said after coaxing her new friend from the car. The girl's long black hair bobbed up and down while she muffled something from behind her makeshift gag. Pawly picked her up and stomped over to the wall.

"I'll be right back," she said after setting Sally down on the pavement. "I don't want these creeps to—"

The Camaro's engine roared to life. An instant later the car sped toward her, engine racing. She lunged forward into a long stride and pushed off the car's front bumper. She managed to stomp over the windshield and hardtop but tripped over the spoiler attached to the trunk lid. After stumbling to a stop short of the alley wall, she turned to see moonlight glinting off the car's gilded aluminum wheels as it tore around the corner and disappeared.

Tommy would surely have scented her angry pheromones by now, even from the locker room. As would any other werecat within four square blocks from what Pawly remembered their mother telling them. She bit her lip as red haze flooded her vision, a wave of panic washing over her. If her brother was on his way and bringing other people to help, she risked morphing into a furbaby right in front of them.

The alleyway door flew open and slammed up against the wall. Pawly made a fist with her claws and jammed it into her jacket pocket. "Hey, there they are!" came Tommy's voice as he darted out of the building. The twins' mother followed close behind, along with a man she didn't recognize sporting a Navy sailor's "Dixie Cup" atop his head.

The woman knelt beside Sally while the two young men held back a respectful distance. Pawly's friend screamed after their mother yanked the tape from her mouth. The girl cried and wheezed and carried on as she threw both arms around the woman's shoulders. Pawly let out a long exhale and the red haze retreated.

"You're safe now, dear. I'm Pawly's mom. And I'll get you back to yours right away," she cooed into Sally's ear and patted her back. "Can we go now? Or do you need a moment?"

The girl turned her head toward Pawly and sniffed. "I don't...I don't want to think about what might've happened had you not been here. Thank you." Then she worked her way free from their mother's embrace and stood. "I'm...I'm okay now," she said, wiping at the mascara running down her cheeks. "Let's go."

Mom and Sally walked past, arm in arm. "You two wait here with Jae-jueung," the woman said over her shoulder to the twins. "I'll take her inside then bring the car around."

Pawly turned to find Tommy glancing down to where she had pocketed her fist. His narrowed eyes confirmed Pawly's own suspicions—he had likely scented her and the blood both from inside the rink.

You okay?

Pawly nodded and drew her lips into a thin line. *For now. Dunno how long.*

Taking measured breaths as she stared down at her feet helped Pawly center herself, just enough to take the edge off. At length the sandy-skinned stranger broke the uneasy silence. "Sorry for my brother's heavy-handedness," he said as he unbuttoned his pea coat to reveal an enlisted Navy sailor's uniform beneath. "My family felt it necessary to vet your and your brother's capabilities. But I strongly doubt Father will approve when he hears of Myung-Duk's heavy-handed tactics." He pulled off his Dixie Cup and ran a hand through his jet-black hair, cut to regulation length. "When your mom gets back, I was planning to sit all of you down to discuss what the rest of us had in mind."

"Yeah," Tommy added. "J.J. here told Mom he'd treat us all to a soda."

Mention of the sailor's nickname jogged her memory back to the last time she and her brother had seen Jae-jueung. The summer before the twins entered junior high, her brother teasing her for crushing on

J.J. all the while. Now here was J.J. again. And he had...grown. Grown *handsome*, in fact. The sailor's uniform only served to make him all that much more devastatingly dashing.

"Oh, okay," she said, feeling the heat on her face and neck creep toward her hairline. "Hey, were you all working that out while I was standing there waiting by the—"

A sharp pain lanced through Pawly's stomach. Without thinking she yanked her hand from her pocket and clutched at her abdomen. She flinched with a yelp after her claws poked through her clothes and into her skin. A glance up at J.J. revealed neither fear nor loathing on his features as he beheld her monstrous appendages. Instead, she found empathy. Acceptance. At least until the red haze blotted out his face like the moon did the sun during an eclipse. She had to go. Now.

Without a word, Pawly turned on her heel and tore off down the alleyway. Rounding the corner, she vaulted the brick wall and bounded off across the grounds of the neighboring park. She leapt up onto the lowest branch of a large elm and sank her claws deep into its bark, right before the scent of a nearby squirrel made her visions of red fade to black.

CHAPTER TEN

SZCZECIN, POLAND. THE FOLLOWING MORNING.

RITZI'S HAND DREW TO his forehead to shield his eyes from the sun while he pulled the kitchen door closed. Residual lack of sleep and stress had resulted in an uneven shed following last night's hunt. Ritzi had decided he needed to wax, in fact, before chancing a return to polite society. The stiff breeze took his breath away when the angry skin on his face and neck flared up in protest.

"Didn't expect *you* up yet, young man!"

He started and the screen door handle slipped from his hand. His father stood at the end of the walk beside the corner of the house, one eyebrow cocked.

"Papa, I...I didn't—"

The screen door slamming shut cut Ritzi off. He licked his lips and tried again. "I didn't hear you about. I thought you were sleeping still."

"I had just crawled back into bed after a trip to the bathroom when I heard you come in last night. Decided to take my morning tea with the neighbors so you could rest." His father held up both hands to show off a clump of wilting chives and a bunch of long black radishes. "After mentioning my son was here visiting from the States, they insisted I take these for our breakfast. Help me put together some *kanapki*?"

"Uhm, thanks, Papa, but no. I'm on my way into town to meet, ah...someone."

His father's eyes went wide for a moment before the corners of his mouth turned up into a sly grin. "Is that why you've been sneaking down the hall to Anthropology whenever we're on campus? Oh, never mind, not my place to pry." He gathered the herbs and vegetables into one hand then nodded toward the sidewalk. "Off with you, then. Just don't make any evening plans. Tonight will be a late one as it is if we're to keep to schedule. But I can handle things tomorrow by myself if you might be, you know. Busy."

Ritzi had only ever allowed himself a handful of dates, the last one years ago. None, he remembered, had knotted up his insides nearly as tight as they felt in that moment.

Forty minutes later, Ritzi sat on a city bus, his insides knotted up for a completely different reason. Tardiness on the part of others irritated him, so Ritzi took pains to avoid being late himself. But his hasty trip to Szczecin's center had failed to account for the myriad pieces of construction equipment lining *Obrońców Stalingradu* on both sides.

By the time he spotted addresses above the storefronts again the bus had already overshot his destination by two blocks. Ritzi yanked on the pull cord and focused on his breathing while the bus shuddered to a stop. His mother had trained him and Alex both in her technique nearly every day since arriving in America decades before—inhale through the nose and exhale through bared teeth, keeping the jaw set. The guy standing in front of the bus's back door took one look at Ritzi's face and couldn't get out of the way fast enough.

After the bus rumbled away, Ritzi spied "9:55" in red pixels marching across the sign above a bank's storefront. He pulled out his cell phone and scrolled back through his text message history. Past a flurry of messages back and forth to his father and sister and brother, he found the one he was looking for.

Arrive Lotnikow Square 1000. Text then.

Ritzi jogged the two blocks back to the square, cursing under his breath all the while. Upon his arrival he groaned and clasped his knees, focusing on his exaggerated breaths *iiiiiiiin* and *ouuuuuuut*. After composing himself, he tapped out a reply in Polish on his cell phone:

Here now. Where are you?

The thing chimed within seconds after Ritzi pressed the SEND button. He squinted at the number, recognizable by its unrecognizability, just as Blaznikov had told him to expect before they parted company the previous night. Each text Ritzi would ever receive from him would come from a different number. Frequently from a different country.

Obiecianki - cacanki

"'*Eggs and oaths are soon broken*'?" Ritzi muttered while he scanned the storefronts surrounding the square. "Just what the hell is that supposed to...?"

His gaze fell upon "*Złamane Jajko*" in red neon, flashing on and off above the lintel of one of the storefronts. *"The Broken Egg." Of course.*

He pocketed his cell phone and strode off across the square toward the restaurant. The smell of hard-boiled eggs and fresh baked bread tumbled out at Ritzi a moment later after he pulled open the restaurant door. Pangs of hunger stabbed at his insides as he shuffled up to the hostess station. A large clock hung beside the grill on the far wall, its big hand halfway between twelve and one.

"*Panie Doktorze,*" came a loud voice. Ritzi's gaze followed it to where a man waved from a corner booth. His bushy graying hair and long, scraggly beard made him resemble an aging Rasputin. Despite having never seen Blaznikov in his human form before, Ritzi couldn't help but recognize the man's mirthful, penetrating gaze.

His host motioned for Ritzi to take a seat on the bench across from him as he approached. "Forgive my being late, *Spadar* Blaznikov," Ritzi said in a low voice and sat down.

The elder man shrugged and went back to slathering what looked like watered-down raspberry jam atop a round crepe-like pastry. To Ritzi they resembled *naleśniki* in a bakery storefront window along Milwaukee Avenue from his old neighborhood. But these were smaller, thicker and darker.

"You will enjoy *syrniki*," Blaznikov said between bites while Ritzi flopped a short stack of the cheese-filled crepes onto the plate in front of him. "Have what you like. *Varenye*?"

His stomach answered for him while his host slid the bowl of preserves across the table. "Oh, thank you," Ritzi said and scooped up a heaping spoonful of the red syrupy fruit.

"You will need something to wash it down, yes." Blaznikov picked up the iron teapot at the end of their table and filled Ritzi's cup. "Tell me, is brother-in-law recovering well from his injuries?"

Ritzi's throat muscles clenched around the mouthful of raspberry-drenched crepe he was trying to swallow.

How the hell would he *know...?*

Feeling his first bite coming back up, Ritzi clamped a hand over his mouth. Blaznikov said nothing while Ritzi launched into a coughing jag, finally managing to swallow in between cautious sips of piping hot tea. "Y-you know him?" he croaked at length.

"We have met. During Korean operation, yes, together with American SEAL team."

Ritzi patted at his lips with his napkin, cleaving unto whatever dignity he had left. "I don't remember him ever mentioning you."

"Befitting one of his security clearance, no? Though never came an opportunity I could reveal true nature in confidence. But that is not for why I seek you." Blaznikov set one elbow atop the table and rested his chin on his fist. "I must speak about your sister. And her children. About our, oh, how might you say? Our...*condition*. Yes."

Ritzi slammed his empty tea cup down on its saucer and leaned forward across the table. "*Spadar* Blaznikov," he said in a hoarse whisper, "I hardly think this is the time or the place—"

"You worry too much." Blaznikov refilled Ritzi's cup and cast a nonchalant glance around to the diners seated at their neighboring tables. "No one here pays us any attention. If they did? I would know."

Ritzi settled back into his seat, pining for a refill of a much stronger variety while the implications of the elder man's statements turned in his mind. Talents afforded him and Alex by their Kindred heritage manifested in different ways. His premonitions enabled him to help their father implement methods to delay their bodies' imminent breakdown, continuing the research his father had begun years before. With hers, Alex could tell whether someone was lying even before they opened their mouth. That Blaznikov was speaking of his own Talents in literal rather than metaphorical terms was concerningly plausible.

"Picked out your sister's scent from your brother-in-law," he went on. "Business brought me to Szczecin; primal urges brought me to the woods behind your father's house. Good fortune brought me there just as you and he were working. Where I recognize her scent. And two others, yes? Your nephew and niece."

Ritzi gawked, fork and knife lost in his hands. From what he remembered of his grandfather's tales growing up, none of Blaznikov's Forest Clan kinsmen had ever denied their Affliction's bloodlust its due. He had once told Ritzi, without Alex around to hear, how bloody schisms among Kindred whether to kill humans had driven his parents to take him and flee in the first place. Better than a third of Białowieża's Kindred left their native forest for the isolation of the high seas—safe until the Soviets massacred them.

But Ritzi understood the man sitting across from him might this very moment be the missing link he had been searching for to help Alex and the twins. If other werecats from his family's genus were indeed still alive and well...

His host said nothing, fixing him with an unsettling stare as he slowly sipped at his tea. "I don't suppose your interest in my family is merely intellectual," Ritzi said at length. He gulped down one piece of *syrniki* after another, hoping that by filling his stomach with something besides acid it would settle down. "What do you...need from...me?" he asked between mouthfuls.

Blaznikov set his cup aside. "Your mind," he replied, raising a finger to his temple. "I know of your research with your father. Americans deport him to Poland, then you lose your lab in Chicago. I can help." He paused and crossed his arms. "Gaining resources comes at a price, yes. I have made many enemies through the years, you see. Needs must always be discreet, so."

Ritzi stared down at his half-empty plate in silence. His father had been there when Ritzi administered the *in vitro* treatments to Alex himself, there as he hugged and cried with Barry after sharing their good news—his children would never suffer under the Affliction like their mother and Ritzi had.

But then they did.

He started as someone grabbed his hand. "Halflings, your niece and nephew, yes? I saw the scars on their father's back. From your sister, for sure," Blaznikov said, the corners of his mouth turning up. "Impressive. Not many human men could survive long taking one of our women for a lover. Tough guy, him. But this bodes well or bodes ill for their children? You do not know. No one knows."

Ritzi's mouth flapped open and shut, but no words came out.

"Let me help you help them," Blaznikov said after a long moment, giving Ritzi's hand a squeeze. "You have science. I have money. And facilities. Let us each benefit the other with what he has." With his free hand, Blaznikov slid what appeared to be a business card face down across the table toward Ritzi. "Contact the proprietor here after you return to America. He will make arrangements, yes. Tell no one."

Ritzi picked up the card and turned it over, taking notice of the bold block letters in English on one side and in Korean on the other. They spelled out the name and contact information of a grocery store proprietor in Albany Park, located not far from his old neighborhood. "What does this fellow have to do with—?"

The musical ringtone from Ritzi's cell cut him off. "My apologies, *Spadar* Blaznikov. I need to take this."

The elder man nodded and took a sip of his tea. Ritzi stood up and stepped over to the lunch counter while hurriedly fishing his cell phone out of his pocket. "*Eomeonim*, what's wrong?" he said after a glance up at the oversized wall clock. "It has to be past three in the morning where you are."

"It is. Give me the combination for the padlock on your sample freezer and I shall go."

Ritzi cupped his hand over his phone's mouthpiece. "What? Why? What happened?"

"Later I will explain. Need more catalyzation proteins to inject Alex with."

Ritzi knit his brow. "But she just *had* a treatment before I left. She won't be due again until—"

"Overexerted herself chasing Pawly down. Raged after Noh Myung-Duk and one of his *kkangpae* accosted Pawly's new friend at the skating rink. Now please, the numbers?"

He blurted out the combination, which his mother repeated number by number as she spun the dial.

"Thank you," she said after he heard the lock pop open. "Alex will be okay. I shall see to it. More talking soon."

His phone beeped after she terminated the call. Ritzi pulled the thing away from his ear and glanced over toward the booth he had been sharing with Blaznikov.

It was empty.

In three strides he stood beside their table again, finding only a pile of *złoty* notes lying atop their table beside the Korean grocer's business card. An engine revved on the other side of the wall an instant before Ritzi glimpsed a silver town car with tinted windows zipping past the restaurant's corner window. The car's rear window rolled down while the driver waited for traffic to clear. There sat Blaznikov, pointing to his eyes with his index and middle fingers before stabbing them toward Ritzi.

"I will be watching you."

The driver spotted an opening. With a squeal of tires, the car blasted out of the alleyway and sped off down the street.

Ritzi stuffed his cell phone and the business card into his pocket. Then, avoiding eye contact with everyone, he shuffled out of the restaurant. Once outside the chilly air bit at his nose, causing him to hunch his shoulders by reflex. He sighed and strode off at a brisk pace, opposite the way he had come, toward the nearest bus stop.

He entered the empty shelter and sat down beside the remains of yesterday's newspaper. Leafing through the tattered pages, Ritzi couldn't help but think of Alex. For a time after their arrival in the

States before their father secured tenure at Loyola, his little sister had been the family breadwinner. Their mother's Korean underworld contacts had highly sought after Alex's Talents, after all. Now his family needed to rely on the Noh family *jopok* and the *kkangpae* working for them again. Or did they? What could Blaznikov offer him and his family that they couldn't?

And, more importantly, what would it *cost* them?

A low rumble announced the city bus's arrival. Ritzi stepped aboard after the thing clattered to a stop and plunked down into a pair of empty seats several rows behind the driver. He drew the business card from his pocket after the bus pulled away from the curb and stared at it. Bouncing along the potholed streets between him and his father's house, Ritzi mulled how Faust must have felt after first laying eyes on Gretchen.

Chapter Eleven

Door County, Wisconsin. Day after Thanksgiving.

PAWLY RAISED HER HEAD and sniffed at the air. As her family's long holiday weekend progressed, she had gotten better at scenting prey on the remote islands near their cabin. Relentless training from her mother and grandmother in the weeks following her first transformation had helped restrain her rage. But it was every bit a part of her as her predator's instinct, as the red haze swirling around the perimeter of her vision reminded her. And it would not be denied its due. To sate it, she would hunt. Because she feared for what she might do if she did not.

That would, however, require her to kill something. And that required her to actually *catch* something first. She cursed herself, having torn through the underbrush in her haste. Turkeys now trotted away in all directions across the clearing, none in any particular hurry. Their clucks and cackles mocking her, surely.

With a snarl, she took off after one that lagged behind the others. It darted its head left and right around the base of an oak tree upon reaching the clearing's edge, as if unsure which way to go next. Pawly leapt, fangs bared, ready to tear the thing's head off at the neck. But instead, she plowed headlong into the tree's decidedly solid trunk.

Fuck, that hurt!

Pawly rubbed the sides of her head with both hands. She blinked away stars and tears until a strained cry mewed forth from her mouth. Snow crunched underfoot nearby as Tommy bounded across the clearing toward her, his footfalls sounding to her enhanced hearing like a herd of stampeding cattle. She clenched her jaw shut and wiped her forearm across her eyes, her pride not about to allow her brother to catch her crying.

The wind matted Tommy's gray and white fur to his face as he approached, dropping to one knee several yards away. He fixed Pawly with wild eyes, not looking at her so much as *past* her. To her left.

Red haze obscured Pawly's vision once again, responding to her brother's low growl. She dashed into the bush and caught the turkey's panicked stink, instantly sending drool dribbling down her chops. Tommy followed turn for turn as she tore off after the bird, weaving around rocks, trees and decaying logs.

Tommy's directions coming in grunts and growls, Pawly homed in on her target like one of the laser-guided shipborne missiles their Dad had told them about. Though she would have had no idea how not to comply if she had desired to ignore his urging. By instinct, she knew which way to turn, how fast to run. The euphoric tingling consumed her once again, but this time she remained conscious. Present. In the moment. And she delighted in it.

Pawly drew her arms over her eyes the instant before she barreled through a bramble bush. In the next she swiped at the air in front of her with both hands and snared the bird. Her claws sank deep into its flesh, tearing it in two as she collapsed to the ground.

Tommy yowled and pounced on the bird's top half after it fell from Pawly's grasp. He tore the bird's throat out with one savage bite, with two more he had its chest cracked open. But before he could go for a third, he tumbled into a nearby thicket and disappeared. Then came a loud *thud* followed by Tommy's pained cry.

Pawly turned back to find their mother stooped over the part of the bird her brother had let slip from his hands. The older woman *tsk*ed and thrust her hand into the bird's carcass. A moment later she stood and held her fist out to Pawly. "Here. Take a bite." A slimy lump fell from her mother's fingers, blood spattering as it landed in Pawly's cupped hands. "Go on."

She made a face and picked up the still-quivering heart between her thumb and forefinger. Two inches from her nose, everything went red. Pawly sank her teeth into the heart an instant before her face slammed into the snowy ground.

"I said to take a *bite*, dear, not to try and scarf down the whole thing. Your brother needs to...oh, never mind. Just watch and learn."

A moment later her spinning world slowed enough for Pawly to sink her claws into the bark of a nearby tree and pull herself upright. Her mother hauled Tommy to his feet by the neck of his trisuit and hand fed him what was left of the heart. The change was almost instantaneous. Tension drained from his face like water down a shower drain. Pawly's hackles lowered until the sound of footsteps approaching put her on high alert once more.

"It's okay," her mother said as she reached down and picked up what remained of the turkey's carcass. "Turn to your right and take a whiff."

Pawly did as asked while her mother sucked the meat from the turkey's bones. A faint scent like the hyenas she remembered from last summer's trip to the Brookfield Zoo grew stronger before their uncle parted the brush across from them. "What...what happened?" he said between gasps.

"You were supposed to be watching Tommy, right?" She belched and tossed the newly cleaned bones over her shoulder into the underbrush. "So, you tell me, Ritzi. Did stuffing yourself day and night at Papa's house finally catch up to you?"

He shot the twins' mother a look while the whiskers on either side of his nose twitched. "I didn't want to be rude, Alex. And I was hungry, okay?"

Mom stepped over to the remaining half of the dead turkey and chucked it toward their uncle. "Fine, you can have the rest," she said in a singsong voice.

Ritzi caught the turkey in one paw and shot her a look. "How do you feel?" he said, sliding up beside her brother and putting his free arm around his shoulder. "Are you all right?"

Tommy rubbed at his face and shook his head. "I...I guess so. I don't recall much before Mom fed me that...whatever it was just now. Something warm and slimy."

"What's the last thing you *do* remember?" their uncle asked before taking a big bite out of the turkey's carcass.

"Well, I was trying to get back the scent of that deer we came along earlier." He raised his arm and pointed at Pawly. "But when we made it to the clearing, I got a snootful of the turkeys Sis and Mom were chasing. Then I saw red." He shook his head. "I don't know what happened after that."

Their mother clicked her tongue. "This isn't at all how it's supposed to work. Ritzi?"

Silence reigned, save for the sound of tiny bones snapping while their uncle chewed. "Papa said to expect stuff like this," he said at length before taking another bite.

"Expect stuff like *what* exactly?" their mother said and crossed her arms.

"Unexpected happenings. Behaviors we wouldn't immediately have an explanation for. Oddities we'd have to research further."

Pawly bit her lip. "You...you mean there's more?" she said and looked down at the gray fur covering the back of her hand. *Just when I thought it couldn't get any worse.*

"No, no." Their uncle examined the turkey stripped carcass for any remaining morsels of meat and, finding none, chucked it into the tall grass beside him. "I don't think the behaviors you two exhibited just now are necessarily bad," he said, taking Tommy and Pawly by their shoulders. "Alex, do you remember what Grandfather told us shortly before he died? About how the Affliction impacts siblings?"

Mom pursed her lips for a moment. "Something about how their strong bond manifests itself throughout their lives."

"Yes. And the closer the connection between them, the stronger the manifestations. Especially while hunting."

She clapped her hands to either side of her face. "Then the bond between twins like Pawly and Tommy ought to be strongest!"

Her uncle nodded. "Yes. But they first morphed well past when anyone would have expected them to. And they hadn't indulged their bloodlust before then, either. I can't say exactly how it would affect them."

"I felt like Tommy could see the prey I was chasing," Pawly said in a small voice. "And he could tell me exactly where to run and how fast."

Their mother reached over and tousled Tommy's hair. "That's just your Eyes of the Lynx coming into focus."

"True. But neither Papa nor I ever expected one sibling could use their Eyes to guide and direct the other." Their uncle leaned forward, gazing back and forth between Tommy and Pawly as he tugged at his ruff. "Then again, the twins have unique genes. Maybe I should head back to the boat so I can—"

"Oh, no no no. Pawly, Tommy, find your father on the beach and tell him we'll be along shortly." Their mother leapt atop a snow-covered stump and breathed deep through her nose. "C'mon, Ritzi," she said a moment later, baring a toothy smile. "With the ice and weather as it is, I doubt we'll be back before spring. Besides, my fingers nearly went numb from gripping my seat all the way here from Pilot Island. I didn't come all this way to *not* take a kill!"

With a twinkle in her eye, she bounded off, kicking up a cloud of snow behind her. Their uncle regarded the twins with a shrug and followed.

Pawly crossed her arms and watched them go. After a moment her brother patted at her shoulder. "Gives me an idea, sis."

She knew that look. Like the time they ran out of ice melt and he suggested they douse the driveway in gasoline. And that *she* should strike the match. "To do what, exactly?"

"How we might show those creeps from the Noh family just what we think about their getting rough with Sally." He nodded in the direction of where their family's launch sat moored to its makeshift dock. "C'mon, I'll tell you on the way."

Chapter Twelve

Two sides of Ritzi's mind fought for control of his consciousness. One, his primal urges to track, to hunt, to kill. Just as his sister was doing this very moment.

But the scientist part of his mind informed him to note her movements, her affect, her scent. Alex's musk was especially strong, even overpowering the panicked stink of the deer they pursued every time she got upwind of him. Following their arrival in America, he had witnessed many of her transformations as their adoptive parents learned how to better contain them. He couldn't remember the last time Alex had behaved in such a feral manner. With how far she hunched forward, he wouldn't have been at all surprised for her to try to run on all fours.

She yowled and leapt for the canopy. Bounding limb to limb after the panicked deer, Alex managed to work it toward the cleft of a rock face near the middle of the island. Before she could corner the thing, it broke left and sprinted alongside the rock. Which, he quickly realized, was exactly what Alex had wanted it to do. She whirled around in mid-air and pushed off against the rock face, launching herself like a missile toward her doomed prey.

His predator's mind asserted its will after Alex ripped the buck's throat wide open with her fangs. The thing's death throes goaded Ritzi forward after the doe, ducking and weaving around trees and rocks as he gave chase. He might have lost the deer in the thicket had it not turned and bolted toward the shoreline. Before long the forest floor's soft earth gave way to rocky beach. The exhausted doe's hooves flailed about, trying to find purchase, giving Ritzi the opening he needed. He leapt up and pushed off a low-hanging branch to launch himself toward the doe's back.

At the last second, he thrust out his arms and sunk his claws deep into its neck. He drove his heels into the rock below his feet and curled his body around the doe's trunk. An instant later he lay atop the dying doe as blood gushed from the hole in its throat. It let out a final mournful bleat then laid still.

A shadow fell all around him an instant before pain exploded across his back. For a brief moment he was airborne until he crashed into the choppy Lake Michigan surf headfirst. Frigid water bit at the skin beneath his down fur like an enormous school of microscopic piranha.

Ritzi righted himself and pushed off with his legs, driving the sharp rocks lining the lake bottom deep into the tender skin between his paw pads. He broke the water's surface with a ragged gasp and whirled about to get his bearings. Another breaker swept his feet out from under him. He fell forward into the water face-first. With his claws he managed to pull himself along the bottom into shallower water. The howling wind took his breath away as he stood, his soaked pelt and trisuit offering little protection from the stabbing cold.

Blaznikov sat on the shore next to the doe's eviscerated carcass, chewing. "Thank you," he said as he held what remained of the thing's heart up to his mouth and tore off a hunk. "For being such a good host," he said around a mouthful.

Ritzi rubbed at his biceps and glared at the other man. "What...what are *you* doing *here*?"

"You return to America over two weeks ago, *Panie Doktorze*. Have yet to call Jin Bak at the grocery in Albany Park. So, I wanted to check in. Vet the twins' skills. Being them 'late bloomers,' yes."

"Wait. You *saw* them hunt?"

"If that is what you call it," Blaznikov said with a laugh and clasped Ritzi on the shoulder. "Like newborn babes suckling at their mother's bosom. Helpless. Dependent on caregivers for everything." The elder man held out in his open palm with the remnant of the doe's heart in the center.

Ritzi took it and greedily gulped it down.

"You and your sister will soon wean them, yes? So, you could do without interruptions. I will be one no longer today." Without bothering to wipe the blood from his hand, Blaznikov drew his wrist up near his face and pinched at the sides of his watch. "Can only talk now because she is upwind of us, focused on her own kill. Pity, though. I would like to see more from you all. *Chłopiec* seems to see through his sister's eyes. An interesting development indeed, no?"

A roller crashed ashore a dozen yards up the rocky beach from them, followed by a metallic screech. Ritzi turned and gawked at the bow of a silver-gray cigarette boat. He turned back a moment later to find an empty spot where Blaznikov had been standing. He whirled around in time to see the man land on all fours atop the boat's deck fore of the windscreen. Water churned behind the thing as it slid back from the shore into deeper water. A hatch in the blackened cuddy cabin roof popped open and Blaznikov scrambled inside. Blaznikov faced Ritzi as the boat put out, pointing his index and middle fingers toward his eyes. After stabbing his finger toward Ritzi, he ducked into the cabin below and out of sight.

I will be watching you.

After turning into the choppy surf, the boat's pilot throttled up. The hatch cover closed an instant before the boat plunged headlong into a breaker and disappeared.

Ritzi drew his arms to his shoulders and shivered.

Chapter Thirteen

Chicago, Illinois. The following week.

"**W**hat's taking them so long?" Pawly whispered.

"Aw, pipe down, willya?" Tommy replied in kind. "It's not like we'll miss them or anything. Besides, you and I ought to see them long before J.J. is ready anyway."

Pawly leaned back against the trunk of the tree and hugged her arms to her chest. She slid up her sleeves and rubbed at her forearms, more out of boredom than anything. Despite the temperatures being below freezing already, she wasn't cold. Because, well, *fur*.

Tommy stepped down the length of the tree limb and out over the ski trail, one foot in front of the other with his arms out at his sides like a tightrope walker. His toe claws would keep his feet securely placed even without the steel wool they had both wound around the bottom strap of their spats.

Showoff.

Across the snow-covered trail, the twins' uncle crouched down atop a stout tree limb. He stared off into the distance, as if looking for something among the treetops. Her mother silently landed on the limb beside him a moment later.

Pawly gasped. *Where did* she *come from?*

Her uncle and mother shot her a cross look before turning their attention back to each other, muttering too low for even Pawly's advanced hearing to make out. Then came the voices of their classmates—talking, laughing, carrying on as the lot of them shuffled along on their skis. Loud enough that they were sure not to notice her, or so her and her family and J.J. all hoped.

Pawly pulled a pair of black leather driving gloves from her pocket. She thrust her hand inside and wiggled her fingers until, one by one, her claws emerged through the seam at each fingertip. After doing likewise with her other hand, a shrill *psst!* drew her attention back to Tommy.

His eyes were wide open, his eyebrows raised. *You ready?*

She glanced across the trail to find their mother crouched atop the same limb their uncle had been a moment before. Mom was alone; surely Uncle Ritzi had dashed off to tell J.J. that the skiers were in position and to make ready with the lights. Just as they had planned.

A Chicago Parks & Recreation Department part-timer before enlisting in the Navy, J.J. would be standing by beside the remote electrical panel awaiting word from the twins' uncle to kill the lights illuminating the trail. Tommy would guide her every move once darkness surrounded their classmates below. Together they would put their link and their Talents to the test, with J.J. observing them through a pair of night vision goggles,

Pawly turned and met her brother's gaze, her brow knit. *Yeah, I'm ready.*

With a twitch of his whiskers, Tommy turned toward a utility pole up the trail from them where they knew J.J. waited. He held his hand up high, waiting for the first of them to pass beneath.

She sprang the instant the muscles in J.J.'s arm went limp. By the time the lights went out, Pawly was already airborne over the trail. Thrusting out her legs, Pawly pushed off a gnarled old oak. Darkness concealed her acrobatics; hooting and hollering amongst themselves, surely none of her classmates would hear chunks of bark or patches of snow falling.

Pawly hit the ground running. She would need but mere seconds to complete her task. Even the few of her classmates who had thought to pack a flashlight would be unable to get theirs out in time to glimpse her. She twirled and twisted in among them, working her fingers into pockets and purses and packs as she passed. Between each one, Pawly dropped her loot with a flick of her wrist into a pair of dump pouches, one strapped to each hip.

By way of Tommy's grunts, groans, and growls—none loud enough for the other kids or their chaperones to hear—he directed her to the other side of the trail within a heartbeat's time.

She turned and sprinted back the way she came, moving through another rank of their classmates. She swept side to side across the trail until she had worked through them all. Sortie complete and satisfied none were the wiser, Pawly vaulted back into the canopy.

The lights came back up an instant after Tommy waved his arms above his head. Pawly landed near his perch and sank her claws into the trunk of the tree. She clicked her tongue in disapproval after following her brother's gaze straight to Bella Dropiewski's butt cleavage. Even a snooty, rich bitch like Bella didn't deserve her pig of a brother leering at her.

With a gasp, Tommy leapt back toward Pawly. The limb shook, dropping the snow covering a clump of leaves near the limb's tip onto the exposed skin above Bella's belt line. An ear-piercing squeal echoed through the forest a second later.

Certain the snowball now dripping down her ass crack had been courtesy of a certain male classmate, Bella scooped up a handful of snow and returned fire. The ball smacked Alan Driscoll square in the face, cutting him off mid-sentence. Within moments, bedlam ensued, snow flying everywhere.

Pawly clenched both fists. "You...you did that on purpose!" she hissed in a loud whisper and took a step toward her brother.

"No, it wasn't me, honest! I just—" Tommy disappeared from sight, his pleading cut short.

An instant later something hauled Pawly off her feet to her left. She yelped and writhed about, stabbing pain radiating across her chest and back from her left shoulder. Had she fallen from the tree and hit her shoulder on something?

"I'm liable to drop you, dear, if you don't stop squirming!" came her mother's saccharine-sweet voice.

Pawly felt her shaky feet touch the ground once more. She stood there, clinging to her mother for support, looking around at a remote part of the forest preserve near a riverbank. One she hadn't ever re-membered being to before.

Uncle Ritzi landed beside them, cradling Tommy in his arms. The gobsmacked look on her brother's face matched her own incredulous thoughts—*how the hell did they* do *that?*

Pawly had more or less gathered herself by the time J.J. came trot-ting up beside them, goggles dangling around his neck and hoodie pulled up over his head. He chuckled seeing Tommy stumble forward, their Uncle Ritzi's quick grab the only thing keeping her brother from falling flat on his face. "Well, let me see!" he said, holding a small pail out in front of him.

She drew in her breath and drank in the intoxicating scent of J.J.'s sweat mixed with his cologne. Until her mother cleared her throat.

"What? Oh, yes. Right." Pawly smiled sheepishly and jammed both hands into her dump pouches. "Here," she said, dropping one handful of loot into the pail and then the other. She did so twice more before her pouches were empty. "That's all of it."

J.J.'s light reflected off the sides and bottom of the pail, illuminating his face as he rifled through Pawly's ill-gotten gains. "Lip balm, chewing gum, breath mints, loose change, a rabbit's foot...and *condoms*?" he said with a hearty laugh. "Someone's sure to get really *un*lucky tonight!"

Her Uncle Ritzi leaned forward and placed his hands on his knees. "How do you feel?" he said, staring eyeball to eyeball with Pawly as he sniffed at the air around her.

She breathed deep, extending her arms out to her sides as she exhaled. "Aside from my shoulder hurting after Mom tried to rip my arm out of its socket, wonderful, actually."

"You'll get used to it," her mother replied. "We'll keep building up your endurance at the *dojang*. Pretty soon even your uncle and I will have a hard time keeping up with you."

J.J. set the pail down beside him and turned toward the twins' mother. "See to it as soon as you can, Alex. We can put 'em to work right away." He leaned over to the twins and winked. "Nabbing cell phones and PDAs from people with *really* curious call histories and address books. Willing to pay big money to keep them confidential."

Their mother and J.J. talked a moment longer while their Uncle Ritzi took the twins' pulses. "Your mother shook the branch you were standing on without you even realizing," he said as he placed the back of his paw against Tommy's forehead. Then he did likewise for Pawly. "That's how fast you'll need to be, my dear, to help keep your Rage in check. Though your link ought to help you do just that in record time."

J.J. said his goodbyes, wagging his eyebrows at Pawly as he shook her hand.

"Now listen to me, you two," their mother said, pointing upstream as she addressed the twins. "Go that way about a half a mile. Veer left to steer clear of the parking lot, hop the bank, and head straight to River Road. *Halmonim*'s waiting for you there in her minivan at the entrance to the picnic area. Your uncle and I will meet you back at home."

The twins did as they were told—as far as the parking lot. "Wait. I want to take a little detour. This way!" Pawly cried and took to the treetops.

Tommy growled and followed along behind. Within minutes they crouched atop a stout tree limb overlooking another trailside parking lot opposite Lawrence Avenue from them. By itself in the parking lot sat a black Chevy Camaro with gilded rims. And a dent in its hood the same size as Pawly's foot.

She clicked her tongue. "Figured those assholes were around here somewhere. Parked in the one lot we ran out of time to check earlier, natch."

"You think they're here to mess with Sally again?" Tommy asked as he stood and squinted toward Myung-Duk's car. "Seems pretty foolish of them to try something when she's here with her entire class, I'd say."

"That's just it. Sally wasn't *with* her class when I was among them just now. Neither was Caesar. But I did hear some of the kids talking about waiting for a couple stragglers to catch up."

"You...you don't think—"

"Come on, Sally's sweet and all, but you know well as I do she can hardly walk and chew bubble gum at the same time. How do you *think* she'd do on skis?"

Tommy's mouth fell open. "Oh, no. Oh, sis, oh...we gotta go find them," he said, wringing his hands together. "They could be—"

"They could be *already*, dumbass. But even so, they're likely only in danger if Myung-Duk and his mook take them somewhere. *That* we can do something about. Here and now."

After waiting for traffic to pass, Pawly jumped down and bounded across the street. She took to the tree line again before landing atop the Camaro on all fours. Her eyes went wide after peering down through the driver's window. There, in a center-console cup holder plugged into the car's cigarette lighter, a cell phone.

A thump from above her head drew Pawly's attention back up to the elm tree where she had leapt from a moment before. "Now what?"

"Come down here and help me, dammit!" she said in an icy whisper.

Tommy landed beside her and squatted low. "Help you do *what* exactly?"

"Kill two birds with one stone. Practice lifting cell phones *and* making sure these pricks will think twice before coming after Caesar or Sally again." Pawly scanned the parking lot back and forth. "Look for a rock or something we can use to break the—"

The hollow *click* from below her froze Pawly in place, followed by the sound of a car door opening. She looked back over her shoulder in time to glimpse Tommy's legs and hind paws slip out of sight into the Camaro's passenger compartment. She then peered around the open car door to find her brother on his back beneath the steering column, fumbling with something under the dash. "How...how did you...?"

Tommy held up one hand and wiggled his fingers, a shit-eating grin on his face. "Lockpicks at my fingertips! Aaaaand..." He paused and jammed his free hand back up under the dash, then pulled it free with a grunt. "Right proper wire cutters, too. That car alarm won't go off now, though I think I fragged the ignition while I was at it. Oopsie."

She whistled, inspecting the frayed snarl of multi-colored wire clenched in his fist. Pretty neat trick, she had to admit. "Grab the phone and let's scram."

"My hands are a little full at the moment." He jammed the wire into his pants pocket and sat up.

"Fine, get moving and I'll catch up," she said and snatched up the cell phone. "Let's make sure we don't leave any footprints in the snow on the way out."

Tommy climbed up the door frame and leapt out of sight with a grunt. Atop the car's roof once more, Pawly smiled and pulled the door closed with her legs. She shook her head and dashed off into the canopy after him. Her brother might be a dork, but he was a pretty smart dork when he wanted to be. Except for when it came to remembering to put the damn toilet seat back down.

The twins said nothing more as they double-timed their way back to the riverbank. Tommy vaulted the river first, landing atop a gnarled oak limb on the other side. Pawly rolled her eyes and launched herself skyward, gazing down at the moon's reflection off the water's surface as she flew. She stuck her landing on the same limb with ease, right where Tommy could see. Or so she thought he would, confused as she discovered his perch vacant.

"Hey, where did you—*oof!*"

The impact knocked Pawly's wind clear out of her. She tumbled head over heels until she landed in a heap on the forest floor. Someone hauled her to her feet before she could even raise her head. And slammed the back of it against a tree, one that sure as hell *felt* like hardwood.

Spinning stars spiraled out of her view to reveal the face of their mother glaring at her. The corners of Pawly's mouth drew into a smirk. "Mom, we've gotta stop meeting like this."

Their mother bore her fangs and drew close. Her hot breath on the fur inside Pawly's ear sent it into a twitching frenzy. "Did you *really* think I wouldn't call *Eomeonim* to tell her when to expect you? After you didn't show at the picnic area, she called me. Just what part of 'go straight home' were we unclear on, exactly?"

"It-it was my idea," Tommy said from somewhere out of sight to Pawly's left.

She turned just enough to glimpse him pinned to the tree beside her, their Uncle Ritzi's arm to his throat.

"I wanted to exercise our link some more, so we figured it wouldn't hurt anyone if we…"

His voice trailed off after their mother raised her hand.

"That was extraordinarily stupid of you both," she said, shaking Pawly's shoulder for emphasis. "Besides, I just got done telling J.J. that before you two sortie on your own you need to prove to *my* satisfaction that you're—"

"Alex! Do you smell that?"

Their mother's body tensed in response to their uncle's hoarse whisper. She turned her head up and sniffed at the air. "Yeah. I sure do."

The new scents informed Pawly the same as they had her mother. Myung-Duk and his man were close.

Her eyes narrowed as she turned back to Pawly. "Your father and I will deal with you two after we get home. C'mon, Ritzi!"

Tommy beat his sister to the punch. "But, Mom, we want to help—"

"You can help by going home and *staying* there. Leave those *kkang-pae* thugs to your uncle and me. We'll make sure they don't bother Sally or Caesar or any of your other classmates."

Their uncle nodded and jumped to the next branch without a word. "Right then," their mother said before she sprang. "You two, get moving!"

Pawly pursed her lips while their mother and their uncle disappeared into the underbrush, neither so much as snapping a twig.

Chapter Fourteen

————— • —————

RITZI LANDED ATOP A stout branch about halfway up the gnarly oak's trunk. On all fours, he shimmied as far as he dared and drew aside the brown leaves. Below him, in the clearing he spied the twins' school class gathered around a trio of wooden picnic tables. The kids tossed snowballs at each other and passed around cups of hot cocoa, laughing and screaming and carrying on without a care.

Breathing deep, Ritzi delighted in the cocoa's wonderful aroma—until the realization of what he *couldn't* smell made his stomach knot. He sprang from his perch toward the next tree, then the next and the next. Limb by limb, Ritzi worked his way around the clearing within mere minutes.

The *kkangpae* weren't here, of that Ritzi was certain. Various scenarios flashed through his mind as he touched down beside Alex, standing with her back to him in a small wooded glen well out of earshot of the clearing. None afforded him any certainty as to where the thugs had gone.

"Okay, we gotta go and tie up some loose ends here, *Eomeonim*. You and the twins get home as fast as you can. No, we haven't seen their friends. We will though. Sure...okay. Tell them we'll scoop you all after we get back." Alex alternated her cell phone between her mouth and the base of her ear. "Don't worry, Ritzi and I made sure those two know better than to try to sneak out on us again. And just who do you think we learned *that* from?"

After saying goodbye to their mother, Alex hung up. Relief smoothed out the lines crisscrossing his sister's face. Neither he nor Alex needed worry about the twins' classmates or anyone else seeing them in their ailuran forms now. Pawly and Tommy being safely away also eliminated the risk of a raging outburst drawing undue attention to them or their family.

Alex's face bunched up the instant she met Ritzi's gaze. "Did you spot Myung-Duk or that punk he brought with him?"

Ritzi shook his head. "I've canvassed the entire area. No trace of either of 'em. Or those Ruiz kids, for that matter. Though I'd thought Noh's *kkangpae* would have been more interested in the twins than in them."

"Well, let's put that very question to them then. C'mon!"

Alex launched herself into the treetops before Ritzi could reply. He followed suit, the fur around his mouth doing little to warm the cold night air he drew deep into his lungs. The burning sensation in his chest became his focus, helping check the anger welling up inside of him at the constant threat his family had lived under for decades now. From when they had first come into their own, he and Alex had hidden their true selves in the shadows. And Ritzi was growing right sick of it. The secrecy their family had by necessity surrounded itself with led to a lonely existence apart from their clansmen. Which is why despite Ritzi harboring reservations regarding Blaznikov's offer, the elder man's being himself Kindred weighed in his favor.

There were other families who lived the same kind of life as Ritzi's, but for different reasons. Over the years his family had joined one such in something of a marriage of convenience. He and his kin didn't much care for the gangsters nor for their tactics; Ritzi supposed the feeling was indeed mutual. Most soldiers of the Korean syndicate were born into their respective *jopok*, just as Alex and Ritzi had been born werecats. But others had chosen to join a *jopok* of their own free will, had chosen to stay and do their masters' bidding. And it was toward them he so desperately wanted to give full vent to his fury.

In through your nose, out through your mouth. Locate your center, no room for doubt.

Their mother's mantra from years ago ran through Ritzi's head as he and Alex closed in on where the two *kkangpae* plowed their way through the underbrush. Any animals in the vicinity would have scattered at the first whiff of their scents, both strong enough for Ritzi and Alex to zero in on them without stopping to check.

Ahead of them, the Ruiz girl—Sally, if he remembered right—flailed about in the snow, trying to keep her skis under her. She and the boy Ritzi took to be her brother jabbered back and forth in Spanish as they waved their arms all around. Their red-faced exchanges only frustrated the hapless girl all the more. Not even a few wobbly strides forward on her skis and she would spill again.

As they reached the *kkangpae*, Alex passed Ritzi and crouched down atop a limb above the men's heads. She belted out an angry yowl, causing Myung-Duk's man to cry out by reflex.

The boy stabbed his sister's bindings with the tip of his pole, freeing her boots from her skis. He did the same and hauled her to her feet. The two of them tore off down the trail toward the picnic area.

Myung-Duk glanced over his shoulder, cursing under his breath. "Come on!" he yelled to his man before taking off after the kids, the two of them raising ruckus enough to start a stampede. Alex snarled and followed the *kkangpae* with Ritzi right behind her. The two men were their prey now.

Drool streamed down Ritzi's jowls. Normally, while on a hunt, he avoided the reviling sensation it produced by rubbing the side of his face against passing tree trunks. But he knew the effect his beast-like appearance would surely have on Myung-Duk's hired man, a human who, for all he knew, had never seen their kind before. The sight of Ritzi's wild eyes, of saliva dripping from his chin and jaw, would surely leave an impression on this punk. One that made clear anyone who violated the families' code of silence *would* be dealt with. Severely.

Alex snarled and waved one hand toward the trail leading back to the nature preserve's parking lot. The scents of the twins' classmates were gone, as were those of anyone else. It was just the four of them now. Alex kicked up snow and dead leaves as she touched down ahead of the two men, blocking their escape. Ritzi landed beside her an instant later and locked eyes with Myung-Duk's hired man. The fellow skidded to a halt, his eyes going wide for a mere second until his training kicked in. Years of hazing by *jopok* leaders had surely conditioned him to remain calm and detached whenever faced with danger. But the man's pheromones gave him away to Ritzi's nose—he was terrified. Ritzi indulged himself, gnashing his teeth in true Lon Chaney fashion. The man recoiled while slimy lines of drool flew from Ritzi's chops.

"This one's a kitten compared to me." Alex toyed at the claws on one hand with her thumb and narrowed her eyes at the man's partner. "Raising kids requires patience, though I'm still not especially good with it. Help temper my urge to rip your ugly faces both off by being…"

Ritzi glanced toward Alex following her unexpected pause. Her chin dipped toward the ground for but an instant then jerked back upright. Had she overexerted herself? He hardly could imagine so. Their hunts would routinely go on for hours, ending even before Alex would be breathing hard.

As if interpreting her hesitation as weakness, Myung-Duk seized upon the opportunity. "You wouldn't dare," he said and crossed his arms.

Alex bore her fangs at him. "Try me."

A trace of movement drew Ritzi's attention. He growled low and fixed the first man with a searing glare. The fellow's hand stopped beneath his jacket, mere inches away from the bulge protruding from beneath his shoulder.

"Hold it!" Myung-Duk said and slapped the fellow's chest with an open palm. "Look, our family has business with the girl's stepfather. You need to respect that," he went on with a nod toward Alex. "Armando Ruiz still owes me for setting up a market for his broken-down rusty machinery in North Korea. And now he's hawking his overpriced scrap metal right in our family's backyard, calling on Great Lakes ports aboard that leaky old scow belonging to your father-in-law's brother. Why I want to talk to his stepdaughter, to tell her to tell *him* to stop being so reckless. Not to mention stupid."

The fur on the back of Alex's neck stood straight up. "I will not allow you to harass schoolchildren, Myung-Duk," she said with deliberate slowness.

"Those brats are not your concern."

"They are. And would be even if they weren't our own kids' friends." Alex's fingers twitched at her sides as she took a step toward the men. "From this moment on, consider both of the Ruiz children to be under our family's protection. Like it or not."

A wisp of pungent anger tainted the man's self-assured, musky scent. "Well, if that isn't gratitude for you. Without our support, you *and* your brother would have been homeless here not even a month off the boat."

Ritzi's winced after his claws punctured his own paw pads. Following their arrival in Chicago, their mother leveraged her connections from both ends of the Korean Peninsula. She aided her destitute and shell-shocked family by enlisting the Noh's help. And their *jopok* hadn't let them ever forget it. Being in their debt might well indenture generations of his family's progeny into their service. Accepting Blaznikov's funding made more sense to Ritzi going forward, the elder man bound by ancient edict not to harm or oppress his own kind. The Noh family had no such compunctions.

Alex fixed Myung-Duk with an icy glare. "Which is why we shall take this matter up with Sung Jin himself. I can't imagine he would ever—"

"No! We are handling his affairs now. And if you choose to interfere in them further, well, whatever happens, *happens*."

Her entire body tensed. The man had no idea the switch his words had just flipped in his sister's brain, but Ritzi did. Her eyes went wide as she sank the claws of one hand into the collar of his jacket and drew the other back behind her head.

As Ritzi rushed Alex, he glimpsed the man's accomplice reaching into his jacket. *Oh, shit, the gun!* "*Aniyo!*" Ritzi yelled in mid-leap. He jammed his toe claws into the frozen ground beside Alex and turned to face the shooter. An instant later, Ritzi felt the bullet's shock wave. Right before pain erupted across his chest and shoulder.

He felt himself falling backward. Consciousness left him while the gun's report rang in his ears.

Chapter Fifteen

"IT IS OKAY. YOU two can come in now."

Pawly exchanged looks with Tommy before she squeezed past him and into the guest bedroom. She set the phone in her hand down on top of the dresser and scratched at her scalp through the towel wrapped around her head. On the bed before them their Uncle Ritzi laid on his back while their grandmother tended him. Bedsheets covered him from the waist down. Swatches of blood-stained fur poked out from beneath the bandages wrapped around his shoulder and chest.

A groan from their right drew Pawly's attention toward the chaise lounge beside the window. There lay their mother, pushing herself up with one hand. Her ears, nose, and mouth had returned to human form. What remained of her claws raked gray clumps of fur free as she rubbed at her face and neck with her free hand. "Hey," she said, a smile crossing her face. But it fled the instant she looked past the two of them toward the bed. "Oh. Shit."

"You need not worry," their grandmother said as she knelt beside their mother. "He will be all right. Bullet did not penetrate deep. Sleeping now but he should wake soon."

Something between a gasp and a squeak escaped Pawly's throat before she clamped her hand over her mouth. Her mother glanced over at her and her brother before turning back toward their uncle. "That bullet was meant for *me*, you two. Myung-Duk's man was surely trying to defend himself and his boss from what he believed to be some sort of monster. This is what can happen when people outside our inner circle see us for who we truly are. Do you understand?"

Pawly nodded. Out of the corner of her eye, she saw Tommy doing likewise while he fumbled at the towel around his waist.

"Good. Because you're both grounded. You go to school, you come home, you go to Mass. That's it for a *month*. Because clearly you need to learn that our Affliction isn't some kind of fucking sideshow act."

"But, Mom! I...I don't think that..."

Pawly's mother shot her a look, as if to suggest juggling bottles of warm nitroglycerin might be only slightly more foolish. Out of the corner of her eye Pawly spied Tommy studying the joints between the floorboards. She stared up at the ceiling and sighed. Their mother stood up and threw an arm each around Pawly and Tommy, nearly pulling her robe off her shoulders. The pungent scent of the twins' remorse must have overpowered the smell of soap and shampoo.

"And I'll drag you both into the basement by the scruff of your necks and chain you to the wall if either of you even *think* about sneaking out," their mother said as she tousled Tommy's wet wavy hair, sending droplets in all directions.

"What do you remember, *ttanim*? From last night?"

The three of them turned as one toward the twins' grandmother. She had finished tending their uncle and leaned back up against the wall, one foot propped up beneath her.

Their mother stared down at the clumps of fur scattered around the floor by her feet. "Ritzi and I intercepted Myung-Duk and his man. Told them to back off, to leave the twins and their classmates alone. Myung-Duk said Sally's stepfather was in his debt, so that's why he's been leaning on her of late. I was about to help the smug bastard take up breathing through a slit in his throat." She sighed and shook her head. "Then I redded out. I don't remember anything after that."

"Your maternal instinct is strong." The twins' grandmother crossed her arms across her chest. "Pawlina. Tomasz. Your mother's reaction does not surprise. Nor should it you. Strong emotions can trigger a rage episode. You must be mindful."

Yeah, Halmonim. *Understatement of the year.*

Their grandmother preempted any further discussion with a wave. "We can talk more, later." She glanced up at the clock and stepped past the twins out into the hallway. "Police called on Brookfield Zoo. Must go to the park now. Young man's body was found there. Victim of a wild animal attack."

Pawly and her brother said nothing as their grandmother pulled the door shut and stepped away down the hall. Their mother sighed and stomped over beside the bed. "I don't understand, Ritzi. You said my rage would never relapse. And that my kids would never...never ever..."

The twins both winced after their mother punched her foot through the footboard up to her ankle. Cursing under her breath, she pulled it back, splintering the solid oak with a sickening crunch as if it were foam board. "Pawly, Tommy, listen to me. Myung-Duk might well also be leaning on Sally to try and bait you, though I can hardly guess why. He could still be sore for Papa and me running out on them, I don't know. He's been one to carry a grudge for as long as I've known him."

She hobbled over to the twins and took a knee. "Look, I know you care for your new friends," she said, looking up as she took one each of the twins' hands in hers. "But we can't risk you endangering them further by—"

An insistent beat cut her off, followed by a light melody line. What Pawly recognized as a trendy K-pop song trilled from the phone atop the dresser. She couldn't make out the caller's name displayed in *Hangul* but managed to silence the ringtone with a swipe at the screen.

Pawly exchanged a nervous look with Tommy and licked her lips. She opened her mouth once, twice, three times until words tumbled out. "Mom, we have an idea…"

DAYS LATER.

*H*ANA! DUL! SET! NET!
Tora…
Hana! Dul! Set! Net!

Pawly had come to love *ki-cho* kicks. The familiar burn in her thighs exhilarated her, especially after being cooped up in the house all week. The only time she and Tommy had left was to go to school, to shovel the sidewalks around their building, or to go train in the family's garage-turned-*dojang*.

Tommy stood at her side, switching his stance in perfect time with hers. Their grandmother scowled at them from one side of the room. Their mother barked out their training cadence with more than a little bit of an edge in her voice. Each in their own way, they made clear they were still pissed at her and her brother both.

To her right were Sally and Caesar. Pawly was grateful her mother had allowed her and Tommy, though they were both still grounded, to continue training with their friends. In the weeks following Sally's near abduction, Pawly's mother and grandmother had made it their mission to equip both Ruiz children so they might better defend themselves. All the while refusing any money from Mr. and Mrs. Ruiz, despite their protests. No matter how badly Pawly's family might have needed it.

Pawly stole a glance toward Sally, long enough to see the difficulty the girl was having keeping pace. She had her mother's curvy figure and, by her own admission, didn't often engage in physical activity. It showed.

Despite the girl's inexperience and lack of conditioning, Sally had yet to complain. But sweat dripping down the sides of her face and her ragged gasps for air told Pawly her friend had had enough for one night.

Their mother appeared to pick up on Sally's not-so-subtle cue as well. She ordered them to kneel and bow before the Korean and American flags hanging on the wall before their little class. Pawly glimpsed movement near the side door as she rolled backward over her shoulder and leapt to her feet.

"Sally, Caesar. You will dress out now. Then go home," their grandmother said.

The twins' friends both nodded and headed off toward their respective changing rooms.

Before Pawly could follow Sally, their mother took her and Tommy one to an arm by their shoulders and squeezed. "Oh no, not you two. You're due for some *special* training," she said with an evil grin, eliciting a groan from the both of them.

The back door creaked open. J.J. grabbed it before the wind did and tugged it firmly shut behind him. He pulled off his Dixie Cup and slipped out of his pea coat before making eye contact with their grandmother. "Teacher most honorable, forgive my intrusion please," he said in Korean as he strode around the outside wall of the *dojang* toward her. He stopped a respectful distance away and bowed slightly at his waist. "Father wishes for you to accept his greeting."

"I was saddened hearing of your mother's passing, Jae-jueung," their grandmother replied in kind and narrowed her eyes at him. "But must the Noh family continue to disgrace mine by refusing to recognize *my* headship? I doubt you're here to register for a class or to make a social call, so you must be here to talk business. Noh Sung Jin sends his youngest, hardly more than a whelp himself."

"Please do not misunderstand us, Most Honorable Opoworo. Regretfully, my father will be back in the homeland settling Mother's affairs until the end of the month. Normally Myung-Duk would have come as his representative. But after the other night, I...I mean, we..." His voice trailed off as he cast an unsure look toward the twins' mother. "The rest of the family thought that might be unwise."

"Your brother's man left me no choice, J.J.," their mother said in English and nodded in the direction of the house. "My brother is in there if you want to ask him yourself. May even show you the bullet wound if you ask nicely."

"Myung-Duk and his man were foolish to provoke you," he said, open palms at his shoulders. "I'm not here to defend them nor stir up more trouble. Though Father is hurt deeply, Honorable Katczynski, because your family saw fit to call us using my brother's stolen cell phone."

"We wanted to send a message. That we have means to work toward our families' mutual benefit," their grandmother said, resuming her halting English. "Or toward their undoing. Your choice."

"Message received. One resembling overt retribution, my uncle told me before I left to come here," he said with a shrug. "Who could know who you might turn over the phone to? The media? The police? The FBI?"

"I can appreciate your concern, truly." Their mother turned and glared at Pawly and her brother. "Though you should know *these* two acted with neither our knowledge nor approval. Which is why their father and I have grounded them."

"Oh! So, looks like you'll be in here training a while," J.J. said to Pawly with a cheesy grin. "Would be glad to help you practice your *cha gi.*"

She coughed and stared at the floor, feeling the heat rise to her face. Would that she would like to throw her heel up on his shoulder so he could lean those buff forearms on top of her—

"But for the moment, some details remain regarding our new business venture we need to hash out."

The twins' mother exchanged looks with their grandmother and crossed her arms over her chest. "Just what do you mean, 'details?'"

"Pawly. Tommy. You will go with your friends now," their grandmother said without taking her eyes off J.J.

"Good idea, *Eomeonim.*" Their mother disappeared around the corner into the alcove which served as the *dojang*'s office. "You two, take your friends and go grab a hot one." A file cabinet slammed shut, their mother emerging a moment later. She handed Pawly a twenty and two fives before glancing up at the wall clock. "But be back here by nine-thirty sharp. Or else."

T HE BUS'S DOORS WHOOSHED shut just after the twins and their friends scrambled aboard. A moment later the bus was rumbling down Milwaukee Avenue, headed toward the coffee shop and bakery Sally and Caesar had introduced Pawly and her brother to the weekend before last. It was their new friends' favorite hangout and Pawly had been eager to go back. She had mentally rehearsed begging their mother into allowing them to join Sally and Caesar there after class.

Waste of a completely good sales pitch, she mulled, mentally filing away her fawning entreaty. *Or maybe not. Chance to use it'll come up soon enough for sure.*

"Wow, girl, you were spacing there," Sally said and nudged Pawly toward the aisle.

"Guess we're both still in shock our mom actually let us out of the house," Tommy said over his shoulder, seated next to Caesar in front of the two girls. "And on a Friday night, at that."

"Oh, is *that* why we nearly missed our bus?" Sally said over top of her steepled fingers. "Here I thought you were just fixated on that hunky sailor. Who is he, anyway?"

"He's...a family friend," Pawly replied, feeling the heat in her face rise to her hairline. She stared down at the floor in the hope she might avoid Sally's notice.

Her friend burst out laughing a moment later, signaling Pawly's epic fail.

"Oh, so you think that's funny? Well, just for that, I'll make you watch me drink an entire double caramel macchiato. I've been think-ing about one since the last time you brought us to Groundswell."

Sally let out a long sigh. "It's not fair! I put on pounds just *thinking* about one. Those things have more calories in one cup than I think you two must take in together in a whole day."

Pawly shrugged. She and Tommy would need every last one of them. And all the caffeine. What punishment their mother was ready to dish out under the guise of training later that night, Pawly could only guess. "I'm sure they'll make you one sugar-free with no-fat cream if you want. Hey, Ceez, what'll you have? My mom's buying, so knock yourself out."

Caesar tugged at his chin for a moment. "Well, you were all on about caramel macchiato, so maybe I'll—"

His cell phone's ringing cut him off. "*¡Hola, Papi!*" he said after tugging the thing free from his pocket and flipping it open. "*¿Que es...? Oh, ay. Ay, ay, ay. Si, un momento...*"

His voice trailed off as he reached up and yanked the bell cord. Pawly was on her feet even before the bus began slowing down. "Is everything all right?"

Caesar jabbered on in Spanish, alternating back and forth between conversations with Sally and his father on the phone.

"I don't know," Sally said at length as her stepbrother said goodbye. "His dad demanded we tell him where we were and who we were with."

Caesar flipped his phone closed. "Yeah. And all he would say when I told him was that he was nearby and would come get us. Then he hung up."

Tommy reached over and patted at the back of Sally's hand. "You going to be all right?"

She stood and met his gaze as the bus lumbered up to the curb and stopped. "I'll let you know. Text you before I go to bed, okay?"

The doors opened. Before Tommy could answer, Sally and Caesar stepped out and disappeared into the throngs lining the sidewalk in front of a block full of dance clubs.

P AWLY HEARD SHOUTING AS she walked up the alley toward the *dojang.*

A man's voice, stern and angry. Yelling in Korean.

She burst through the door, Tommy right behind her, the two of them nearly colliding with J.J.

"Are you hearing me, Alex?" boomed Myung-Duk's voice from the front of the training area.

She turned to find him kneeling beside her mother's prone form. "Mom! No!" she cried and bolted toward them.

"Pawly, wait!" J.J. yelled, his eyes wide. But the red haze already frothed at the edge of Pawly's vision. She plowed headlong into Myung-Duk, sending them both tumbling into the far wall. Adrenaline surging through her body like electricity, Pawly sprang to her feet. Her breath came in angry gasps as she pinned Myung-Duk's shoulder to the wall with one hand. A claw emerged from the end of one finger. Myung-Duk yelped while she drew it along the base of his neck. Fur sprouted from underneath her jacket sleeve and across the back of her hand. "I will *end* you if you've even so much as—"

"No, don't!" Tommy and J.J. yelled from behind them.

To Pawly's left she glimpsed her grandmother stepping around the corner, a spray bottle held out in front of her. A stream of liquid struck Pawly's left cheekbone an instant later, scattering foul-smelling droplets across her face and neck. Her vision blurred, her nose burned, the room began to spin.

"*Tomasz!* To the house!" her grandmother yelled over her shoulder. "I will call for help."

And then Pawly's knees buckled. She wouldn't remember hitting the floor.

Chapter Sixteen

— · —

Dawn. The Next Day.

T HE SOUND OF A door slamming open thrummed off the ware-house walls, jarring Ritzi awake.

"Hello? Anyone in there?"

With a groan Ritzi lifted his head from his folded arms and squinted at his watch. Dim light streamed through the clerestory windows high above his head. Was it really morning already?

"Yes, Janie, I'm..." was all he managed before stabbing pain from his still-healing shoulder took his breath away. "I'm here. Behind the sprinkler room."

Footsteps echoed throughout the wide-open space as Ritzi grimaced down at the mess strewn about his rudimentary lab bench. Thick, green goo holding the catalyzed proteins in solution had trickled out of an upended beaker and off the thin sheet of cheap vinyl, adhering solidly to the plywood beneath. An idea had come to him in the middle of his investor presentation the night before. Janie had volunteered to see the suits off afterward so he could rush over here and try it out. Before he knew it, the evening's last Green Line train had come and gone. So, Ritzi had settled in to work until daybreak came, then planned to catch the first train back to the city—which he would do now, just as soon as he restocked his reagents. And hauled his ruined work surface out to the trash.

Ritzi wiped at the corners of his eyes with his thumb and forefinger, berating himself. His research had progressed little since his ouster from Loyola's industrial incubator, despite the generous offer from Janie's brother to allow him to work here. Even his efforts together with his father in Poland had tendered less-than-optimal results, due in part to Papa's reticence to conduct their experiments at the lab where he taught. Without the tight controls a proper, well-equipped lab environment offered, the volatile compounds in concentrations necessary to produce optimal results were as likely to blow up as they were to yield anything useful. Papa refused to take such risks at the university. An incident there would certainly draw scrutiny, the sort that put discovery of their kind's secret existence intolerably at risk.

But, now that he and Papa had reason to suspect Alex's body was breaking down, time was of the essence. He couldn't afford any more setbacks, couldn't afford any more delays. Maybe next time he would cut the reagents at only half the current rate? If a fire did break out here in the warehouse, at least he'd still be able to knock it down with an ordinary fire extinguisher before it could—

"Alex and Pawly were both rushed to the hospital late last night. Thought you should know."

Nat emerged from around a stack of pallets, a sour look on his face. Ritzi stood and fished his cell phone out from the jacket of his blazer, draped across the back of his lab stool. "Then why didn't you just...? Oh."

His phone's tiny display informed Ritzi he'd missed fifteen calls and seven text messages in addition to having four voice mails awaiting him. He swore and fumbled through the damn thing's menu to reactivate the ringer. "What happened? How are the girls?" he said and jammed the thing into the pocket of his rumpled khakis.

"J.J. came to the *dojang* to try and mend fences with Alex and *Eomeonim*," Nat replied. "Then Myung-Duk barged in and..." His voice trailed off as Ritzi drew his hand across the front of his throat.

Nat stepped over to the open door and glanced out toward the alley before pulling the door shut. "Janie's not here, if that's what you're worried about. She let me in and then said she'd be in her office if we needed anything. Asked us just to lock up back here when we left."

Ritzi sighed and walked back to his lab bench. "Okay, go on, please. And I'm so sorry about missing everyone's calls."

Nat nodded. "Alex collapsed for some reason right before Pawly came in. She saw Myung-Duk there with her and went ballistic. *Eomeonim* hit Pawly with the carfentanyl, then dialed 911."

Ritzi sucked in his breath. "*She* called them? Why would *Eomeonim* risk exposing us by calling the paramedics?"

"A calculated risk, I suppose," his brother replied with a shrug. "Had the benefit of getting rid of the Noh brothers but quick, too."

Ritzi rubbed at his forearms. "'*Calculated* risk'? What about the chemicals? What about the piles of shed fur everywhere?"

"Alex passed out before she morphed, and *Eomeonim* took Pawly down before she could. Any erupted fur had retreated back into her skin by the time the ambulance showed up."

Ritzi's brow furrowed. "Do you think anyone at the hospital might be suspicious?"

"*Eomeonim* managed to ventilate the room and administer all the naloxone in her kit beforehand, but we otherwise lucked out. The ER doc looked over Pawly and Alex then chalked it up to severe dehydration from strenuous physical activity. They should be on their way home soon." Nat looked over at the ruined plywood and made a face. "Can I...er, help you with that?"

Within five minutes, the two of them had put away the reagents and heaved the plywood sheet into the dumpster beside the warehouse's roll-up door. "Now, is there anything *you* need to tell me?" Nat asked as he and Ritzi climbed into their mother's minivan.

Ritzi blinked. "I...I don't know what you mean."

Nat pulled a folded piece of paper from the van's center console. "*This* is what I mean," he said, waving the paper beneath his brother's nose.

Ritzi took the paper and unfolded it. It was a copy of one of the investor profiles he'd handed out during his presentation, featuring Blaznikov's smarmy smiling visage at the top beside his own. "Still not following you."

Anger flashed behind Nat's eyes as he jammed the car into gear. "Just what the hell're you *thinking*?" With his free hand, he snatched the picture out of Ritzi's grasp and crumpled it into a ball. "Did you know this son-of-a-bitch is wanted in six countries?" he said, tossing the paper out the window.

Ritzi's mouth fell open. "No, I...I didn't..."

Nat let out a disgusted sigh and tromped on the van's accelerator. "A lot has changed since our folks brought you and Alex here from Poland. I get that. But Dory says Blaznikov posing a threat to our family is *not* one of them."

Ritzi stared down at his feet in silence. "The peril Alex is in may be every bit as great," he said only after Nat turned the van onto the freeway on-ramp. "And as for the twins, who can say? As of this moment, no one. Not even Papa and me."

Nat shook his head and merged into traffic. "Even so, you're going to have a hard time convincing Barry of that. Along with the rest of us, for that matter."

N AT PULLED UP TO the curb past the house's driveway and killed the engine. As he and Ritzi exited, a taxi backed out of the driveway and tore off down the street. The two of them trotted around to the small backyard and found their mother leading the procession toward the back door. Dory helped Alex along; Tommy did likewise with Pawly. Aside from being bleary-eyed and a bit wobbly, neither his sister nor his niece seemed any the worse for wear.

Inside their mother's kitchen a moment later, Ritzi clutched his sister and niece to him tight. They sighed and sobbed together until their arms all started to go numb. "Where's Barry?" he managed at length.

"He's with Top and Sheila," Dory answered. "In the mood he was in, I didn't think it wise he come home right away. They're just getting settled into their new place up the block, so they took Barry there for coffee."

Ritzi glanced back and forth between Alex and her father-in-law. "What...what do you...?"

Alex patted Pawly and Tommy both on the shoulder and nodded toward Dory. "You two go with Grandpa D and wait for us in the living room. Now."

The twins nodded and shuffled off behind Dory. Alex threw open the storm door and yanked Ritzi out onto the back porch. "What Dory was *trying* to say," she said in a loud whisper after pushing the door closed behind them, "is that right now Barry would just as soon kick your ass as look at you. Hopefully Top and Sheila can distract him long enough to calm down. Because your even *talking* with Blaznikov amounts to no less than—"

"What are you wearing?"

Alex's eyes went wide for an instant before her brow knit. "What the hell does that have to do with—?"

"Was this what you were wearing before you passed out?" Ritzi replied, tugging at the shoulders of her hoodie.

"No, we were just finishing class. I was still in my *dobok*."

"So where is it now?"

"Wherever you guys parked *Eomeonim*'s minivan, I guess," she said, looking around. "She came to the hospital with a change of clothes for Pawly and me, then asked Nat to come get you. He took our duffel with him. But what difference does that...?"

Alex's voice trailed off as Ritzi sprinted down the driveway to the street. He threw open the van's rear gate to find a black duffel behind the back seat, silkscreened with the *dojang*'s logo. After yanking open the bag's zipper, Ritzi turned the bag upside down and gave it a good shake. Alex and Pawly's strong, sour scents wafted up from the sweat-drenched garments as they tumbled out onto the floor.

Ritzi grabbed a black top with gold fringe around the hem and held it up to his face. A deep breath through his nose told him what he needed to know.

Oh, shit. There it is.

Among the garden-variety sweat and grime on Alex's *dobok*, Ritzi's sensitive nose picked out the unmistakable residue left over from her body's deconstruction. The peculiar scent seemed to manifest during times of great duress, and tonight had purportedly been such a one.

Ritzi and Papa had been hoping against hope their conclusions were wrong, but now he had irrefutable, empirical evidence. That Soviet sub captain had goaded Alex into transforming at an earlier age than expected. And the twins had transformed at a later one. Such irregularities placed them in mortal peril.

Her body is breaking down. Maybe even faster than Papa and I had first thought.

Ritzi shook his head and grabbed the other *dobok*. Wadding it up, he thrust his face into it and took a deep breath. He swore and shook out the thing before trying again. Then he used the garment as a handkerchief, blowing his nose to make sure his nasal passages were clear. He scented the *dobok* a third time and confirmed what his nose told him but his mind and heart both loathed to acknowledge. Faint though it was, Pawly's *dobok* gave off the same scent as Alex's had, no matter how much he longed to deny it. With a scream, Ritzi tore at the corners of Pawly's top and ripped it in two.

Instantly, his conscious mind squashed his rage back into the depths of his psyche. Their father's previous experiments might well have ruined Alex as a control, but he could take a different tack. All he needed to do was focus. Maybe Ritzi's clan hadn't been the only Kindred leaving Białowieża following the Allied victory in Europe. Maybe others had too, ones his elders simply hadn't spoken of. They might provide a suitable control; all he had to do was find them.

His gaze flickered back and forth between the halves of Pawly's *dobok* in his hands. A plan formed in his mind—harvest traces of her DNA from the cloth, do likewise with Alex's, compare and contrast them to help him figure—

The *dobok* fluttered free from Ritzi's hands as he whirled around and slammed up against the side of his mother's van. After blinking away stars, he found Barry standing nose to nose with him, a look in his eyes every bit as feral and wild as any one of Ritzi's kinsmen over-come by their Affliction's madness. All the more terrifying given Barry was related to him by marriage and not by blood.

"What have you *done*?" Barry screamed, his spit making Ritzi's cheeks damp. "Why would you lead that...that *monster* straight to us?"

He gulped. "I didn't know! I didn't think that my—"

White-hot pain shot through Ritzi's left eye before his head smacked the window glass behind him. His legs gave out and he crumpled to the pavement, holding his eye with both hands. A hand gripped Ritzi's chin and jerked it upward. Steam from Barry's hot breath surrounded his face as he took a knee in front of him.

"Yeah, you're right," Barry said, his nose an inch from Ritzi's. "You *didn't* think. Didn't think how this asshole Blaznikov rolls. Maybe now you won't be so inclined to forget." He slid the patch over his own left eye up onto his forehead, revealing an empty socket where an eyeball had once been. "Because I sure as hell won't," he continued in a harsh whisper as Ritzi's eye throbbed.

"Barry!"

Ritzi peered over toward the sound of footsteps running their way.

Barry stood and began to scuffle with whomever had ap-proached them.

"I figured this is where you would be," said the dark-skinned man in a booming voice. "Sheila told you to go on and make yourself at home. *Not* to go on and get yourself on home."

Barry stabbed a finger in Ritzi's direction. "This fucking guy here sold my family out to the asshole who tried to kill you and me!" he said before pointing to his eye patch. "Another cunt hair to the right and we'd've *both* been shark bait."

Ritzi's chest clenched. Blaznikov's words over breakfast weeks before played on an endless loop in his mind. *We have met. During Korean operation, yes...*

"Your man here ought to have his say, Bear." Top nodded toward Ritzi. "Cut him some slack in the meantime, willya?"

Barry turned to his former shipmate, crossing his arms across his chest. "Ritzi cuts himself slack enough. Cutting corners. Slacking off. Putting us all at risk." He glanced over at Ritzi then turned away, his shoulders slumped. "You of all people should know better. I spent a lot of time flat on my back aboard ship in the infirmary on the way home from Korea. Thought about how much of my kids' lives I'd already missed out on. I...I won't let anyone or anything take them from me now that we're together again."

"'Only easy day was yesterday,' right shipmate?" Top asked, clasping his old friend's shoulders. "We'll see to it no one ever does."

The corner of Barry's mouth curled. "And *you* had better see to it their Affliction doesn't either, Ritzi."

Top helped Ritzi get to his feet. "But you'll need to be able to see straight first," he said before Ritzi could answer. "C'mon, let's get you inside and find a bag of frozen veggies to put over that eye."

Chapter Seventeen

Two days later.

PAWLY GRUNTED AND THRUST out her arms in front of her. The hand cart bumped and banged across the warehouse floor's uneven concrete until it crashed into another cart parked against the wall.

"Everyone all right down there?" came Sally's voice from above a moment later.

"Yeah, we're fine," Tommy shouted toward the mezzanine. "Kill the lights, we'll meet you at the door." Then he turned and glared at Pawly. "Will you stop? Being grounded is bad enough without having to put up with your petty tantrums."

She crossed her arms. "But it's not *fair*!"

"So you've told anyone unlucky enough to get within earshot for days now. It's getting old, sis."

Pawly harrumphed and followed Tommy to the door. Lights inside and outside the warehouse went dark one by one. Darkness enveloped the pier all around them, save for the single bulb above a rusting metal sign beside the door reading RUIZ MACHINERY SALES.

She gazed out over the water and sighed. Off in the distance to her left lay Navy Pier, crisscrossed by tens of thousands of Christmas lights. To her right rose the steel cathedrals surrounding Indiana Harbor. Between the two they lit up the night sky like daylight, obscuring the meteor showers Tommy and Sally had both hoped to see. But they would have their chance once Uncle Bobby put out for deep water. Pawly's window to glimpse My Chemical Romance's Winter Wonderfest concert from atop the pilot house on the way past Navy Pier was closing by the second.

Sally clattered along the catwalk toward the metal staircase beside the entrance, whistling as she went.

"Hear that?" Tommy said as he jabbed his thumb in her direction. "You an' me are just paying our penance, sis. But while you cop a 'tude, Sal here's trying to make the best of it. She should be in Florida at Universal Studios with Caesar and his mother. Not stuck here with us just because her stepdad's freaked out from the Nohs harassing her."

Pawly's gaze wandered to the end of the pier. Spotlights mounted above the bridge of their great uncle Bobby's tugboat lit up the barge deck fore of it, where Mr. Ruiz and the other adults crawled over the trolley crane's massive assemblies. They tugged and twisted at the bindings lashing the equipment fast to the barge's deck, giving each one its final inspection prior to casting off. Sally's stepfather had insisted on accompanying the twins' Grandpa D and great Uncle Bobby during the ferry move to Green Bay. The paper mill awaiting them, shut down following the appearance of a fatigue crack in their own crane's main beam, would ensure both families' struggling businesses ended the year well into the black.

She jammed her hands into her pockets and leaned against the warehouse's metal wall. The peeling paint crackled and popped under her weight. "Suppose he doubts her assailant being mauled by a wild animal right afterward was mere coincidence either," she said as she drew back. Pawly made a face at the tiny flecks of paint covering her right side and brushed at her jeans and hoodie. She had wondered whether Sally thought of the two of them like that. Their mother had, after all, insisted Pawly and her brother shadow the girl night and day during their voyage.

But the wistful look on Sally's face, as she emerged from the warehouse and closed the door behind her, suggested to Pawly otherwise. As if her new friend looked forward to their being stewards and deckhands all weekend, like it was all some sort of grand, swashbuckling adventure. Although from the shit-eating grin plastered across Tommy's face, Pawly figured he had a very different kind of adventure in mind.

The demure smile Sally returned while she keyed the deadbolt closed hardly tempered Pawly's suspicions. She cleared her throat, earning her a nervous chuckle from the other two. *Blargh.*

"Well, at least we can hear MCR pretty well," Sally said and shoved her bare hands beneath her armpits. "The sound really carries across the lake."

"I'd been wanting to see them for months, and now *there* they are." Pawly nodded with her chin toward Navy Pier before pointing down at her feet. "And here I am."

Tommy clicked his tongue. "Uncle Bobby said we could check 'em out once we got underway, didn't he?"

"Ooooh, yeah!" Sally's eyes twinkled as she pointed to the top of the pilot house. "Just like the water taxis, but up higher. We'll have the best seats in the house!"

Pawly drew her lips into a thin line. They would miss the show if they didn't shove off soon, along with the fireworks. That didn't seem to deter Sally, who appeared determined for the three of them to have a good time. Whether or not Pawly wanted to seemed to mean little.

"And then we'll have the best view of the meteor showers anywhere once we're away from..." Sally's voice trailed off as she waved her arms around her. "Once we're away from all this. I don't get to go into the woods like you guys do up in Sconnie."

A smile crooked across Tommy's face. "I'll ask my folks if we might remedy that come spring."

"Wow, that'd be wonderful!" she replied, drawing her hands to either side of her face. "Hey, maybe we can spot the Aurora Borealis! That'd be *so* romantic, don't you think?"

Pawly stepped over to one of the wood pilings dotting the edge of the pier and leaned up against it. No, she wasn't *one* bit jealous. Why wouldn't a couple of astronomy geeks want to hang out together? But the way Sally looked at Tommy, the way he looked back at her, Pawly found herself thinking back to when J.J. appeared in the *dojang*. She longed for a chance to see him again, if only to demonstrate just how good her kicking technique *really* was.

She drew back into a crouch and twirled into a low, spinning kick with one leg, then sprang up into a high spinning kick with the other one. Her impromptu practice had the added benefit of not having to watch Tommy and Sally make goo-goo eyes at each other while they took turns pointing up at the sky.

A guttural snarl from down the pier gave Pawly a start. She turned and scanned the length of their barge, but saw nothing but parts from the massive crane and the looming shadows behind them. When she glanced over at Tommy, he met her gaze with wide eyes. *You heard it too?*

A human-sized silhouette traced an arc through the air above the tug's wheelhouse an instant before disappearing behind the funnel.

Another dark figure followed close behind. Then came the sounds of a feral melee. Gnashing teeth, an angry yowl. Sally went on blathering about Arcturus rising, completely oblivious.

The breeze changed direction, sending a strong, masculine musk straight her way. This scent was sharper, sourer than she remembered Tommy's or her uncle Ritzi's ever being. *Holy shit. Another werecat?*

A sharp *crack* rang out, louder than a gunshot to Pawly's alerted senses. One of the boat's radio aerials clattered to the wheelhouse deck. A wisp of shadow streaked through the air above her head. The intruder turned to face her after it landed, twitching its tufted ears before bounding off into the night.

Pawly turned toward Tommy and shook off a sudden chill.

Sally, silent for the first time all night, stood beside him looking all around as if trying to pinpoint from where the sound had come. The girl possessed mere *human* hearing—had she been too far away to know for sure? Pawly could only hope.

She met her brother's gaze and nodded toward Sally. *Watch her. I'll go check—*

Hands clamped themselves with superhuman strength over Pawly's mouth and shoulder. Then they shoved her face first into the graffiti-riddled shipping container behind her. The hand over her mouth drew her head gently to one side. The stars parted and her mother's fur-covered face came into focus. "*You're* not in trouble but Sally might be. You and Tommy get her aboard and below deck. Stay there until your Uncle Ritzi says otherwise. Got me?"

Pawly nodded once while her mother sniffed at the air over her shoulder.

"Good," her mother replied and patted her cheek. "*Halmonim* and I will meet you ashore in Green Bay. Now go!" With a grunt, she launched herself atop the container and disappeared.

Pawly held her cheek, still warm where the fur covering her mother's hand had caressed it. Her mind raced, torn between going after the werecat intruder and abiding her mother's wishes. The tug's prime mover rumbled to life, settling her on the task at hand while thick smoke belched from the funnel. She stepped out from behind the container and met Tommy's gaze. *Get all that?*

With a slight nod in reply, her brother reached down and took Sally's hand in his. "C'mon, my telescope's stowed beneath my rack ahead of the engine room. Help me set it up?"

"Uh, sure. Okay," Sally replied with a nervous smile.

Chapter Eighteen

Later that evening.

Ritzi closed the cabin door and stepped over to the bulwark. Gingerly, he laid his elbows atop the cap rail, the dull ache in his shoulder forgotten as thousands of stars twinkled back at him from the dark canopy above Lake Michigan. He leaned into the rail with his right side and blew out a long sigh.

What could Blaznikov's game possibly be? The man had been harassing their family on and off for generations now, Ritzi had come to learn, getting up to all sorts of illicit things in between. Which had made him rich. And all that much more dangerous, to hear Dory tell it.

So, what had enticed Blaznikov to show up here? Now? Dumb luck had seen to it the elder werecat showed up while Armando Ruiz was in the head. Then again, Blaznikov could well have been watching them already, waiting for an opportunity to taunt at his fellow Kindred. Or to test them.

He rubbed his temples, then closed his eyes and breathed deep through his nose. Ritzi exhaled slowly through his mouth while his shoulder muscles relaxed. Tension from the last several weeks of chaos slipped away, carried off with his breath into the cold air, but only somewhat. It would have to do until he returned to dry land, until he began his meditation routine once more.

Though it was going to take much more than that to exorcise his worry for Alex. He had no idea what had become of her after she'd taken off after Blaznikov. And would her going toe to toe against another werecat hasten her body's imminent breakdown? Though his sister was as tough as she was fast, if anything were to happen to her, he would hold himself responsible. Not to mention that Barry would, too. Despite Ritzi's promise to never again entertain the idea of working for Blaznikov, now knowing what his family had shared with him about the man.

Flashes of light around the edge of his vision drew his attention back to the wardroom. He half expected to witness smoke pouring forth from the galley as the kids fled some mishap of their own creation. But all he saw were Pawly, Tommy, and their friend Sally, seated around the table as Dory's younger brother Robercik held court. Bobby was the quintessential Great Lakes ship captain—weathered skin, lined face, long bushy salt-and-pepper beard, unruly graying hair sticking out every which way from beneath a black wool sailor's cap. And, like generations of Great Lakes mariners before him, wont to regale any and all with stories of his seafaring exploits given any opportunity.

Ritzi, Barry, and Alex could each recite Bobby's repertoire of tall tales from memory by the time they reached adulthood. The near two decades since had undoubtedly allowed their captain to grow his collection both in size and incredulity. Sally's eager, bubbly nature suggested to Ritzi she was a trusting and somewhat naïve type of girl. The rapt attention she paid to Bobby was neither feigned nor forced.

But could he say the same for the twins? For all he knew, they were just trying to duck out of scullery duty.

Or, maybe, the twins were trying to distract themselves from the disconcerting answers Ritzi had given them whenever one or the other managed to get him alone. *Yes, Pawlina, you likely saw another werecat. Yes, Tomasz, there* are *other werecats scattered about the world over. Yes, differing ideals about how to live among humans led to bloody schisms between our ancestors' clans.* And Ritzi had no idea whether the influence of one particular rival clan elder nudged his family toward deliverance from their Affliction or their destruction by it. Though application of Occam's Razor led Ritzi to what he believed the most likely conclusion—that the twins worried about their mother as much as he did.

The sound of a sliding window caused him to look up the ladder toward the wheelhouse deck. Dory stuck his head out the window and shouted toward the cabin roof above his head where Armando Ruiz and Nat stood beside the mainmast. The three of them sniped back and forth as they finagled a replacement radio aerial into place and tested it. Either Alex and Blaznikov snapped off the original during their scuffle earlier, rendering their ship-to-shore unusable until it was replaced. Despite Bobby's reluctance, Alex had insisted the boat put out anyway while she drew Blaznikov away. Dory had been quick to concur.

Ritzi went back inside the wardroom, a smile coming to his face as his gaze fell on Bobby. Dory must have sent him below to check on their meal preparations, affording himself a few minutes of quiet in which to effect repairs. Though the mariners who used the bands regularly would lament Lake Michigan's most notorious rag chewer being back on the air, the family needed to ensure reliable communications with the Coast Guard and other vessels should they encounter rough weather or another calamity as they steamed toward Green Bay.

Armando and Nat confirmed his suspicions when they slid one after the other down the ladder and entered the wardroom. They exchanged knowing nods; Bobby hadn't even bothered to acknowledge them. The throaty growl of the boat's enormous diesel engine two decks below their feet dropped a half octave, then another, then another. Ritzi's gaze darted between Nat and Bobby and Armando. Their surprised looks suggested they didn't know why Dory and Annie would suddenly throttle down either.

Boots clomping down the wheelhouse ladder garnered everyone's full attention until Annie burst through the cabin door. "This just came through from the National Weather Service in Milwaukee," she said, thrusting the piece of paper in her hand toward Bobby. "Dory told me you needed to see it right away."

Brow furrowed, Bobby took the note and squinted at the letters printed there. A strained gasp escaped his mouth after his eyes shot open. "Open Lake Forecast *I* read before we shoved off didn't say nothin' 'bout any..."

He jammed the paper into the pocket of his pea coat and stomped over to the wardroom door. After snatching a pair of binoculars from their hook beside him, he threw the door open and scanned the horizon back and forth. "I want all of you to stow our grub and then get below, just to be on the safe side," he said as he lowered the binoculars to his chest. "We're in for some weather."

Forty minutes later.

Ritzi knelt down in front of Sally, gripping a bunk upright to steady himself. Their 115-foot boat pitched and rolled beneath his feet, making slow yet sure headway through the storm. "All right. Let's see if those potatoes are ready yet."

The girl sat on the floor with her back to the bulkhead, straddling a large metal stock pot. Pawly and Tommy looked up from where they sat shoulder-to-shoulder with their friend, the three of them wedged between opposite bunks at the front of the forecastle. Bobby had insisted upon their arrangement for safety's sake, so as to prevent the kids from being bounced around.

He winked at them with approval. Ritzi had been aboard ship on rough seas before, and these didn't especially worry him.

Sally had panicked after Bobby ordered them below, certain she would be sick. She needn't have worried, clearly. Regardless, the twins had seen to it the girl's hands and mind remained occupied carrying out their evening meal's preparations. If they were at all scared themselves, they weren't letting on to anyone. Even to Ritzi, whose nose detected no trace of fear's stink on them.

"They should be," Pawly said as she whittled away at the block of cheese which she had carried below with her. A pile of slices lay in her lap atop a paper plate.

Rye bread slices stood stacked up in a cardboard box set upon the floor before Tommy's crossed legs, each pair separated by a square of aluminum foil. "Sal here's been mashin' and mixin' away like a champ."

Sally let go of the masher's wooden handle, allowing her hands to drop to her sides. "A champ whose arms are about to friggin' fall off," she said and leaned back against the bulkhead.

"Don't worry," Pawly said with a wry grin. "Tommy'll be glad to hand feed you if your arms are still tired by the time we eat, won't you?"

While Sally and Tommy blushed, Ritzi swiped his finger through the potatoes and popped a dollop of them into his mouth. "Oh, that's good," he said, smacking his lips together. "The sauerkraut ought to be mixed through the potatoes evenly before we bake the sandwiches, and these are quite fine. Thank you, Miss Ruiz."

The hatchway leading topside creaked open. A pair of boots clomped down the ladder while the hatch slammed shut.

Ritzi leapt to his feet. Before the footsteps reached their compartment door, he opened it find Sally's stepfather standing in the passageway with a big smile on his face. "You're holding up better than you thought, *cariño*. What were you all on about earlier, saying you get seasick in a rowboat?"

"She's been a big help to us down here, for sure," Ritzi replied before Sally could answer, waving an arm toward the foodstuffs set out before the kids. "And I believe we'll all feel better with something on our bellies. Not thrilled at the prospect of eating our sandwiches cold, though."

The other man pursed his lips. "Why would we?"

"We're not to go topside until the storm blows over. Even to use the galley oven."

"Nonsense. Wrap the sandwiches up in that foil and box 'em up," Sally's stepfather said with a nod toward Tommy. "I'm on my way to the engine room to check our oil levels. Five minutes on top of the exhaust manifold in seas like these? Make sure to turn 'em once and they'll surely be crunchy on the outside, gooey and warm on the—"

A sickening hollow screech from outside the compartment door cut him off. His hand shot up and gripped the handrail running the length of the overhead before the boat lurched to starboard.

"The load, Armando!" crackled Dory's voice through the PA speaker above their heads. "The crane trolley on top slid all kittywampus after that last breaker over our bow. Threw the whole thing off balance!"

Armando cursed and bounded up the hatchway ladder two rungs at a time. At the top, he threw open the hatch just as a wave crashed into the side of the barge lashed fast to the tug's bow. He yelped and yanked the hatch closed, but not before the frigid spray drenched him head to toe.

"No shit the load's off balance!" he shouted back into the mouthpiece of the squawk box beside the hatchway door. "List like that and another roller's liable to send it and the barge straight to the bottom."

Ritzi gulped. Earlier he had watched Nat, Annie, and Dory secure the barge to the tug under the expert supervision of Armando and Bobby. If the barge went down, their boat would certainly go with it. Along with all of them. Lake Michigan's water didn't need to be deep to be cold. And lethal. Ritzi had no desire to discover how much.

He winced as Armando's fist slammed up against the compartment wall. "Come about then!" he barked into the squawk box, grabbing a turnbuckle ratchet and a longshoreman's hook from the rack behind him. "I'll...I'll go cut 'er loose." With that, Armando turned and scrambled back up the ladder.

"Don't do it!" Sally screamed after him before giving chase.

Pawly stumbled across the compartment to the ladder. "Wait, Sally!"

Armando, on deck already, glowered at Sally after she popped up through the hatchway behind him. Stepfather and daughter screamed at one another to get below until the howling wind drowned them both out. Metal scraped against metal with an ear-splitting shriek when the load aboard the barge shifted again. The boat lurched hard to port in response, tossing them all to the floor.

Ritzi blinked away stars and gazed back up at the hatchway door, finding no trace there of either Armando or Sally.

"No!" Pawly cried. The pungent odor of her fearful pheromones sent images of the *Baltic Wayfarer*'s final hours afloat coursing through Ritzi's mind. The last thing he remembered before the Soviet sub commander pistol-whipped him was the wild, feral look in his sister's eyes.

The same one he saw now in her daughter's.

Chapter Nineteen

P AWLY *KI-HAPED* AND SLAMMED her open fist against the hatchway door at the top of the ladder. It flew open and clanged against the cabin wall as she bounded to the gunwale and peered out over Lake Michigan's churning water. A flash of lightning illuminated her view from horizon to horizon before blackness covered everything once more. "Sally!" she cried, her hands cupped to her mouth. Then started after something brushed across the bare skin of her face.

She gasped and stared down at the gray and black guard hairs sprouting swiftly across her hands and wrists. *Oh no! Not now!* "Sally! Sally, can you hear...?"

Her voice trailed off as deafening silence enveloped her. Pawly clenched her eyes shut and palmed her temples, intent on clinging to her consciousness with her own two hands if need be. Her eyes flickered open, revealing only a dark void. She squeezed her head and screamed as her other senses abandoned her—smell, touch, even taste. The void dampened every sensation, squashed every thought before it could even form. Consumed her wholly, extinguishing her very existence.

But then a prick of light burst forth, like the first star at dusk on a clear night. Her vision widened as she turned, and at its center lay an enormous Chinook salmon. The largest one Pawly had ever seen come to spawn wriggled about on the stream's rocky bank. She padded her way along the shore, oblivious to everything around her, eyes fixed on her prey. It taunted her with wide eyes, flapping at the water with its huge fins, trying to escape.

The ground beneath her feet pitched and weaved with every step. But this catch would be hers, despite even the stupid ground attempting to thwart her. The fish purged its air bladder as Pawly approached, its soft moans crescendoing into terrified shrieks. Killer's blood coursed through her body with every heartbeat. Her prey must have been able to sense it, knowing she was about to be *its* killer also.

Pawly's awkward dance, though, tried her patience. Her stomach gurgled; drool dribbled from her jowls. Growling in frustration, she hunched up against a rock and compressed her body like a spring. Seconds stretched on as she waited. Saliva dripped from the tips of her fangs as she made a show of licking her lips. She flexed her toes and prepared to pounce. Time slowed to a crawl while the water broke ashore with a low rumble.

Now!

In that moment came a throaty roar, seemingly from everywhere. It penetrated Pawly like electricity, shorting out her huntress' instinct. Conveying one message and one message only—her alpha was *not* happy.

A booming thunderclap startled her, followed by breakers crashing across the bow of their boat. A hollow *clunk* from somewhere to her left drew Pawly's attention toward her brother's fur-covered form, clawing at the air between him and their uncle. Ritzi gnashed his teeth and pressed her brother up against a bulkhead, one hand wrapped around his neck. Sally's stepfather Armando lay face up on the deck plates beside them. Blood poured from a gash across his face.

Oh, God! Did Tommy...no, no he couldn't have...

Ritzi spied her and roared again, his tone and pitch suggesting Pawly heed some warning she didn't yet understand. A scream from where the fish had been a moment before made Pawly turn, just in time to see Sally's prone form disappear beneath a wall of water crashing over the boat's stern. The breaker retreated an instant later back into the raging surf, taking Sally with it.

Without even a backward glance, Pawly leapt atop the gunwale and dove headfirst. Her nose and paw pads went numb in the frigid water. Air trapped by her thick down fur would protect Pawly from the water's ferocious cold for a time, but Sally wouldn't last two minutes out here. Even less if the girl had already gone into shock. She had to work fast.

After breaking the surface long enough to fill her lungs with air, Pawly dipped her head under and kicked back and forth with all the energy she could muster. Thrusting water behind her in long, sweeping motions, Pawly did likewise with her arms once, twice, three times. At ten, she stuck her head above the water. Her ears twitched back and forth as she listened for a scream, a whimper, a cry—anything that might help her locate Sally. The stale air in her chest needled at her lungs, but she didn't dare breathe. Not yet. Not until she found where...

There!

Pawly blew out her breath. After drawing in more air, she paddled with all her might in the direction from where she'd heard Sally gasp and sputter. A plunging breaker dragged Sally beneath the surface once more as soon as Pawly heard her. She wasn't about to let it keep her friend for long.

Within seconds Pawly reached her. Sally's limp body drifted downward, the little trail of bubbles floating toward the surface getting shorter with each passing second. Pawly shot out her arm and snatched a fistful of the girl's pants. Her claws sank into the sturdy denim, snaring them. Good. They were in this together, now. They would both survive or both drown. And to hell with the latter.

Her legs burned as Pawly thrust their way to the surface. They burst from the water in time for her to glimpse their boat's starboard side, pounding its way through the waves away from them. Pawly had jumped from the port side amidships. In human form she could never have swam such a distance so quickly, even in calm water. In human form, she might well have been dead by now.

Just as Sally was sure to be if she didn't hurry up.

The wind howling at Pawly's back chilled her right through her down fur. Her legs, submerged in the frigid water, burned as if they were on fire. But if she stopped kicking, even for a moment, the massive rollers all around them would surely suck them under. And if she failed to approach the boat's deck at just the right angle, the crushing surf would piledrive them both into the hull headfirst.

Pawly cried out as she struggled to keep Sally's head above water. With the girl's chin in the crook of one arm, Pawly kept them afloat by paddling with her other. But she needed both arms to swim and needed them *now*. Her body tensed up, overwhelmed by the cold water surrounding her and the red-hot adrenaline within.

After adjusting her grip beneath Sally's shoulders, Pawly overreached and tugged hard on the girl's belt. With a grunt she tossed Sally onto her back and fumbled with the belt's buckle until she worked it free from her jeans. Thrashing her legs to avoid sinking further, Pawly threaded the belt around the girl's wrists and cinched it tight. She poked one claw through the belt's canvas webbing, creating a new hole to keep its grip snug. Then she looped her friend's arms around her head and tied off the long end around her forearm. After the girl's hands drew tight across Pawly's neck, she breathed deeply and dove forward.

She managed to get them halfway to the boat before running out of air. After nudging Sally's hands aside with her chin, she gulped down another lungful and resumed her frantic paddling. They plummeted into the valley of a massive swell while the boat rose up atop another. It loomed over them like a skyscraper during an earthquake, an instant before crumbling to the street below atop the fleeing throngs.

Having mistimed the waves, Pawly screamed into the frigid water, foolishly expelling her air. Arms and legs thrashed about as she tried to get as much water between them and the boat's keel, but she was going nowhere. Her heart raced; her lungs burned. As she glanced back toward the hull, a bright orange life ring skittered across the water past her left shoulder. "Grab on!" someone shouted above the din.

Pawly threw her arm over top of the rope. It drew taut, sliding through the crook of her arm until the life ring snugged up against her side. After jamming her arm into the ring, pain exploded across her side and shoulder. Pawly and Sally burst forth from the water and bellyflopped onto the deck plates. Needles of ice stung clean through to Pawly's skin, her soaked clothes and fur frozen solid by the frigid air.

But none of that mattered. They were safe. Pawly lay there and moaned, still clinging to the life ring. Every part of her throbbed in pain, the numbness barely taking the edge off. She opened her eyes and found Uncle Ritzi on one knee beside her, gathering Sally's unconscious form up in his arms.

He stood and folded Sally over like a coat in the crook of one arm before offering Pawly his other hand. "Can you stand?"

"Th-think so," she managed to spit out before her uncle pulled Pawly to her feet. He led her along the deck toward the hatchway behind the galley. "Look out!" he cried, clutching Pawly about her shoulders with his free arm an instant before another roller crashed down upon them.

A loud *creeeeeak* came as the waters receded, followed by a hollow *thunk*. "This way!" Uncle Nat shouted before Ritzi thrust his hip into her back. Steel scraped against steel once more as the hatch slammed shut. Darkness enveloped them.

Their ragged breaths echoed off the walls inside the cramped compartment. Nat wriggled free of the tangled heap he lay in together with Ritzi, Sally, and Pawly and switched on his light. "Annie is tending Armando now," Nat said and motioned them toward the passageway. "Come on."

Ritzi leapt to his feet and stomped off in the direction Nat had indicated, Sally still in his arms. After drawing up alongside them, Nat checked Sally's vitals and swept out her mouth. Ritzi turned sideways and gingerly stepped through the compartment door to keep from jostling the girl more than necessary. Behind him, Annie sprang from the head of the bunk where Armando lay to the one opposite. "We'll take it from here, Ritzi," she said, waving to where he ought to put Sally down.

"Are they...will they...?"

"It's too soon to tell." Annie nodded toward Ritzi. "But I'm certain the only reason they have a chance at all is because of you and Pawly."

Pawly blinked. "Wait...didn't Tommy—?"

"No, he had nothing to do with Armando's injury." Nat knelt beside the elder man and wrapped a fresh bandage around his head. "Took a mooring bit to the face after a breaker bowled him over. That's all."

"Come, Pawly," Ritzi said, shoving past her through the hatch. "Tommy's already topside. I'll need help from you both."

Chapter Twenty

R ITZI'S FOREARM PROVIDED LITTLE protection from the tiny ice balls pelting his face. What didn't hit him from above bounced off the railing in front of him and struck him from underneath. He squinted straight into the squall, finding Tommy had taken up post on the deck of the barge nearest to their tug's bow.

Pawly had disappeared behind the crane trolley balancing precariously near the barge's port side. When the wind ebbed for a moment, Ritzi made out her tiny form clambering her way toward the operator's cab. She paused as the barge climbed a roller, continuing on after cresting it. Once atop the cab, she stabbed her toe claws into the rubber blocks beneath an electrical equipment cabinet and drew herself up to her full height.

The window behind Ritzi rattled and banged as Bobby lowered it. "Are you ready?" he said after sticking his head out.

Ritzi nodded.

"Steady as she goes," Bobby said over his shoulder to Dory, standing at the boat's helm. After bowing his head and crossing himself, Bobby turned back to Ritzi. "Your show, mate."

With a huff he turned away and leaned up against the railing. Bobby had gambled and gambled big in a last-ditch effort to save his business—the same business which helped Ritzi's adoptive father keep a roof over his children's heads until the dean of Loyola's biology department hired him. And here Ritzi was, together with Pawly and Tommy, trying to keep Bobby and Armando both from financial ruin. Yet another burden he found himself forced to shoulder, despite never having agreed to do so. Though if they didn't stop the barge from capsizing and taking the tug to the bottom with it, it would hardly matter. Ritzi leaned over the railing and gave voice to his anger with a roar.

Pawly and Tommy snapped into action. She scrambled to the top of the crane trolley's superstructure while her brother hefted the coil of rope beside him.

Ritzi wobbled as another roller crashed across the barge's deck, drenching him with frigid water for the third time in as many minutes.

Tommy shook out his fur and swung the rope around his head. The grapnel tied to its end made a larger circle with each pass until Pawly yowled and jammed her hands together out in front of her. Her brother leapt atop one of the barge's massive wooden spuds and let the grapnel fly.

The gale drew the line taut behind the grapnel as it flew from one side of the barge to the other. Pawly caught it in both hands and whirled around to keep the thing's momentum from bowling her over. Then she wound up and hurled it back to him. The twins pitched the grapnel back and forth the length of the barge and back again. After that, Pawly set to lashing the rope to the eyelet at the end of a steel cable.

Tommy wound the rope around the deck winch nearest him and took up the slack. After a wave from Pawly, he cinched up the rope with the windlass, pulling the steel cable over and around the crane's components splayed across the barge deck.

From his perch, Ritzi darted his gaze back and forth between the rope and Pawly. She bounded along over top of the equipment, keeping watch over the rope as it pulled the cable through. Any sign of the cable binding up or the rope chafing against a sharp edge and she would signal, which Ritzi would relay to Tommy. The barge shuddered beneath the shifting weight of the equipment. They would have only one shot at saving the load, along with their lives.

After the cable eye reached him, Tommy jogged the winch until he had a length of cable wrapped around the windlass' drum. Then he slammed the gearbox into low and the windlass took up the remaining cable at a snail's pace. The heavy structural members of the crane creaked and groaned as they slid away from the edge of the barge, back toward its center.

Bobby whistled. "Holy shit, it's working!"

A smile spread across Ritzi's face. It was indeed. Or so he thought, until metal screeching across metal shattered his happy illusion. He gasped and glanced down to where Tommy peered over the windlass at the slack cable strung across the barge deck; he must've heard it, too.

The line's tension had caused the crane jib to slide into the trolley and bind up. Without raising one or lowering the other, pulling the cable taut again might snap them both in two. And breaking such large and heavy pieces loose could well result in the twins being crushed between them.

If that wasn't alarming enough, any part of the crane sufficiently cracked or warped to work itself out from underneath the cable might slide free across the barge deck. Should all the members skid to one side, the next big roller would surely flip both barge and tug right over. And Ritzi had no desire for him or anyone else aboard to end their night sleeping with the fishes.

"Dory! Maintain course and speed," Bobby said as Ritzi turned around to face him. He had pulled his rainsuit's overcoat back on and was fumbling with the straps of his life preserver. "C'mon, mate," he said with a nod. "We've got to get down there and help them."

Ritzi opened his mouth to say something, but Tommy's yowl cut him off. More like a cry of excitement than one of warning. He spied his nephew pointing off their starboard bow toward the horizon, face barely containing his smile. When he made eye contact with Ritzi he held up his five fingers on one hand. Then he held his hands above his head and brought them together. After that, he thrust both arms in the direction he'd been pointing and mouthed what looked to Ritzi like *give 'er hell*.

"What's he tryin' to tell us?"

Ritzi glanced in the direction Tommy had indicated but found no answer to Bobby's question. The blackened sky flashed white for an instant, revealing a wall of water bearing down on them. His eyes went wide as a thunderclap shook the deck plates below their feet. Ritzi clutched the railing and turned away to keep the force of the crashing wave from blowing him overboard.

"The fuck's with you, now?"

Bobby's voice dragged Ritzi back into the present moment. Another breaker crested across the horizon, a monster at least four times the size of any they had ridden out tonight. And it was heading their way. Why had Tommy spotted it before? Why hadn't *he*? Ritzi vowed to investigate later, so long as they all managed to get out of this alive.

"Bobby, aim our bow that way!" Ritzi said over the din and thrust his right arm out over the water. "Cut the power on my signal, then be ready to re-engage."

Bobby sucked in his breath at the sight of the massive roller. "Hard to starboard!" he shouted over his shoulder and grabbed the PA mic.

"Annie, Nat, get everyone below deck secured *now*. Dory, stand ready for flank speed on my mark. And everyone, hang the fuck on!"

Dory blinked. "But...but, that'll—"

"Do it!" Ritzi yelled.

Dory growled and cranked the wheel over to his right as fast as he could. When it clanked up against its stop, he shouted "We're hard over!"

Ritzi stared up at the towering wall of water roaring toward their boat. "Holy shit," Dory mumbled from behind him.

"Sta-a-and by..." Bobby bit his knuckle until Tommy dropped his arms. "Flank!"

The boat rode into the valley ahead of the roller and powered into it just as the wall of water broke over their bow. When the force lifted both vessels into the air, Tommy worked the winch as hard as he could.

Ritzi hunched down and wrapped both his arms around the railing. The claws on his fingertips scraped along the brass as he struggled to keep his footing. After the wave blasted past, Ritzi shook his head to clear water from his ears and glanced up toward the barge's bow.

The cable pulled free and yanked the crane sections into a straight line right before the barge came crashing down atop the water's surface. Everyone grunted and hollered and held fast as their boat did likewise.

Tommy pumped his fist in the air and let out a whoop. By divine Providence, the boat—along with all of them—had remained upright.

Pawly untangled herself from the frame members, her claws sunk deep into the wooden dunnage beneath.

With a wave, Ritzi beckoned them both back to the bridge. Tommy secured the winch and shuffled his way back toward the wardroom.

Ritzi entered the pilot house and fell into a chair shoved into the back corner. "Good work, everyone," he managed to mumble before passing out.

"**R**EVEILLE! REVEILLE! ALL HANDS, heave out!"

Dim gray daylight filtered through the cloudy skies above, assaulting Ritzi's eyes as he blinked them open.

Barry knelt beside him. "Heave out and trice up," he said in a gruff voice as he shook Ritzi's shoulder with one hand.

Ritzi moaned and sat up. A panoramic view of the Green Bay waterfront spread out before him through the pilot house windows. "What're you doing here?" he said, rubbing at the loose fur covering his face. "I thought you were in Washington on Navy business."

"I was. Until your mom called to say Alex had collapsed after chasing off that shitstain Blaznikov. Let's just say my CO understood the urgency of my immediate leave request."

Ritzi started, yelping as a clump of fur pulled free. "She did? Where is she? What happened? Is she okay?"

"Yes, she did indeed. She's at the house, where your mom is tending her. And...we don't know. No reason I can figure Alex would've collapsed. Near as me and the rest can figure, she'd barely even worked up a sweat."

Barry stood and hurled a bundle at Ritzi, almost knocking him out of his chair after it caught him in the face. "Put these on." He nodded toward the now-empty barge in front of them. "Have something on the deck you need to see."

Ritzi grunted and tugged a watch cap free from inside a wadded-up pair of coveralls.

"There's a balaclava inside," Barry said as he stepped over to the helm. "Figured you'd need it. You look like shit."

Barry stared down at the barge's deck while Ritzi suited up, his back to him. "I drove your mom's van up here to spot Nat and Annie. They were going to pick up that Ruiz girl at the hospital here and drop her off in Milwaukee on their way through."

"Bit of a hike from Jefferson Park, don't you think?"

"That's where they airlifted her stepfather last night after taking him and Sally off at Kewaunee. Her mom'll be there waiting." Barry turned his head just far enough to peek at Ritzi out of the corner of his good eye. "Nat and Annie'll have that long to try to tease out of Sally just what she knows. About Pawly."

Ritzi stood and zipped up the front of his coveralls. "Nat said Armando was out cold by the time the twins morphed," he said, pulling the balaclava over his face. "Lucky for us, huh?"

Barry's face hardened. He stomped over to Ritzi, coming nose to nose. "Don't count on it. Dad and I have reason to believe we're *not* the only ones who know Sally saw the twins in their ailuran forms." Barry gripped Ritzi by the wrist and led him from the pilot house. "C'mon. See for yourself."

Ritzi swallowed his lips and followed Barry down the bridge ladder. Together they climbed over the bow fender and onto the barge deck, not a word passing between them. Barry stopped in the doghouse doorway and pointed to where Dory sat at the chart table, fiddling with a small black object about the size of a box of business cards. "Dad tells me Bobby spotted this thing atop our port side spud. I arrived after Bobby left to get groceries, so while we've been waiting, I shimmied up and got it down."

"What is it?" Ritzi asked, stepping forward to get a better look.

Dory held the thing out toward Ritzi. "Some sort of battery-powered surveillance camera, near as I can tell." He tapped at the top of the device with one finger, near where a jagged stump of fiberglass rod protruded forth. "I think it might've been equipped with some kind of encrypted satellite uplink feed. Likely the antenna sheared off during the storm sometime."

"Right where Alex thought it might be, too," Barry said. "Leading Blaznikov away from our family was her first priority. Then she collapsed before she could tell any of us about him planting the camera. By the time she came to, you guys were almost to Kewaunee."

Ritzi blinked. "I...I don't understand. Why would Blaznikov..."

"But wait, don't answer yet!" Barry proclaimed in his best TV commercial announcer voice. "That's not all!"

Barry stepped over to a pair of frayed steel cables lying on the barge's deck and took a knee. "Look here," he said, taking the end of one in his hand. "These strands frayed when the cable snapped. But these *here* were cut and cut clean. By someone who knew exactly what they were doing."

Ritzi gasped and drew his fingertips to his mouth. "Sabotage, Barry? But why would he—"

"Holy fuck, man! Why do you *think*?" Barry cried and threw down the cable. "And everyone says *he's* the smart one," he muttered, shoving Ritzi aside as he stomped off toward the boat.

Dory laid a hand atop Ritzi's trembling shoulder. "We think Blaznikov set us up. Apparently so he could watch the twins in action. I don't know what his game is, Ritzi. But your actions have forced us to play."

Then Dory turned and followed Barry, saying no more. Ritzi watched them go until both men climbed over the fender and disappeared. He pulled down the opening of his balaclava and rubbed at his chin, absentmindedly tugging at a clump of shed fur. With a sigh, he set the clump flying away in the stiff breeze. After watching it waft off across the harbor and out of sight, Ritzi turned and set off after them.

Bobby appeared to have just arrived back from the grocery store, though Ritzi didn't recall hearing their scooter approach. Together with Barry and Dory, they passed sacks of food and other supplies to one another like an abbreviated bucket brigade. Ritzi made his way back to his bunk from the other side of the boat, his path taking him past the boat's tiny shower amidships. He paused, hearing Pawly humming to herself from inside over the sound of running water. Most of her clothes and her jacket lay in a heap on the passageway floor beside the door. The wind picked up outside where someone had propped open their starboard side sea door, whooshing throughout the boat's passageways. Giving Ritzi a face full of the sweet, sour scent he'd come to loathe.

Coming right from Pawly's clothing.

Ritzi gasped and rifled through his niece's clothes. Every scrap reeked, just as strong as Alex's had been. Not only had Pawly's body manifested the telltale signs of imminent breakdown, their bout of physical activity last night had hastened the process.

No, that couldn't be right. Surely, his mistake.

He tossed Pawly's clothes aside and barged into the berthing compartment he shared with Tommy. The same smell, just as strong in here. "Fuck!"

"Whazzup?" his nephew mumbled from his rack as Ritzi combed through every article of the boy's clothing lying about the compartment floor. "Uncle Ritzi? What...what're you doing?"

What *was* he doing, anyway? Ritzi didn't know. Didn't know what he was doing. Didn't know how he was going to save the twins. Didn't know how he was going to save his sister. Didn't know whether Barry would ever forgive him. Didn't know whether Barry might one day hunt him down and torture him. Slowly. The compartment walls came closer, closer, all four sides, all at the same time.

"You okay, Uncle Ritzi?"

He turned to find Tommy peeking out at him through his berth curtain, rubbing at his eyes with one fist.

"No, I...I..."

Tommy's face washed out red, as did everything else in sight. Ritzi reached out and fell forward, catching himself against the compartment wall. He hyperventilated through clenched teeth, his fangs piercing his bottom lip. His claws scratched and screeched along the walls as he fumbled his way along, out of the compartment and down the passageway. He wreathed the latch handle and burst through the door, emerging out onto the boat's deck. Though overcast, he still had enough light to make out shapes. Like the two men approaching him, both calling his name.

He cursed under his breath and launched himself ashore.

R ITZI LEANED BACK AGAINST the tree and patted at his stomach. He belched and picked at his teeth with one claw. Steam rose from what remained of the fresh deer carcass mere feet away from him in the clearing. He sighed and drank in the scents of the small wooded area all around him, Green Bay's homes and businesses and factories hardly a stone's throw away. But one strong, masculine scent in particular, wafting its way along via the gentle breeze, set the hairs on his back all on end.

He jumped to his feet as Blaznikov emerged from the tree line, once again wearing only his *mawashi*. The man stopped a few paces away, regarding Ritzi with a thoughtful look while scratching at the streak of silver fur above his forehead. The tufts of his ears twitched before his face cracked into a toothy grin. "You are a gracious host once again. Yes." Then he knelt and plunged his face into the deer carcass. After ripping every scrap of meat from the ribs, he looked up and fixed Ritzi with a mischievous smile. "Jin Bak at the grocery has still not heard from you. Rude of you to dally so long."

"I've been...busy."

Blaznikov drew the tips of his fingers to his chest. "I am busy man, too, yes."

"So I've heard. Doing whatever it is you do to get yourself on six countries' Most Wanted lists."

"Oh, how do the Americans say...to make omelet, must break eggs? It is like that."

Ritzi narrowed his eyes at him. "Then what makes you think I'm at all interested in working with you still? Knowing I'd put my family at risk in doing so?"

Blaznikov's ears laid back against his head as he crossed his arms. "What choice do you have? I can help you help the twins. Your sister, too. And prevent unnecessary bloodshed. Yes."

"'Bloodshed?' What bloodshed?"

"Your father and I agree on little. But we are both loath to risk exposing the clans' existence." Blaznikov studied his palm and flexed his fingers, causing his claws to extend and retract one by one. "Armando Ruiz and his daughter are both risks. Which we cannot permit to continue."

"He doesn't know anything. He was unconscious just before the twins morphed. Armando Ruiz poses no risk."

"Perhaps," Blaznikov replied with a shrug. "But you cannot say the same for the girl. I saw her myself in the video. Saw your niece morph and rescue her. Yes."

Ritzi said nothing as Blaznikov drew his wrist to his face. "Are you there?" he said, brushing aside the fur covering his watch.

"Go ahead," crackled a man's voice from the thing.

Myung-Duk? What the hell is he—?

"Have you located the Ruiz family?"

"Affirmative."

Ritzi gasped.

The man glanced up at him and smirked. "Where are they now?"

"In Milwaukee. Just pulled onto I-94 headed south. We're a couple cars behind them."

"Describe their vehicle."

"Late model Ford F-350 crew cab. Royal blue with lots of rust. Diesel engine. Woman driving has her foot to the floor on her way down the ramp. Can hardly see through the smog."

Ritzi gulped.

Blaznikov smiled. "Do you see the girl?"

"Affirmative. Looking out the rear driver's side window. Kou and Pang would like a word with her."

"The two whose brother was mauled in the park after she and her brother ran from you?"

"The same."

He locked eyes with Ritzi and smiled. "Do not let them see you. Follow them. Until I tell you otherwise. That is all."

The watch buzzed with static a moment and fell silent. "So, what fate might befall your niece's friend? We should discuss, no?" Blaznikov poked at the fur on his wrist once again. He jabbered in Russian for a bit with the man who answered, preening the long hair beneath his jowls with his other hand. Then he flipped the watch closed and narrowed his eyes at Ritzi. "My driver comes. And this time, you *shall* join me for a drink."

Chapter Twenty-One

Pawly cupped her cheek with one hand and sighed. Without moving her head, she glanced back and forth and counted in silence. Cars sped through the intersection in twos and threes, first in one direction then the other.

Tommy leaned farther forward and *tsk*ed each time she stomped down on the brake pedal.

"You're no expert either," their mother said over her shoulder. "Both of you need more practice."

He grumbled and leaned back as Pawly tromped the accelerator.

"Like a clock, like a clock," their mother said while Pawly completed her turn, letting the wheel slip through her hand. She could almost feel her skin burning beneath Mom's withering stare.

Replacing her hands at the ten-and-two positions on the steering wheel, Pawly could have sworn the car's passenger compartment had been ten degrees cooler mere moments ago.

Her brother had driven them all to O'Hare to see their Uncle Nat and Aunt Annie off. After saying their goodbyes at the security checkpoint, Pawly, Tommy, and their mother had almost made it back to their car when Mom's phone rang. The airline had grounded their uncle and aunt's flight to San Francisco via Denver, but offered to put them on a non-stop if they waited around for another four hours. So, their mother returned to the terminal, the twins in tow, to join them. It would be rude for Nat and Annie to wait alone, she had said.

Pawly could hardly blame her. Their family was disappearing one by one. Last year, Grandpa N's deportation. Today, Nat and Annie's trip back to the Chinese border with North Korea to rejoin their months-long research expedition. Days before, following their voyage from Green Bay and despite his new billet at Great Lakes, their dad's being called to Washington before deployment to yet another undisclosed theatre. And, holed up in a warehouse across town after finding his own way home from Wisconsin, any of them having seen Uncle Ritzi more than enough times to count on one hand with fingers left over.

Four blocks past the stop sign Pawly made a right and then a left onto their street. Their mother had been tight-lipped on the ride home from the airport, save for reminding Pawly as they sped along the Kennedy about the construction and weekend closure at their usual exit.

Their mother's sudden gasp as they approached their house made Pawly jam on the brakes. Fire rushing up both arms took her breath away before claws burst forth from her fingertips, embedding themselves into the faux leather wrap around the steering wheel.

"Sorry," Mom said, her hands planted atop the dashboard in front of her. "I did not mean to startle—"

"Hey look!" Tommy pointed past Pawly's shoulder out the right side of the windshield. "There's Miss O!"

Indeed, it was. Janie Olszewski, their uncle's former admin, slammed the driver's door of her tiny roadster. Their mother reached around the car's center console and waved her hand toward Pawly, low enough so the other woman couldn't see.

"Is Ritzi here?" she said as she approached their car.

"I...uhm...I'm, not sure, really," their mother replied. "Not sure at all, you know."

Pawly managed to work her claws free while her mother stammered out her answer, then jammed her hands into her armpits as if to warm them. Or, at least, that's what they'd all want Miss O to think.

"We've been out all afternoon. And Ritzi wasn't here when we left," their mother went on as she squinted at the car's clock radio. "Wasn't he at the warehouse with you?"

The other woman clicked her tongue. "He was until he left, but that was hours ago. He called afterward and asked me to swing by here after I closed up instead of his apartment. I'd've been here long before now, but an accident on the Circle downtown had traffic bottled up in every direction. Still wanted to bring him this." She held a paper shopping bag out to their mother. "Odds and ends left over from the move."

"Move? Ritzi didn't say anything to us about a move."

Janie's eyes went wide. "You mean he never told you?" she blurted out before a pained expression came over her face, as if debating whether to betray her former boss' trust or spill for his own good. "He said he'd found a new home for all his materials and equipment. Needed to get it all out of our warehouse right away so he could set up shop with some outfit overseas."

Their mother opened her mouth to say something but the sound of a car horn from behind cut her off. "Hop out, you two. Take this bag of your uncle's things and head inside. I'll be right in after I park the car around back." She took the bag from Miss O's hands and nodded.

"Thank you, Janie. For everything. I'll make sure Ritzi gets this. Now, if you'll excuse us..."

Miss O nodded and walked back toward her car.

When Pawly opened her door an instant later, their mother thrust her thigh into her side. Pawly stumbled out into the street while their mother yanked the door closed and gunned the car's engine. It tore off down the street while a truck went around on the opposite side, the driver giving them all a dirty look as he passed.

Pawly jammed her fists into the pockets of her jeans and invisibly flipped the guy off. A claw on each hand tore through each pockets' insides like it was tissue paper. She yelped, causing Tommy to snigger before he turned and trundled off into the house. Pawly fell in behind him, her mind racing as she plodded along. Where had Uncle Ritzi gone? Was he okay? Was this all somehow part of Blaznikov's angle? What was their mother thinking?

"Wait," she told Tommy when he slipped off his shoes inside the kitchen door. "Let's see if we can sniff out where Uncle Ritzi went. I'll check upstairs."

He shrugged. "Whatever. I'll start down here. Sweep the living room on your way out the front door and check the fence line. I'll duck out back and meet you by the garage."

Pawly did so, though any whiff of their uncle's scent in the house was already hours old. She found no trace outside either, but did, making her way along the fencerow, find plenty of thornbriers. Certainly, he hadn't come this way. Their uncle would have certainly left behind traces of his scent all over everything if he had. Much like Pawly was doing now, cursing under her breath every time a thorn poked its way through her jacket sleeve. Or whenever a burr lodged itself firmly in her hair.

Tommy exited through the kitchen door just as Pawly emerged from the bramble patch. She snarled at his amused expression. "Not one word, got it?" she said, carding at the end of one pigtail with her fingers.

"Have you found him?"

They both turned. Their mother rounded the corner of the garage and approached them.

"No, not yet," Tommy said while Pawly shook her head. "And we've looked everywhere."

Their mother let out a dejected sigh. "No, you haven't. Come with me."

The twins followed her into the garage, to the far corner of the *dojang*. She opened up the equipment locker and pushed the *jool bong* hanging on a rod at chest height to one side. Then she laid her palm flat on the wall and slid it from side to side until her fingers found a seam. She followed it down to a small hole and stuck her finger inside. A little door flipped open, revealing a keypad with numbers on it and a little red light above.

"One. Nine. One. Nine. Three. Nine," she said as she poked the buttons. "For the day Hitler's Germany invaded Poland—1st September 1939. Just like you learned in World History."

The back of the locker slid open and their mother stepped through. She waved for the twins to follow. Together they made their way single file down a narrow staircase. At the bottom to Pawly's right, a single lamp hanging above a small table in the corner lit the cramped space with a dingy glow. Beyond the half-opened door behind the table, Pawly spied a toilet and a sink. A sofa took up the entire wall opposite her. If it were a pull-out, pulled out it would just fit.

Pawly's mind reeled. How long had *this* been here anyway? Did it have to do with Grandpa D's being a ranking CIA official? Or had their family's soured relationship with the Nohs turned violent at some point? And had anyone planned to tell her and Tommy about it?

The stirring final measures of Poland's national anthem trilled forth from a speakerphone situated at the center of the table. Their mother stepped over next to it while a man's voice announced Polsat had reached the end of their broadcast day and that they were going off the air. "Hello? Anyone there?" their mother said into the speakerphone over top of the test pattern's piercing monotone.

"*Marsz! Marsz, Dąbrowski! Z ziemi wloskiej do Polski!*" came their grandfather's slurred voice in reply.

"Indeed Papa, 'Poland Is Not Yet Lost,'" she replied in Polish, a sad smile crossing her face. "But you *are* drunk."

"Alex, my dear!" Grandpa Niko replied in kind. "It's...it's your brother's fault, you know. I told him we...we shouldn't break open any of the *siwucha* I left for you all, but he insisted. Say, when'd you get here? An'...an' where's Ritzi?"

"He's not here, Papa, just me. The twins and I came looking for him."

"Oh, no. No! I was...was just talking to him. He couldn't have..." Through the phone drifted the sound of chair legs scraping across a tile floor, followed by a loud *thump*. Grandpa N regaled everyone with an assortment of Polish cuss words before breaking down. "Oh, Ritzi! My son, my son!" he said between sobs.

Pawly gulped, her stomach turning.

"Papa! What about him?" their mother said in a shaky voice.

"I...I tried to talk 'im out of it, Alex. Ritzi said he...he said he had to go. Wouldn't say where or how long he'd be. Only that he'd come home as soon as he could. And that he...he loved us. All of us. Even...even Barry..."

Grandpa Niko cried anew while their mother pulled out the chair beside Pawly and took a seat. She shoved the book in front of her aside and poked at the speakerphone's mute button. "After you slide open the door into the locker upstairs, it should shut ten seconds behind you. Go on into the house, I'll be along soon." Then she poked at the phone again and cooed to her distressed father in Polish, as if to calm him.

Pawly felt Tommy's hand on her elbow, tugging her toward the staircase. As she turned, she glimpsed the open book lying atop the table in the spot where their mother had slid it out of her way. Pawly recognized it as the Holy Bible her uncle had kept atop his office desk, opened to the twenty-third chapter of Luke's Gospel. Someone had highlighted a single verse toward the left page's bottom right, reading:

> *"For if men do these things*
> *while the tree is green, what*
> *will happen when it is dry?"*

Chapter Twenty-Two

North Korea. Eighteen hours later.

RITZI DREW BOTH HANDS to his mouth and dashed toward the trash can beside the banquet room door. The other Party officials sat stone still, transfixed by the grotesque images flashing across the screen set up at the front of the room. None flinched as Ritzi threw up every bit of the sumptuous brunch served mere minutes before, not an hour having passed since he and Blaznikov had arrived at Chŏngjin's tiny airport.

Undaunted, Blaznikov paced back and forth the length of the banquet hall. "As you can see, progress of our ailuranthropic human augmentation program to date is…unflattering," he said, addressing his North Korean benefactors in a flawless *Chosŏngŭl* dialect. "Inexplicable mutations and resultant threats to safety and security required our scientists terminate these subjects' test regimes early." Along with the subjects themselves, Ritzi knew went without saying. Not that any said subjects would have had the presence of mind to resist. He hoped their dying moments had brought each a sweet release, realizing their misery was at an end at last.

A similar thought had crossed Ritzi's mind high above the Pacific Ocean the night before. Aboard a chartered jet between the Aleutian Islands and Vladivostok, Blaznikov had detailed the program's spectacular failures going back to its inception a year earlier. But nothing, he realized as he gathered himself and stood, could have prepared him for the horrific realities he'd just seen. Nor for the cold, calloused manner in which Party leadership viewed the entire macabre enterprise. Reflected by the man at the place setting next to him, greeting Ritzi with a shrug and a breath mint as he returned to his seat.

Blaznikov droned on, describing each successive experiment's inevitable result. Ritzi's heart sank lower with each passing minute. To help his sister and the twins avoid such horrors themselves, he and his father had come to realize he would need a new control. The longer he thought about his loved ones' peculiar scents, the more he convinced himself previous treatments and therapies had ruined them for such a purpose. So, he would need access to another population of werecats.

Like, for example, the one Blaznikov told him about, rumored to still roam the mountain ranges bordering China and Russia to the north. The very ones he might be able to access one day—if he did exactly what Blaznikov and his benefactors among the assembled Party officials told him to do. Though if he didn't, they had made clear Ritzi would forfeit the lives of his loved ones. Starting with the Ruiz girl.

The screen went dark for a moment. A highlight reel of sorts queued up, featuring the twins' exploits during last week's near-fiasco while underway on Lake Michigan. Blaznikov raved about their displays of strength and agility while they responded to the calamity that he himself had manufactured. Ritzi grimaced and watched the twins save their boat, its load and their lives all over again. Numerous *oohs* and *aahs* from Party officials suggested they found their all-night motorcade north from Pyongyang to be eminently worthwhile.

"We can expect great things from Doctor Opoworo here, based on the research he and his father have already conducted," Blaznikov concluded, stepping up behind Ritzi to slap his shoulders with both hands. "Anything to add, Doctor?" He squeezed, Ritzi winced.

"My...my research," he began once their eyes were upon him, "will certainly progress now with your support." Ritzi's lips and jaw felt constrained, like he was trying to speak around a rolled-up sock stuffed into his mouth. Didn't help that he was struggling to remember his Korean on the fly, either. "And for that...for that I am grateful."

The contingent of Party officials and scientists appeared to approve of Ritzi's acceptance speech. They returned their attention to the screen after Blaznikov called up a slide presentation containing implementation targets and funding schedules. Ritzi steepled his hands and laid his chin atop them, staring straight ahead while his mind raced. He felt like a dog that had caught the damn car. *Now what the fuck do I do?*

"Dr. Opoworo, answer his question please."

Ritzi shook his head and glanced around to discover everyone in the room scowling at him. "I'm...I'm sorry. Could you ask it again?"

A man in a starched, olive-drab uniform adorned with red and gold piping stomped over to Ritzi's seat. "You will renounce!" he said and slid a paper across the table.

He blinked and looked down at a letter. What Ritzi tenuously grasped from the *Chosŏngŭl*, the English beneath it made patently clear. They were asking him to deny his American citizenship and pledge his allegiance to the Great Leader. His mouth fell open as he lifted his head. Blaznikov hadn't said word one about anything like *this*.

The man drew a pen from his chest pocket and clicked it open. "Do it," he said and jabbed the pen toward Ritzi. "Do it now."

Blaznikov nodded and rubbed at the back of his neck. Yes, Ritzi had wanted the opportunity to finish his research more than anything else. To save his sister. His nephew. His niece. One of his conditions in agreeing to any of this was his identity must remain a secret from anyone outside of this room. But signing a document like this would compromise his bargaining position, would torpedo any and all forms of plausible deniability. Officially and irrevocably, he would render himself an enemy of the state of his own adopted homeland. How could he help his loved ones if he couldn't get himself or whatever treatments he might come up with *to* them?

His world imploded, pulling the red haze from the edges of his vision along with it. Ritzi sprang from his seat and bolted down the hallway toward the exit. The soldiers stationed by the door levelled their rifles and shouted.

He couldn't make out a word they said.

DAWN. THE FOLLOWING MORNING.

AS HE AWOKE, RITZI's stomach growled like a roaring bear roused from hibernation. He turned his head toward the little city beyond the tree line. Doors slamming, engines turning over, voices while families woke up, ate breakfast, shuffled off to work and school. Paying *him* no mind whatsoever. Good.

He had been on the run from Blaznikov's goon squad for almost a day already, making his way west overland toward Mount Paektu at the Chinese border. He wasn't sure if he was feeling nervous or feeling relieved the North Koreans had yet to reveal themselves. They were sure to come; of that Ritzi was certain. His past biomolecular research and African tissue synthesis pilot project experience would be key to their human augmentation operation. Were they tracking him somehow? Trailing him, just out of sight? Toying with him like a lynx might a plump and tasty snowshoe hare?

His stomach growled again. Ritzi swore, wanting more than anything to change and take a fresh kill. But then he might be spotted still covered in fur and sporting pointed ears. Reports from freaked out locals of a monster in their streets would bring soldiers and special agents running. But then again, so would their spotting a Caucasian male walking around without an escort.

Since coming to after his initial rage had passed, he had so far managed to keep a low profile on the way from Chŏngjin. Stars shining bright in the clear night sky had enabled Ritzi to make good time through the forests. Avoiding open spaces like highways and railroad grades all the while.

Luck had afforded him an opportunity to filch a change of wardrobe and a blanket from backyard clotheslines in a remote farming village, right before helping himself to a small bunch of radishes and carrots from a community garden. He had ventured toward the livestock pens just long enough to snag an empty burlap sack and a pair of raggedy work boots from beside one of the barn doors. Even under cover of darkness Ritzi had not dared go further, no matter how much the thought of sinking his fangs deep into the neck of a chicken or goat had caused him to salivate.

The first rays of sunlight filtered down through the canopy above his head. Across the valley, Paektu's snow-covered peak lit up as if it were on fire. Though he couldn't remember its name, Ritzi recognized the town beyond the tree line from the last time he'd summited the mountain from the Chinese side. Which was, praise be, where he hoped to be again before nightfall.

Ritzi unwrapped himself from the blanket and shook his shed fur free. The goosebumps covering his skin made it easy for him to wipe the rest of his shed away before he dressed. He donned his undergarments and pulled the stolen shirt over his head. It came down just past his belly button.

Huh. Won't have to worry about tucking it in, I guess.

He would not have been able to, at any rate. The pants hung down as low on his hips as possible without falling down, and the cuffs still didn't quite reach to his ankles. He groaned and knotted his scarf around his waist. The gray wool was a close enough match to the villagers' clothes that Ritzi didn't quite look like he was wearing a cummerbund.

His stomach growled a third time. If this kept up, all the North Koreans would have to do to track him would be to stick their heads out of a window and listen. Which made Ritzi wonder all the more whether Blaznikov had let him run solely to prove a point.

Though Ritzi had a point of his own to prove—he didn't *need* the North Koreans. Fuck 'em. And fuck Blaznikov, too, for that matter. He'd carry on his own research, accompanied by the Ruiz girl and her whole family so he could personally assure their safety. Once he found his way back to America, that is. Or maybe to Poland? Yeah. There both he and his father could work to save Alex and Pawly and Tommy. Work harder than they ever had before. Sure, he and Papa were out of money. But he'd think of something! All he had to do now was get the hell out of here.

He needed to climb Mount Paektu, but figured he ought not on an empty stomach. Despite the vegetables from last night and the couple squirrels and rabbits Ritzi had managed to run down, Ritzi's flight had sapped his energy. The more sluggish he became, the easier it was for the animals to elude his grasp. Taking a deer or a boar would have been nice, but Ritzi had yet to see one. This was North Korea, after all. For certain, they had appeared tasty to someone else long before Ritzi had landed. Appeared the only source of protein to fuel his mad dash across the border was dumpster diving if he wanted to avoid detection. Peachy.

All of Ritzi's things went into the burlap sack, including the tatters that remained of his suit coat and slacks worn during his meeting the day before with Party officials. Ritzi tossed the sack over one shoulder before pulling the brim of the bucket hat down low over his eyes. With a halting gait and a hunched back, Ritzi set off toward town, hoping the natives wouldn't notice him being taller than most by a half a head at least.

Hours later.

Ritzi's taste buds confirmed what his nose had already informed him: he was eating dog meat. Charred dog meat at that, likely why the cooks had thrown it into the trash in the first place. But he didn't care. As hungry as he was, it could as well have been choice sirloin.

He sat hunched over in the bottom of the dumpster behind the restaurant the busful of European tourists had come out of, tearing flesh from the bone in bite-sized chunks. One went into his mouth, another into the too-small pockets of his stolen clothes for later. His mind wandered back to when his adopted parents would take him and Alex to pick blueberries as children, north and west of town near the Wisconsin border. Wandered so much, in fact, Ritzi failed to notice angry voices approaching until they were right beside his foul-smelling hideaway.

Ritzi's throat clenched around the chunk of meat he was trying to swallow, almost making him gag. He stuffed his fist into his mouth and bit down hard to help keep himself quiet. Two pairs of footfalls, belonging to an older man and a child. From their fast-talking Korean dialogue Ritzi learned the kid had tried to lift merchandise from a street vendor setting up shop for the day's market. *Whack! Whack-whack! Whack!*

A thump. And then crying. Followed by the man's solemn promise to use his knife without hesitation if the kid ever again showed up near his stand. The child's crying continued as the man's footsteps trailed off down the alley. Ritzi counted to thirty once he could no longer hear them. Then he poked his head up over the lid of the dumpster and peered down toward the alley floor.

There, a sobbing girl wobbled from side to side as she got to her feet.

Ritzi vaulted out of the dumpster and landed near where the girl had knelt a moment before. She started when she saw him and turned away, ready to bolt. "W-wait! I...I have food," he stammered as best he could in Korean. When her muscles relaxed, he knew she understood well enough.

Without waiting for her to turn around, Ritzi stuck his hand into his pocket and drew forth several chunks of the greasy meat. "Here, take them," he said, holding his open palm out to her. "Take them all."

The girl turned and tottered over to Ritzi with wide eyes. Her hand a blur, the girl snatched up the meat then darted beneath a box truck parked opposite the alley from them. She gaped at Ritzi as she stuffed the chunks into her mouth and chewed.

"Soon-Bok!"

Ritzi whirled around toward the sound of a woman's voice behind him, but no one was there. When he peeked beneath the truck again, the girl was gone.

"How dare you beat her!"

A flash of blue and black. Then stars. Followed by a chuffing sound, as if someone were blowing through a tube. Ritzi stumbled backward and banged his head on the side of the box truck. By reflex he sucked in his breath through his mouth, setting his throat aflame. Immediately, he coughed. Ritzi rubbed at his burning eyes with both hands. Blinking produced tears, further obscuring his vision.

Footfalls sounded off from around him. "Take him!" a man said from behind, his voice ringing in Ritzi's ears as loud as a megaphone. He broke into a run without even a backward glance. Before making it even twenty feet, he stumbled over a trash can and smacked the pavement face first. He yelped after someone clamped his wrists together as if in a vise.

"You said the Europeans' bus left already, Kang." A woman's voice. The same one that had accused him of beating the girl.

"It did. Saw it myself. Their escorts must have missed one!"

The woman snarled and hauled Ritzi to his feet. She twirled him around just as a gust of wind whipped a lock of her hair into Ritzi's face. He gasped as he drank in her scent, foreign and familiar both at the same time. *Wait, is she...is she a...?*

"Play along," she hissed into his ear.

Ritzi gulped and nodded.

"For your sake," she went on in a loud voice, "I hope someone aboard that bus is willing to pay. Might just convince me to let you live after attacking Soon-Bok like that."

The man walking up the alley toward them chuckled. "And what'll you do if they don't?"

"Well, my dear Pak, I'll serve this filthy cur his main course," she replied as something sharp and pointy pricked the skin on the right side of Ritzi's neck. "In fact, I think maybe I'll give him an appetizer right now."

"No, please!" the little girl said between sobs as she drew near. "I need to tell you—"

"Shush now, little one," replied the woman. "Would you two please take Soon-Bok back to camp? I'll be along soon."

The men both laughed. "Sure, Lim," said the one named Kang while he led the little girl away.

"Consider your good fortune, pig," said the other to Ritzi from over his shoulder. "If she doesn't want us sticking around to carry you afterward, she can't be planning to hurt you *that* bad. "

Kang replied with a chuckle, "Not yet at least."

LATER THAT EVENING.

RITZI'S HEAD WAS STILL spinning as Lim closed the door behind him. He rubbed at the sore spot on the side of his neck and glanced back and forth the length of the defunct factory's roof. Certain they were alone, he stepped over to the water tower ladder and leaned his arms over one of its rungs. "Is that where we're headed?" he said, pointing.

Lim nodded. "I've made it over the border in two bounds before, but I was completely tapped out afterward. You and I might need three with the load we'll be carrying. Though we'll ought to have no reason to make a return trip."

Ritzi leaned his arms against the ladder rung and took in their commanding view of the countryside. Numbers ran through his head—mass, velocity, acceleration. Lim would be laden with two children and him three.

"From here, we should be able to both make it to the top of the speed skating building. The big blue roof over there," Lim said, stretching out her arm. "The red one beyond it is the train station. Once more off that gray building by the checkpoint."

"And then we're into China."

"If we do it at night so the guards ought not spot us, yes. But if they do..."

"Then we'll all surely be dead before we hit the ground. So, let's say we avoid detection and land safely. What will you do then?"

Lim studied the floor around her feet. "I found these kids crying and lost, wandering the streets after a typhoon's floodwaters swept away their village. They begged me to help them stay together, being kin to one another. And certain one or another of their parents would surely come for them."

"Oh. I see," Ritzi replied, his words ringing inadequate and hollow to his own ears.

She paused and drew in her breath. "We've managed this long, but no one can say how long we can keep this up. I hear in the West there are places willing to take in groups of children, find them homes together." Lim turned and looked out over the Yalu River valley spreading out before them. "But we'll never reach them from here. Maybe, from China, or if we can make it to the South, we can."

"You will go with them?"

Lim shook her head. "I'm practically an adult now, so I'd have to find my own way. After they're set up with a new family, I need to get back to looking for mine. My parents are long dead, but as rumors go a handful of our kind still inhabit the borderlands north and east of here near the…"

Sounds of people clamoring up the stairwell soon displaced the momentary silence. Ritzi glanced over his shoulder toward the access door then back to Lim, but she wasn't there. A tinny *zzzztch* came from his left just as cold metal drew snug around both his wrists. He turned his head and met Lim's gaze.

"Have to keep up appearances," she said, the corners of her mouth turned upward into a playful smirk. "The guards will likely nod off before long. Then the children and I will come for you."

Ritzi craned his neck around while a group of thugs emerged from the doorway.

Lim trotted up beside one of them, a smarmy-looking fellow older than the rest. North Korea's answer to James Dean, sporting slicked-back hair and a black leather jacket. She plucked the matchstick the man had been chewing on from his mouth and pulled him into a passionate kiss. "Look what I brought you!" she cooed after their lips parted.

The man said nothing as he swiped his matchstick from Lim's hand and nudged her aside. After poking the matchstick back into his mouth, he drew a tactical baton from the pocket of his jeans and raised it over his head. The ladder shook after the baton clanged loudly against the rung closest to Ritzi's ear. Ritzi jumped.

"I don't know why those suits here from Pyongyang are so interested in you, pig, and I don't care. All I know is that you're going to make us all rich."

Lim's eyes went wide. "But, Chung, I thought this fellow was a tourist who missed his—"

"Pak and Kang heard they were searching for some American they thought might be headed this way." Chung snapped his fingers. "Told them the guy they'd seen matched their description. So, we called it in and, well, sure enough…"

Into Ritzi's view, a gaunt man with thick glasses and graying temples stepped forward, fumbling with something in his hands. "Ready, Doctor?" Chung said, grasping Ritzi's ears and wrenching his head back to center.

"Yes, keep him still," the man replied before a pin pricked Ritzi's neck. A burning sensation followed, travelling quickly up his carotid artery. By the time Chung released his hold, Ritzi already felt light-headed and nauseous.

Lim gasped. "What are you *doing*?"

"Not taking any chances, that's what." Chung turned and whistled. Soon-Bok emerged through the roof door, her elbows each in the hands of a man on either side of her. A boy about her age followed, accompanied by two more thugs, then the smaller children led around by their wrists—a boy, then a girl, then another girl. All of them crying.

"Won't risk you sneaking off with him to collect the reward for yourself. I know you won't with them right here," Chung said, nodding toward the children. "The suits will be here in half an hour or so to collect the American. And to haul off these runts to an orphanage in Pyongyang."

"That wasn't our deal, Chung!"

A smug sneer spread over the man's face while Ritzi fought against the drug to keep his eyes open. "You're cute when you're mad, you know that?" he said, caressing Lim's cheek. "I only took you and the urchins in because you were useful to me. With the bounty I'll collect for this American, I won't need anyone pickpocketing Mount Paektu tourists anymore." Chung paused and took Lim's chin into his hand. "But *you* on the other hand, have been useful indeed. And will continue to beeeeee—!"

Chung howled as he flailed about, trying to work his hand free from between Lim's teeth. At length he remembered the baton in his other hand and delivered a crushing blow to the side of Lim's head. She tumbled across the floor, coming to rest at Soon-Bok's feet.

He gasped and flexed his mangled thumb. Blood spurted from its end, now just above the knuckle. "You...you cunt!" Chung screamed at Lim's still form. "I'll kill you for that!" He sucked in his breath and stuck his ruined hand into his armpit opposite. "I'll kill you *all* for that! And this high up, no one on the street below will hear your screams."

Lim did a kip-up and spat something into her hand. With a mirthless chuckle, she flung whatever it was back toward Chung. It landed near Ritzi's feet. Even with his vision fading, Ritzi made out the end of the man's thumb.

"Thanks for the tip," Lim said in an eerily calm voice as she smiled and stepped Chung's way, her fangs already halfway to her chin. "Children, listen—you must close your eyes." With a roar, Lim lunged for Chung's throat an instant before Ritzi's knees gave out.

Chapter Twenty-Three

— • —

CHICAGO, ILLINOIS. THE SAME DAY.

THE TRAIN'S DOORS CLOSED behind Pawly an instant be-fore it glided away. Sparks flying from the third rail afforded her and Tommy a glimpse of the deserted platform around them. The train rounded a curve and disappeared, leaving only the crescent moon's silvery glow to light their path. Crews upgrading the Pink Line's stations hadn't made it this far. The rusty luminaires flickered on and off above their heads, of those that still worked at all.

Pawly hugged her shoulders as she and Tommy made their way to the exit. "So where is this place? Is it close?"

Tommy drew out a piece of paper from his pocket and studied it as they walked. The dim light didn't seem to bother him. Or her, for that matter. Though being a werecat might come with some cool perks, their mother's admonitions about their kind's deadly rage tempered any enthusiasm she might have had. Hazy images from the night she first transformed had plagued her since they boarded the train downtown, along with vivid flashbacks from the hallucinations she'd experienced during last week's storm. The sooner they finished, the sooner they'd be back on the train toward home, the sooner Pawly would breathe easy again.

"From what I was able to make out on MapQuest, we take a right outside of the station. Place should be a block and a half down Kedzie Ave. on the left."

Pawly stepped over a pothole at the end of the concrete ramp and stopped in the middle of the sidewalk. Glowing neon lit up the night sky to their left and right, spelling out various Spanish words and phrases. "Are you sure?" She feared for someone taking a petite blonde like her, accompanied by a lanky, red-headed boy like Tommy, for an easy make. Though any would-be troublemakers would suffer their mistake's grave consequences, she loathed the idea of drawing that kind of attention to themselves.

Because for all anyone in their family knew, she and Tommy were downtown at St. Peter's-in-the-Loop with Sally and Caesar for the citywide Catholic Youth fun night. Which they had been indeed, prior to ducking out early to make a clandestine detour through Little Village on their way home. Just as J.J. had asked Pawly and Tommy to when he intercepted them the night before while they walked home from the ice rink. Right after making them swear not to tell anyone, not even their parents.

Tommy strode off down the block and waved for Pawly to follow. "Yeah, I'm sure," he said after she caught up to him. "Caesar told me about this place. He came here a couple months back after his dad grounded him for flunking his algebra test."

Before long he and Pawly stood at the front door of a store advertising money orders, prepaid phone cards, and pay-as-you-go cell phones. Tommy pulled on the bars covering the door's window glass and they stepped inside.

Pawly studied the dust in the corners of the shop's dingy floors. Tommy stammered through his request in Spanish to a clerk standing behind a pane of bulletproof glass. He pulled out a clip of bills from his pocket and peeled off enough to pay for a burner phone. Then they were out of the shop and across the street, making their way back toward the "L" station.

A group of gangbanger wannabes walking down the sidewalk opposite them paused their conversation long enough to check Pawly out. She cursed herself for not thinking ahead—she could have tied up her hair and stuffed it down her collar. Or hid it under a ball cap, one of a dozen still strewn about their home weeks after the family's unpacking. Then maybe she wouldn't look so feminine. Dressed to the nines together with Sally and their friends for a girls' night out, Pawly might've liked such attention. But not here. Not now. She bit her lip while bile percolated up the back of her throat. As much as she longed to answer the punks' unwelcome advances, she and Tommy needed to keep a low profile to stay on schedule.

Pawly looked over her shoulder to find Tommy following behind by a light pole's length. He glanced up from the new cell phone's screen, whistles and catcalls drawing his attention toward his sister. After making a face in the boys' direction, he jammed the thing into his pocket and jogged her way.

She tugged at her sleeve and peeked at her watch. "We want to catch the next Blue Line train," she said when he joined her at the station entrance. "If we miss it, we'll have to wait for a Pink Line train and transfer downtown to get home. We're cutting it close to curfew as it is."

"True enough," Tommy said as they slid their paper cards into the slot on the turnstiles and pushed their way through. "I don't expect

J.J. will get into too many details when he calls. You and I won't hardly be able to work this deal if we end up grounded again, will we?"

"When he *calls*?" Pawly glanced down again at her watch. Only a couple of minutes remained before the Blue Line train arrived at Kedzie station. "Why would J.J. be calling at this time of night?"

"He said to send a text to the number he gave us, remember? Right after we got our hands on a phone no one could trace back to you or me. That's what I was doing just now while you were—"

The cell phone's ringing cut him off. Tommy pulled the phone out of his pocket and waved Pawly over beside him. " I am the Keymaster!" he said in a loud voice when he answered.

Pawly shot him a look.

Tommy shrugged.

"I am the Gate—wait, Tommy, is that you?"

"S-Sally? This isn't your number! Where are you? How did you get—?"

"She's here with me."

Pawly gasped at the sound of J.J.'s voice. "What are you doing? No matter the connection between her stepfather and your family, she's not involved with this."

"A trustworthy source told me recently she's seen you and Tommy sporting fur. That makes her involved already, whether any of us like it or not. We decided to keep her as close to us as you two will be."

Tommy's face screwed up like he'd just chugged a pint of soured milk.

"The three of you will be working together soon enough," J.J. went on. "In fact, Miss Ruiz pleasantly surprised me, having been sent on an errand much like the pair of you. Because *she* managed to find me first."

A metallic squeal drew the twin's attention to the pair of headlights wobbling down the track toward them.

"Sounds like your train is here. Call this same number tomorrow night, this same time. I'll ask Miss Ruiz to do the same."

The line went dead an instant before the train's head end whooshed past. Its last car came to a stop in front of the twins and opened its doors.

Pawly and Tommy shuffled inside. Neither said a word all the way back to Jefferson Park.

Chapter Twenty-Four

*B*LOOD. *ALL AROUND ME. Rivers of it.*

At least that was what Ritzi's nose led him to believe. With tiring effort and agonizing slowness, he managed to crack open one eyelid. His surroundings appeared broken, jagged, as if peering through a pane of crackled glass set in a privacy window.

After scooting his feet beneath him, Ritzi flexed his legs and rose. Once in a standing position, he leaned against one rung of the water tower ladder and blinked. Then again, and again. His vision cleared bit by bit, the hazy lights from the cityscape below the factory roof coming into focus.

He gulped and glanced over his shoulder. The beacon atop the radio mast behind him illuminated the area all around once every second, dispersing the darkness for a mere instant each time. It was all Ritzi needed to make out arms, legs, torsos. Entrails. Heads. Strewn about from one side of the roof to the other.

Dear God, Lim! The children! Where are they?

Heart pounding in his chest, Ritzi turned toward where the stern-faced doctor slumped up against the parapet beside him. "What happened here, Most Honorable?" he said, addressing the man in Korean.

The doctor fixed Ritzi with a vacant stare but said nothing. Ritzi stuck out his trembling leg and jostled the man's shoulder with the toe of his boot. The man's head tumbled down his chest and rolled past Ritzi across the blood-slicked floor until it bumped up against one of the water tower support columns.

A tap on Ritzi's shoulder almost made his heart stop. He whirled around, coming face-to-face with an orange-and-white-striped ailuran with bobbed black hair.

"Just me. Hold still," it said in a hoarse and raspy facsimile of Lim's voice.

She worked at the handcuffs around Ritzi's wrist, her chest heaving. Ritzi blinked and looked the young woman up and down, recognizing Lim's clothes from earlier. Or at least those parts he *could* recognize, those parts not stained a rusty brown by the blood of her victims.

"Are the kids...still here?" Ritzi said as the second handcuff popped open. He rubbed at his wrists while Lim stared out over the Yalu River toward China.

"No. Except for Soon-Bok, I managed to get them all away, though."

Ritzi's eyes went wide. "Four of them? Across the river by yourself?"

Lim shook her head. "I knew I couldn't make such a trip with all of them. I carried the others two at a time to a clearing in the woods." She pointed toward an area beyond the city lights near the river. "We'll hide a while there."

"Do you need me to—?"

"No, we have lost our moment," Lim replied, meeting Ritzi's gaze. "It was a long shot at best. Now we must figure out where we can go to..."

Ritzi glanced down to where Lim's striped tail stood straight up behind her. "I hear them, too," he said, nodding toward the roof door. "Let me deal with the people on the stairs. You grab Soon-Bok and get out of here." He swallowed but the lump in his throat remained. "I'll...I'll figure out a way to find you again. Someday."

Lim bit her lip and bounded off. Ritzi dashed over to the wall next to the roof door and sat down. He yanked off his stolen boots and flexed his fingers and toes, coaxing forth his claws. Fur sprouted from every follicle on his skin while two people thumped their way to the top of the stairs.

"Something's seeping under the door, sir!"

Ritzi heard a hoarse whimper, then another. He scanned the roof back and forth until he spied Lim. She stood over where Soon-Bok lay curled up on the floor, covering the back of her neck with trembling hands. Lim crouched down beside the girl's head and stroked her hair, muttering something in a soothing tone.

The door flew open and crashed up against the wall. A pair of soldiers hustled through and dropped to one knee. Lim scooped Soon-Bok into her arms and looked right into a pair of flashlight beams aimed at her head and chest. Along with their rifles' muzzles.

"Wh-what *is* that thing, sir?" stammered one of them in Korean, clicking off his rifle's safety.

"I don't know, just fucking shoot it! Before it can—"

A roar from behind caused Ritzi's chest to clench. Blaznikov burst forth through the door an instant later, yanking the men off their feet one to an arm as he bounded past. The three of them vaulted over top of a condenser unit and out of sight, landing with a dull thump.

Cloth ripped. Flesh tore. Bone snapped. The men's horrified screams trailed off into grotesque gurgles as each drew his final tortured breath.

Ritzi blinked and looked over where Lim had knelt a moment before. She and Soon-Bok were both gone. He closed his eyes and sighed.

Blaznikov emerged from behind the condenser unit a moment later. Fresh blood covered the elder man's field uniform from his collar to his knees. His eyes narrowed at Ritzi as he stepped close. "We make a deal, *Panie Doktorze*. I find another way for you to add value to my DPRK colleagues. They will not make you renounce your citizenship. I have accepted full responsibility for you."

Ritzi winced as the elder man poked him in the chest with the claw on his index finger.

"See to it I never regret my decision, hm? For your family's sake. Because you and them surely have much riding on native Kindred here."

Blaznikov stood and nodded toward the forest clearing Lim had indicated. "Like that one, I suppose. Much riding on her. Yes," he said before disappearing down the stairwell.

Ritzi choked back a sob and followed.

Chapter Twenty-Five

Chicago, Illinois. The following spring.

WITH FINALS FAST APPROACHING, Pawly was grateful for Tommy's offer to stay home all weekend to help her study. But after being at it all last night and half the day today already, they were well and truly on each other's last nerve. So Pawly didn't mind Mrs. Biggs peppering her with questions on the drive back from Irving Park. She was just grateful for the chance to get out of the house.

A few of Mrs. Biggs' questions Pawly could answer—yes, Mr. Biggs was coming to their house to meet them; no, she didn't know what this was all about. Though as to the rest, Pawly could hardly even venture a guess. Including as to why Tommy had passed at the chance to fly solo to the comic shop *en route* to pick up Mrs. Biggs himself.

Mr. Biggs was out the back door the moment Pawly turned up the alleyway behind the house. He tugged at his wife's car door handle even before Pawly rolled to a stop. The Biggs laughed and hugged one another after he scooped his wife up in his arms and shuffled off toward the house. Tommy was there holding the door open, greeting Pawly with a shrug as she trotted up the steps behind them. As if to suggest that he didn't know what was going on either.

Their Grandpa Dory took over from that point, herding every-one into the living room. Their mother was already there with *Halmonim*, though neither looked up while the twins shoved the ottoman into the corner beside her chair and sat down. The adults all took a seat on the sofa and the easy chair, except for Grandpa D who remained standing. "I want you all to know that I had to fight hard for authorization to tell you what I'm about to," he began as he paced back and forth beneath the portico. "Respect that I likely won't be able to answer many of your questions. And that what I say must be held in complete and utter confidence amongst us."

Pawly smirked and glanced over at Tommy. If Grandpa D was getting on about super-secret spy stuff, neither of them were about to be grounded for anything.

No one said a word while their grandfather recapped what their Uncle Nat and Aunt Annie had told him about the earthquakes along the Chinese/North Korean border. An especially strong tremor had shaken apart a hydroelectric dam which flooded the valley downstream. In a rare move, Pyongyang had joined Beijing in reaching out to the international community for help. The United States planned to give them just that, beginning with a Red Cross team to help care for the thousands of sick and injured people.

"So, Nat and Annie will be joining us there," Grandpa D said as he laid out his plan. "But that's not the only reason why we're going. The Chinese have three confirmed reports now by recent North Korean defectors of human experimentation. No one is sure whether they're soldiers volunteering or concentration camp inmates being volunteered, but we have eyewitness accounts of people bearing fur, claws, fangs."

Halmonim gasped. "You...you don't think..."

"Maybe, maybe not." Grandpa D rubbed at his face. "Our intelligence services are sure this is Blaznikov's doing. And we have no reason *not* to believe Ritzi is aiding and abetting him."

The room erupted into chaos. No one wanted to believe that the twins' uncle could have had anything to do with something so sinister. But Grandpa D remained firm in his suspicions, certain of his sources. That didn't mean any of the rest of them had to like it.

Pawly looked over at their mother. She sat silent, staring out the window with her chin in one hand, her expression unreadable, as if strong, conflicting emotions waged a war for control of her mind. Pawly could relate.

"Everyone, everyone," Grandpa D said at length over top of the din. "Now listen. 'Windfall' is one of these new psychotropic drugs all over our streets, right? FBI believes it originates in North Korea, from commercial scale *Amanita muscaria* cultivation."

Halmonim wrinkled her nose. "Fly agaric mushrooms. Nat and Annie worked with them as undergrads. Together with Ritzi."

"I remember," their mother mumbled without turning to look at them. "He presented their findings at a conference in Warsaw the summer before Annie entered med school."

"Which is what the intelligence community really thinks Ritzi is up to. Because Windfall's appearance here happened less than six weeks after he left home." He drew in his breath and stepped over beside the twins' mother. "I intend to find out for certain what's going on along the border, Alex. And how Ritzi is wrapped up in it. But I'll need your help."

"Me?" Their mother gaped up at Grandpa D before waving a hand at Pawly and her brother. "But...but who will look after them?"

"I will call Niko right away," *Halmonim* said, leaping to her feet. "Will tell him our vacation is postponed."

"You will do no such thing, Sunny," their grandfather said in a firm tone.

Pawly traded looks with Tommy. Her brother screwed up his face, realizing from the look on hers she was up to something. "We'll be just fine here by ourselves for however long you need," she said, her gaze never leaving Tommy's.

Grandpa D beamed as he stepped over and patted the twins' heads. "I know you will be. Which is why I'm going to ask you two for a favor."

Tommy rubbed at the back of his neck. "Okay, what exactly?"

"Top said he was willing for him and Sheila to move in with you here until we return."

Pawly swallowed her lips as she looked back and forth between the two adults. Mr. Biggs motioned to his wife. "So long as that's okay with you, dear."

Their mother stood and took Mrs. Biggs' hand in hers. "Probably a good idea. Barry is sailing to Korea aboard the *Mercy* and called early this morning from Guam. He's got orders to act as an interpreter and guide for the hospital ship's force protection unit, so he'll likely be several weeks."

Mr. Biggs turned toward the twins with a wry grin. "And just think, dear, you would have live-in room service!"

Their mother let out a chuckle. "That's all fine and good," she said while Pawly *tsk*ed and crossed her arms. "But I'm concerned about travelling. Especially with how...unpredictable my Rage has become."

"That's the beauty of it, my dear," Grandpa D replied, his eyes twinkling. "Nat and Annie should be in the air on their way to Scott Air Force Base as we speak. After they equip a MAC flight with all the equipment they'll need, we'll join them there and head back to Korea together. They've assured me they can keep you stable until we touch down in Seoul."

Their mother's brows knit. "And then what?"

"Once we're in theater, Alex, you'll be on your own," Grandpa D replied, fixing her with a stern look. "We'll need you to sortie into North Korean territory to check out the place we believe the experiments are taking place. With a little luck the earthquake and flooding might've set them back far enough to where they'll bunch it."

Tommy shot to his feet. "But that'll be suicide!"

Their mother sighed and hung her head. "It can't be helped. We have to find Ritzi, talk to him, get him away from Blaznikov. Because if we don't..."

"That's really what this is all about, isn't it?" Pawly asked in a small voice.

Grandpa D cleared his throat. "Yes, my dear, it is. I've been given latitude on how best to gather intel the Agency wants regarding DPRK's therianthropic capabilities, so I intend to use it to track down Ritzi. We've got one shot at this. If we don't find Ritzi and convince him to surrender himself, he'll be tried in absentia for treason. Declared an enemy of the state."

Pawly knew if he was, none of them would ever see him again. Worse even than Grandpa N's deportation.

The twins' mother looked at Tommy and Pawly and then back to their grandfather. "How long do you think we'll be gone?"

"I'm not sure. Nat and Annie's work with the Red Cross will earn us a heap of goodwill with the local Chinese authorities," Grandpa D replied, rubbing his chin. "That should allow us greater freedom of movement on their side of the border to move freely. But we'll talk more about this tomorrow night in the bunker after we get Nat and

Annie on the line. Until then, no one says anything to anyone. Got me?"

Their grandfather's steely gaze fell upon each person in the room. One by one, everyone nodded.

"Good. Now I've been hankering for pizza the whole week I've been in Washington. And I can't stand the grease-soaked cardboard that passes for pie there. Who's hungry?"

Pawly and Tommy brought up the rear as everyone filed out of the living room. One by one the adults shuffled through the back door toward the alleyway and their respective cars. Everyone talked at once, but Pawly barely noticed.

Days later.

Pawly's nose wrinkled as she strode toward the front door of her family's apartment house. A spectacle played out before her in the living room window. Over the back of the sofa, she saw the tops of two heads. A pair of hands caressed a tangle of rusty curls, another twirled straight black hair around its fingers. *"We'll be here studying,"* huh? *Yeah, right. Anatomy, maybe...*

Two toots of a car horn from down the street drew her attention toward the back end of J.J.'s yellow Charger. Turn signal flashing, it pulled away from the curb and sped off down the street an instant before the Biggs' black SUV rounded the corner.

Panicked gasps and muttered curses came as Pawly pulled open the storm door and keyed the lock. A moment later she crossed the threshold into their home's foyer.

Tommy peered over Sally's shoulder from the sofa, eyes wide until he recognized her. "Oh. It's only you."

Pawly pulled her purse strap over her head and hung it around the stairwell banister. "Yeah, but the Biggses are right behind me."

"Pity, we had a good volley going there, too," Sally said and booped Tommy's nose with her finger. "Say, girl, Carson's is having a sale this week on summer dresses. Tomorrow after school we could—*¡Quiero Dios!* What happened to your *hair?*"

Pawly chuckled and rubbed at the back of her bare neck with her free hand. The cool air blowing out of the vent in the foyer's ceiling made her skin tingle. "You like it? I'd grown my hair out since second grade. Thought it was time for a change."

"You look so...sophisticated," Sally replied, her voice a breathy whisper.

Tommy flipped his hand at Pawly while she hung her sun hat on one of the hooks. "And I suppose J.J. thinks so, too?"

Sally fixed Pawly with a searing glare. "Did that...that *man* put you up to this?"

"Well, sorta."

Tommy leaned up against the living room portico and crossed his arms. "Yeah, sis, tell ol' Sal here what you told me."

"Well, after that guy last week yanked me around by my hair until Tommy showed up to distract him, I realized I need to play better defense," she said, chin dipping to the floor. "J.J. suggested I chop it off so as to make it harder for anyone to grab hold of me. Figured if Natalie Portman could make it work, I could, too." She turned to

Tommy, hands on her hips. "And you should be grateful, dumbass. 'Wash n' go' means I'll be done in the bathroom that much quicker."

"Pawly? Tommy? We're back!" boomed Mr. Biggs after entering the kitchen via the back door.

"In the foyer," Tommy replied before sharing a quick farewell peck on the lips with Sally.

"Oh, hello, Sally dear," Mrs. Biggs said as she came shuffling around the corner. "They just opened a new Jewel down the street from my OB/GYN so we picked up another pound of ground beef after my appointment." She pointed back and forth between Pawly and Tommy. "You two are cooking tonight, so if you care to make a little extra spaghetti and sauce then Sally's welcome to stay."

"Thank you, Mrs. Biggs," Sally replied as she slid on her shoes. "But my mom and stepdad insist us kids both be home for dinner on Sunday nights."

"Another time then. You're always welcome here." She reached over and wiped a smudge of lipstick from Tommy's cheek with her thumb. "Though this shade looks a lot better on *your* face than it does on his, child," she said, wagging her finger as she trudged into the living room.

Sally's face flushed while she nodded her goodbyes to the twins and dashed out the front door. "Hey, you two," came Mr. Biggs' voice from behind them in the kitchen, "get to browning the beef and cooking the pasta. We forgot to get mushrooms at Jewel, so I'm walking to the Mini-Mart to grab a can or two."

The back door slammed before Pawly or Tommy could answer. "Whew!" Mrs. Biggs said after flopping down on the living room couch. "Pawly, dear, if you decide to start having babies someday, make sure you've got your man trained like that one. I didn't even have to *ask* him to go."

Pawly and Tommy shared a nervous laugh while Mrs. Biggs' picked up the remote and flicked on the TV.

"Yeah, a perfect gentleman," Tommy said and pulled the ground beef out of the bag Mr. Biggs had left out on the counter. He slid up beside Pawly at the sink, eyeing the water flowing from the tap into a stockpot. "Suppose J.J. could learn a thing or two from him."

She shrugged. "Who says I would *want* him to?"

Tommy dropped the flat of ground beef but managed to catch it before it splashed into the stockpot. "You...you can't be serious."

"I'm quite serious. He understands me, you know? He's got something to prove, too. Especially to that asshole brother of his, Myung-Duk. And the rest of his family."

"But...but J.J. is an *adult*," Tommy hissed into her ear.

"Age of consent in Illinois is seventeen. And besides, my body is my business. No one else's."

Tommy clicked his tongue and laid his hand atop Pawly's shoulder. "I can see you've put a lot of thought into this. But don't think you've got to prove something to any—"

"Who the fuck are you to tell *me* I've got nothing to prove, huh?" Pawly batted Tommy's arm away. "We've *all* got something to prove, dumbass. Prove we deserve to *exist* without being exploited." She gripped the counter and stared at the floor, her face so hot she thought her skin might ignite. "And where do you get off lecturing *me*, huh? Look at you, dragging Sally into your orbit. Knowing full well you and me will never be 'normal' again while the two of you paw at each other like a pair of fuckbunnies. You don't think you're not being the least little bit selfish?"

Tommy bit his lip and looked away toward the kitchen window. "You two okay in there?" Mrs. Biggs called from the living room.

"Yeah, we're fine," Tommy replied in a loud voice before leaning over next to Pawly. "So, what sort of job does J.J. have lined up for us next?"

Pawly set the stockpot on the range and lit the burner. "It's big. Some sort of small craft anti-cloaking device thingy being prototyped for the Coast Guard right here at Illinois Tech. It's going to sea trials on Lake Michigan soon aboard a Coast Guard boat seeking out semi-submersibles seized from drug runners. Security around the thingy is pretty tight, but I doubt it's too tight for you and me."

Tommy whistled and fumbled at the ground beef's plastic wrapping. "You weren't kidding. This *is* big."

"I know, right?" Pawly replied, her eyes twinkling. "We can really score big, too."

Tommy furrowed his brow. "Or really lose big. I mean, we could do friggin' *prison* time if we're caught—"

"Everyone in this family is going out of their way to help you and me. We have our Talents, so we need to start using them to help ourselves. And Mom. Uncle Nat and Aunt Annie are going to need money and a lot of it to help her. You and I pull this off, there'll be a lot of zeroes in it for all of us."

"But what about Sally?"

"I told J.J. I'd gore out his Adam's apple with my own two fangs if he so much as breathed a word of this to her."

Tommy chewed on the inside of his cheek and nodded. "Good. I...I don't want her more involved than she already is."

"Better that J.J. doesn't want to split the money more ways than absolutely necessary. Now, here's the plan..."

Chapter Twenty-Six

Chinese/North Korean border. Same day.

RITZI PICKED UP A chunk of wood sticking out of the mud and drew it close to his face. He tilted it back and forth in the setting sun to examine the contrasts which had first caught his eye. One end resembled the color of foundry slag, more black than brown; the rest shone bright red, burnished by surging floodwaters for a day and a half following the dam's collapse. He and his escorts had left Chŏngjin for Hwanggumpyong Island earlier in the day, right after North Korean army engineers reported they and their Chinese counterparts had finished securing the area. An extraordinarily wet spring this year had been the harbinger of an active typhoon season across the Korean Peninsula and into mainland China. In front of Ritzi, the Yalu River rushed past behind the engineers' makeshift levee.

He pursed his lips and squinted at the *Chosŏngŭl* and Mandarin characters spelling out the ruined research facility's name. Each glowed orange in the day's dying light.

"Our window of opportunity to salvage anything of use from your lab is closing, Doctor," said Ritzi's DPRK army liaison, a dour, leathery-faced captain named Oh.

He nodded. "Then I suggest we suspend operations and resume in the daylight."

Ritzi didn't expect Oh's men to find much anyway, which suited him just fine. After all, he'd done what he'd come here to do.

With a grunt, Ritzi chucked the wood toward the river as hard as he could. It didn't even reach the base of the levee, landing like a javelin in the middle of a massive puddle with hardly a splash. By his rough estimate, water leaking through the levee would cover it within the hour. Good.

"Captain! Captain!"

Ritzi looked over his shoulder to find the lieutenant in charge of the engineering battalion running up to Oh. After a hasty salute, the man's wide eyes disappeared beneath the brim of his hat as he bowed. He stood there panting for some while, hands clasped to his knees. Had something spooked him? The wrecked buildings over that way should have been mostly empty. Fortunately, he had finished relocating the *Amanita muscaria* pinning beds to the hold of Blaznikov's merchant ship berthed in Chŏngjin. Preceding Punggye-ri's latest detonation by an entire week, as good luck would have it. Speculation went that the blast had weakened the dam and, along with day after day of torrential rainfall, led to its failure.

"One of my troops," the man said at last, "was mauled by what we first thought was a tiger." When he looked up, Ritzi noticed the man's lower lip quivering. "But when we approached to fend it off, we...we saw a..."

"Will you carry your man out or bury him on site?"

The lieutenant blinked. "He's lost a lot of blood. Our medic says we need to get him to an infirmary soon if he's to have any chance."

"Round up your men and return to base camp," Oh said in a gruff voice. "I will send for a medivac for your wounded and for State

Security to debrief the rest of you. Not one word of this to anyone, any of you. Understand?"

The man snapped to attention and saluted once more. "Sir!"

"If you'll excuse me," Oh said after the soldier scampered off. "I'll be in the car."

"Sure. I'll be along after I scout around the site."

Oh nodded and marched off toward their olive drab utility vehicle. "Better to help our units know where best to start in the morning."

Fur sprouted from Ritzi's skin even before the man was out of sight. He knelt down and pulled off his boots one at a time. Fire flared across his chest and arms, then his legs and groin. He sucked in his breath through clenched teeth. Transformations were a natural part of Kindred life, painful in an exhilarating way.

Before long, he was bounding from one rubble pile to another, thinking more about young Lim than about any salvageable equipment or materials Oh's team might find in the morning. Where had she gone? Did the kids she looked after go with her? Were they all okay? Would they *ever* be?

Blaznikov had told him more about the weretigress after Ritzi's first encounter with her in Samjiyŏn. The elder man's DPRK-born predecessor had tried to broker a deal with the other ailuranthropes from Lim's clan. But one night shortly after refusing his advances, they abandoned their ancestral home in Ryanggang's hill country and dispersed. He had suspected some, likely including Lim and her immediate family, had fled to the mountains near Musan and the Chinese border. Until Lim came to Ritzi's aid months before, Blaznikov had yet to track down one of her kind himself.

Ritzi gasped when he spotted her. Lim lay flat on her back atop a slab of concrete that had previously been a poured wall, her orange-and-white striped pelt dirty and disheveled. He scrambled on all fours across the rubble toward her unmoving form, paying no heed to noise or vibration. As he drew near, Lim let out an angry snarl and turned her head his way. Though her scent was unmistakable, it was different, having sour, musky characteristics to it. Ritzi sighed and stepped to one side so the breeze could carry his own scent toward her.

Lim groaned and slumped down atop the concrete.

"What are you *doing*?" Ritzi crouched down next to her head. "This is a secure area. You...you could have been shot."

"The...the children," she said in a voice raspier than the one he remembered, though not out of character for their kind when manifesting their ailuran forms. "Must find them...they're in the water...they're..." Her breathing was shallow, forced.

Ritzi scooted around to kneel beside her chest and took her head in both hands. "On second thought, don't try to talk," he said as he gazed into her droopy eyes. She was going into shock, which was likely the only reason any of the engineers had survived their encounter.

And he hadn't heard any shooting, either. Lim must have been sick or injured or both long before the engineers spotted her. A quick scan the length of her body showed no tears or bullet holes in her sleeveless gray *dobok*. With a flick of his wrist, Ritzi called forth his claws and sliced away the wrappings around her forearms. He slid around to free her ankles and froze.

Blood oozed from the crotch of Lim's trousers. It dripped from the tip of her tail and trickled down the concrete below her feet. Ritzi glanced over to find a pool forming downgrade in the slab's corner joint. She would need much more than a few bandages. "What...what happened?"

"I...I tried to kill it," she said between heavy breaths. "But...I failed. Now it's tried to kill the children...must find them before...before it can..."

"You tried to kill it? Kill what exactly, Lim? Lim?"

But she didn't answer. She met his gaze with a blank stare, her mouth slightly open.

"No! Lim!" he said and patted at the side of her face. When that didn't elicit a response, he pulled off his shirt and sliced it through with one claw. In a moment Ritzi had wrapped a makeshift cravat around her crotch and cinched it tight around her waist. Then he took her limp body in his arms and stood.

Swirls of orange and red painted the western sky where the sun had been only moments before. His pulse raced and his breath came in short gasps, racking his brain to think of someplace she could get the care she needed without risking capture. Or being shot.

But if Lim didn't get stitched up and some blood into her soon, it wouldn't matter. He swore. *Think, Ritzi!*

A dark purple hue fell across the landscape like a house painter unfurling a drop cloth. He gasped and looked up to see stars leaving trails of light in the sky behind them as they followed the Yalu River's flow. A flap of fabric to his left drew his gaze toward the pale silhouette of someone leaping through the air.

Ritzi's mouth fell open. *Alex?*

He gaped at her as she landed and turned to face him. His mouth flapped open and closed, but no words came out. Did he dare call her name? Would she vanish if he did?

Alex fumbled at the collar of her sneak suit, her whiskers twitching. Dark trails in her cheek fur from her eyes to her jawline glinted in the day's dying light. "I ditched the rest of the soldiers. Come on!" She knelt down into a crouch and launched herself into the air. After landing on a large rock in the middle of the river, she took off again without a backward glance.

Ritzi clutched Lim to his chest and bounded off after her. Alex, surely not here alone, would lead him back to her base camp where help would certainly be waiting. *Hang on, Lim!*

Every few hops, Alex paused to survey her surroundings before resuming her trek. She made her way thusly across the debris field while Ritzi struggled to keep pace. Though Lim could have hardly weighed a hundred pounds soaking wet, carrying her now slowed Ritzi's normal stride more than a little. He took advantage of Alex's hesitations to close the distance between them, knowing losing her would put Lim's survival in dire peril.

At length they reached an encampment. Alex landed in a deserted area between two rows of tents and disappeared into the darkness.

"Nat! Where have you been?" came a voice in English from the tent nearest him.

Annie?

"Sorry, dear, but the mess tent ran out of *moo goo gai pan*," Nat answered.

Ritzi bit his lip, a wave of emotion washing over him at the sound of his brother's voice. He shoved the tent flap aside with his leg and ducked inside. "Though the cooks insisted I wait while they whipped us both up some—"

Nat gasped and dropped the foam boxes tied around with twine which he held one to a hand. Droplets of mud splattered up from the ground where they landed on either side of him.

Annie stood beside her husband, staring at Ritzi with one hand over her mouth.

"What...what are *you* doing here?" Nat managed after a long moment.

He stared at the muddy ground around his feet. What *could* he say? Lim moaned and squirmed.

Ritzi blinked once, twice, then held her out to Nat. "Help her. Lim Young-Hee is her name," he said, his words spurred on by the girl's unconscious prompting. "She's bleeding out through her vaginal area somewhere. Please, she...she saved my life."

"Dinner will have to wait, dear," Annie said and glanced over at Nat. "It would seem we have a patient."

THE HAZY MOON HIGH in the sky shone through a slit in the tent canvas, lighting up Ritzi's otherwise dark surroundings as clear as a summer's day. To his eyes, anyway.

Nat and Annie had shooed Ritzi into an empty bunkroom within minutes of his arrival, ordering him to stay there with the lights out until they came for him. He could hear their voices, Lim's muffled cries, footfalls from the trio of armed guards stationed outside the tent as they mumbled back and forth to one another in English. Operatives from CIA or some other alphabet soup agency, near as he could tell.

He edged closer to the tent flap as the trio shuffled off to complete their rounds. Another pair of footsteps approaching gave him pause, uneasiness turning to panic as they drew near. *Shit, someone's coming! If they see me like this...*

His sister's familiar scent wafted through the air. In an instant Alex burst through the flap and buried her face in his shoulder. She howled into it until her tears soaked through his fur all the way to his skin.

"Alex, I—"

That was all he got out before she drew back her fist and socked him square in the jaw. Ritzi's head snapped to his right and bounced off the freestanding hutch beside him. He fell back against a tent pole and the entire tent shook. Chin in one hand, he slumped to the dirt floor.

Alex stood with fists clenched at her sides while her smoldering eyes bore into him.

"I guess I had that coming."

"Fucking *right* you did," Alex replied, ears sticking straight out from either side of her head. "It's been months since you've been home. Why haven't you answered any of my emails? I'd've sent a real letter but you didn't even leave a forwarding address." She rubbed her face with both hands. "And just why the hell would you come to a shithole like this in the first place?"

Ritzi shook his head and got to one knee. "Blaznikov knew about the Ruiz girl, Alex. Knew she'd seen Pawly and Tommy and me in our ailuran forms. If I cooperated, he agreed to spare her life. Along with every other human he's aware of who knows about us."

She gasped. "Like Barry?"

"Him especially. And I believe Blaznikov has both means and motive to do him harm." *Trust me, dear sister. Blaznikov has already tried to kill him once.*

Alex blew out her breath. "Look, Ritzi, I have to know. Dory and the CIA believe you're involved with North Korea's human experimentation program. Are you? And don't you dare lie to me!"

"No. I'm not doing that," he replied as he got to his feet. "I threw up when I first learned of it, in fact. I've done some other pharmacological work for Blaznikov while here, but I'm done doing that also. I'm coming home to help you and the twins now that I've pulled my hitch. But before I go, I need to repay Lim."

"Is that the tigrine girl?"

Ritzi nodded. "When Blaznikov and I first arrived, Party officials pressured me into renouncing my American citizenship. I tried to escape. A gang of street thugs took me captive in Samjiyŏn, hoping to cash in with Pyongyang." He looked away toward the field hospital's operating room. "That girl was their leader's lover. She freed me to help her carry a bunch of human kids she'd come to love and care for into China. He showed up announcing he'd sold them all out to State Security and she raged, Alex. Tore each and every one of the thugs to shreds."

Alex sniffed at the air and stepped over to the tent flap. "Then we should go."

"Go?"

"Go look for Lim's children, duh," she replied, peeking her head out through the flap. "The ones I heard her moaning to you she was trying to find. Come on, before someone here spots us."

Ritzi clicked his tongue. "Thank you, Alex, but I can manage—"

"Not a chance. I know better than to let you out of my sight again."

ALEX AND RITZI SAID nothing as she led them back to the camp, bounding from rubble pile to rubble pile strewn along the Yalu River's banks. He glanced at the eastern sky, cursing under his breath at the sun's imminent rising moments from now. Every passing minute increased their risk of someone spotting them. And however many minutes since he and Alex had first left the camp in search of Lim's child companions had not been enough to find them. Ritzi hadn't even caught a single whiff of their scents.

They landed together outside one of the tents and went in. "Any luck?" Nat said from where he stood at the sink beside Annie, cleaning themselves up.

Ritzi sighed and shook his head.

"We can try again after we finish our shed," Alex replied in between heavy breaths. "You should still be able to scent them, Ritzi. Maybe Dory can arrange for a boat or something."

"You two have done a noble thing already, trying to save the girl," Annie said. "Her and her unborn child."

"What?" Ritzi and Alex said together.

"That girl you brought here. She was pregnant."

"I..." Ritzi shook his head back and forth. "I didn't know."

"She was *in your arms*, Ritzi. How could you not have?" Alex replied, her brow furrowed. "While I was carrying the twins and I visited you at Stanford, you scented me the moment I set foot on campus."

"The girl was bleeding out when you found her. That might've had something to do with it," Nat said. "Annie and I figure she tried to give herself an abortion with something made out of metal."

Annie shivered. "Jagged, rusty metal at that. Scraped around inside herself as if trying to scramble an egg, what appears to be two or three days ago."

"And her wounds must have reopened following her strenuous physical exertion," Nat went on for her after a long moment. "Couldn't have been long before you found her, near as we can figure. We decided to give her an emergency C-section."

Ritzi stared up at the ceiling of the tent. He didn't remember hearing a baby's cry as he and Alex approached. "Stillborn?"

Annie studied the grain of the plywood around her feet. "We patched the girl up as best we could with the tools we have here. And managed to get four units of blood back into her."

I...I tried to kill it...but...I failed. Now it's tried to kill the child ren...

Ritzi bowed his head and crossed himself, Lim's chilling words from earlier playing over and over in his mind. Eddies in the air currents from Alex's direction suggested she was doing likewise. When at length Ritzi looked up, he found Nat and Annie both standing with their hands folded and eyes closed. "When can we see Lim?"

Alex's face fell. "We...we have something to tell her."

"The girl will be unconscious for hours yet," Nat replied, shaking his head. "After the delivery, we asked her if she would like to see or touch or hold her baby. She...she went berserk. Screaming 'Kill it now! Kill it now!' while trying to shred the baby and both of us."

Annie pursed her lips. "And that was after we'd administered an epidural, even. One of Dory's agents tasered her, after which we administered a strong sedative. She's in the recovery room now. Might even be tomorrow sometime before she—"

"Halt! Identify yourselves!" The deep baritone of one of the guards drew everyone's attention toward the camp's perimeter. Followed by a mix of angry Mandarin and English which Ritzi couldn't quite make out.

"What the hell is the meaning of this?" came Dory's voice.

"Agent Katczynski. I am Captain Xing-hue Mein. With the Ministry of State Security," replied a man nearby in stilted English. "My agents and I are here to search your encampment."

"On what grounds? Our operational clearance comes straight from Beijing—"

"And was never intended for you to grant safe harbor to a child killer."

Dory said nothing.

Ritzi pictured his poker face, attempting to stare down the Chinese intelligence man. "You are mistaken," he said at length.

"I am not, Agent Katczynski. We have a credible report of a North Korean woman being treated here. One eyewitnesses report tied together a group of screaming children and tossed them into the raging floodwaters."

Slides worked back and forth on at least two dozen assault rifles, making it plain the man meant business. "You shall let us pass. And suspend your operation immediately. You and your personnel shall be afforded a twenty-four-hour grace period in which to leave our country. Remain longer and you will be placed under arrest."

Ritzi hadn't taken a step before Alex had her hands on his shoulders. "No, don't!" she hissed into his ear, her voice barely a whisper. "We'll figure out how to—"

Clutching her to his chest, Ritzi cut her off. She shuddered and returned his embrace until he took her by the shoulders an arm's length away. "This won't be forever, Alex." He looked over her shoulder toward Nat and Annie. "Look after Alex and the twins until I make it home."

With that, Ritzi dashed past Alex through the flap at the back of the tent, off to find Lim.

CHAPTER TWENTY-SEVEN

CHICAGO, ILLINOIS. THE NEXT DAY.

PAWLY PLACED THE LAST bug into the crook of the tree and poked the little button on its top. The button blinked red three times then green, indicating its boot sequence had completed and that it was working normally. It went dark a moment later so as not to give itself away once night fell. *Good, that's all of 'em.*

Tommy finished placing his own devices in the tree opposite the boatyard from her. He glanced toward the throngs queuing up at the portal in the chain link fence while Coast Guardsmen swept back and forth across the green behind them picking up trash. The Calumet Harbor station open house had been a success by many measures. Parents and caregivers led their respective broods out to the parking lot—older children huffing and puffing as they shuffled along behind and the younger ones asleep in the adults' arms. And the Coast Guard had succeeded in its mission to promote boating safety and community goodwill.

Tommy met her gaze and gestured toward the fencerow behind her. She spied the scrub surrounding the chain link's corner post and nodded. He leapt up and disappeared into the canopy an instant later.

Pawly took flight herself, landing atop the boat garage. After retracting her claws, she scrambled on all fours across the blind side of the roof, careful to keep out of sight of the installation's security cameras. She pushed off from the roof's edge toward the base of the massive silver maple beyond the fencerow and looked over her shoulder. The station's entire complement appeared to mill about below her as she flew, herding visitors toward the exit. In all likelihood there was no one staring at the security monitors anyway.

She touched down into a halting gait and stepped into the brush beneath the tree. Tommy joined her a moment later. "See?" Pawly said, beaming. "I told you today would be the best time to do this."

Tommy pursed his lips. "Only after I told you about that Elder Scrolls LARPer meetup happening in Calumet Park this weekend to celebrate the latest expansion pack's release. But yeah, we've been lucky. Except for this last bug of mine that got dinglefritzed somehow."

"I've got the programmer right here." Pawly reached into the hole in the maple tree's trunk and unzipped her backpack. "Hand it to me and I'll reflash it," she said, producing the programmer and setting it on the ground in front of her.

"Be careful with that thing," Tommy said, pulling the defective bug from the chest pocket of his sneak suit. "These things are delicate. And you have all the finesse of a friggin' hand grenade."

Pawly blew him a raspberry as she took the bug and wiggled its bottom into the socket atop the programmer. She poked a button on the unit and its tiny display flashed to life. "I have it under control," she said as she scrolled through the application menu.

"I doubt that. You have to turn the bug on, too. Remember?"

Pawly snarled and twisted the top of the bug. Its lights flashed and then went out, just as before.

"No, no, not like that. Didn't you pay attention earlier?" Tommy said as he knelt down across from her. "You have to turn it the *other* way to get it into programming mode. Do you want me to do it?"

"No, I don't want you to do it. I just forgot."

"Well, *remember* then, wouldya? And hurry so we can get out of here before someone sees us."

"Ah, you worry too much," Pawly said, twisting the bug until it flashed blue and entered its programming mode. "None of 'em will ever know we were even here. The Coasties have had their hands full all day and the LARPers are all busy—"

"I wuf yer coshtumes!"

A roar ripped from Pawly's throat. She whirled around to find a wide-eyed little girl dressed in faux fur pelts adorned with polished metal. "Oh, uhm, h-hi," she said, eyeing the girl's quivering lip. *All hell breaking loose in three...two...*

"Aiee! O fearsome one, tiniest *Dovahkiin* to ever seek the Dragonstone! Be not alarmed by my sister's outburst. Practicing we are, yes."

"Practithing? Practithing whut?" the girl murmured, her gaze never leaving Pawly's.

Tommy reached an arm around his sister's shoulder and drew her toward him. "Ridding foul rats from yon Coast Guard boats, of course. Any who dared sneak aboard today, she and I will surely scare ashore."

The corner of the girl's mouth turned up. She raised her hand and pointed at Pawly's waist. "She's ready. She's really scary!"

Tommy snorted and stuffed his fist into his mouth while Pawly gave him her best murder stare. "Why yes," he said, teeth clenched tight around one knuckle. "She is indeed!"

"Miranda! Where are you!"

Pawly and Tommy both turned toward where the woman's voice had come. "Really scary also when parents cannot find their child, yes," he said, giving the girl's shoulder a squeeze. Then he stood and nodded in the direction of a pair of approaching footsteps. "We have work to get now. Run along, fierce one. To the parents who made you so."

"Oh, okay. Buh-bye, nice Khajiit man," the girl peeped before toddling off through the brush. "And you too, scary Khajiit lady."

"Seen again, Miranda," Tommy replied, waving after her. Then he turned and narrowed his eyes at Pawly. "And since you brought it up, I don't think *you* worry nearly enough. Now grab your ruck and let's go. Before we're spotted by someone the police might actually take seriously." Before she could reply, he vaulted up into the canopy and disappeared.

With a growl, Pawly hefted her pack up onto her shoulders and bounded off after him. Her brother zigzagged from treetop to treetop. She trailed behind him following by scent, only able to catch a glimpse of his tail now and again. The two of them had sortied enough times by now that she could tell Tommy was trying to shake her. Like she had cooties or something.

Pawly caught up to him next to the railroad tracks. The tree lines here sat too far apart to attempt a leap from one to the other. Tommy stood out in the open beside a utility pole, waiting for a train to pass rather than try to vault over it. Pawly agreed—doing so over a double-stacker like the one now passing would be unwise. They stood shoulder-to-shoulder, watching the parade of brightly colored boxes whisk past in front of them.

"That was too close, you know. Though I'm beginning to think you like it that way," Tommy said over the din.

She blinked and turned his way. "Just what's that supposed to mean?"

"It means I think you're getting reckless. Whose idea was it to prance around like this in broad daylight, huh? We could've easily been up to our necks in shit back there."

Pawly huffed and crossed her arms. "I still think the crowds were a better cover than darkness, when sound travels farther. Besides, the bugs were *your* idea."

"Sis, think. We can't hardly stake the place out every day without the adults getting suspicious."

"Who said we had to?" Pawly nodded in the direction from which they had come. "J.J. overheard the Coasties at the Navy Exchange say the descrambler's field trials would only take a weekend."

"Yes, but it wasn't going to be *this* weekend. Try to keep up, would you?" Tommy groaned and rubbed at his forehead. "J.J. also said sea trials are scheduled for sometime within the next month or so. We can't possibly duck out every friggin' night without someone noticing, especially once Mom and everyone else are back from Korea." He flexed his fingers and studied his claws, watching them slide in and out of his fingertips. "If we ever have to tell Mom and Dad some morning we need to stay home from school because we haven't finished shedding yet, I want to only do it *once*."

Pawly's own claw tips dug deep into her paw pads as she clenched her fists. She exhaled slowly while pain radiated up her arm. Good, something to focus on other than the burning skin beneath the fur on her cheeks and neck. "You don't think I know that?"

"If you do, you don't act like it. This...this..." Tommy waved his hands in the air in front of him as his gaze met hers. "This is a risky enough game J.J. has asked us to play without your...grandstanding."

"I am *not* grandstanding!" Pawly growled and sank her claws into the utility pole between them. "We're helping J.J. help us so we can help Mom, that's all. We don't have to like it."

Tommy stared up at the sky but said nothing.

"Look, you're a goalie, I get it," Pawly went on. "I'm a forward. You're used to guarding the crease and I'm used to screaming up to the net to take a shot. This is a shot we need to take. For Mom's sake."

"Dad told us never to take foolish risks," he said with a scowl. "He never goes out to get shot at without knowing what he's up against."

She groaned and pulled at her muzzle. "We've been *through* this already! We know exactly what we're up against. Uncle Nat and Aunt Annie need money and lots of it if they're going to help Mom. And they need it *now*, so we need to score big. Would you rather we spend our summer filching wallets and cell phones at the Bumblefuck county fair?"

"Where Billy Joe, Jim Bob, and every other make we're trying to score from has a gun rack in his pickup? Hardly." Tommy stared at the ground and sighed. "I'll be sorely disappointed to discover we *don't* have nine lives after all. And I don't want to dispel that notion anytime soon."

Pawly scratched at the back of her neck. "Nor do I want us whisked off to some secret government lab to start new careers as fucking pincushions. We need to make money, dumbass, big money. And then drop off the grid."

Tommy looked at her as if she'd slapped him. "But Sally and I are..." He snarled and rubbed at his temples. "Look, you and I have been accepted into Northwestern's NROTC program for the fall, right? And I want to try out for their hockey team as a walk-on, too. I've been tutoring your stupid ass all this time just so we could—"

"Oh, for fuck's sake, Tommy! College, hockey, sea duty—that's all stuff *normal* people do," Pawly replied, waving her hands. "We're *freaks*, Tommy. Figure the sooner we both accept that, more the better for everyone."

The last car of the train passed. Tommy bounded off toward Mr. Ruiz's shop, whose back lot outbuilding the twins had been using as a rally point.

Pawly's shed was already underway by the time she dropped down from the outdoor storage racking behind their makeshift headquarters.

Tommy had propped himself up beside the door with one arm while he pulled off his spats. "You go first, since you seem to be going all to pieces," he said and wiggled his toe claws. "I'll shower after Sally and I debrief."

Pawly huffed and stomped past him without a word. For all she knew, Sally would use this opportunity to resume their make out session. This time featuring a live-action *Khajiit*. Tommy would certainly be an eager participant. She rather envied them, in fact, but better she didn't think about guys right now. Even though no girl at St. Connie's would deny that their classmate Allan Driscoll was *hawt*. Their mother had warned her and Tommy both their genetics might impact their sex drives, which could well have lasting effects on their partners. Being a Navy SEAL, their dad had the perfect cover to explain the scars on *his* back.

Sally's enthusiastic greeting trailed off into silence after Pawly pulled a clump of her cheek fur free and held it out to her. The other girl sat gawking at Pawly until she rounded the corner to the shower room. Only after she locked the door behind her did she allow herself to laugh. The sort of laugh one laughs to keep oneself from crying.

Pawly stripped off her clothes and shook them out before stepping into the shower. Warm water helped her slough off her shedding fur, which she flung handful by handful into a plastic colander placed in one corner. One of their dad's ideas, in fact, from back when he first came to know the truth about their mom. Helped keep anyone from having to fish gobs of wet fur back out of the drain later.

Time passed as Pawly dug at her skin square inch by square inch using a plastic pot scrubbie as a loofa. As much as she hated to agree with him, Pawly conceded Tommy had a point. They had to think about their futures. Whatever nerdy science stuff Nat and Annie got up to would at best earn their mother more of the same—a loose grasp on her fate, which would slip away forever if anyone ever found them out. And who knew whether the twins' bodies would turn on them like Grandpa N said their mother's had begun to.

Pawly emerged from the shower room with one towel wrapped around her head and another wrapped around her body. Tommy mumbled something about having enough hot water as he shoved his way past, almost making her drop her gear she'd wadded up into a ball under one arm. She stuck out her tongue at him before the shower room door slammed shut. Maybe running out of hot water would be a good thing. He needed to cool off anyway.

She came around the corner to find Sally leaning back in her chair, hands behind her head and feet crossed atop her console. "No, darlin', y'all don't need to worry your pretty head about that none. Not one little bit," Pawly's friend said in a bad Southern accent into her headset's boom mic. Sally was an avid gamer and did live action role-play whenever she could, even more now together with Tommy. She had an entire repertoire of tricks she used to camouflage her real voice and loved using them. Every bit as she had come to love the job J.J. had given her.

The girl stared toward the dingy window above the door, like she frequently did while on the phone with a "customer." "Wouldn't be no trouble 't'all," Sally went on, "for us'ns to send y'alls cell phone special delivery to the Attorney General's office in Springfield, even."

She swung her feet down from her console and threw Pawly a knowing wink. "But we'd be much obliged if'n y'all gave us a diff'rnt address to mail it to, darlin'. Right after we talk about just how much that pesky shippin' n' handlin' business is gonna run y'all."

Pawly sat down in the chair beside Sally as her friend wrapped up her call. She took her time toweling her hair while the other girl hustled two more poor slobs, one as an Indian named Matra and another as a Russian named Irina.

"Rough day, huh?" Sally said after she pulled off her headset and laid it atop her console beside her keyboard.

"Yeah. Suppose Tommy already told you we were really off our game, trying to work a crowd in broad daylight."

"I don't think J.J. will mind. After all, we took in a small fortune from that assistant DA! Twice as much as we did last week from the massage parlor owner in Chinatown."

Pawly fluffed her choppy bob with both hands and chuckled. It appeared their ruse had worked. Sally seemed to accept the twins hadn't scored on their last job without question. Good. For Sally's own protection, the twins and J.J. had gone to great lengths to ensure she would never know anything about the Coast Guard heist. Just about as far as the people from which she and Tommy filched wallets and cell phones—corrupt officials, leaders of rival gangs, a select group of lobbyists, and other assorted shady figures—might go to keep their cell phone address books and calling histories private.

"Though I'd've been grateful for a few more reasons to make phone calls tonight." Sally pushed herself away from her console and swung around to face Pawly. "Since I've got nothing *better* to do."

Pawly's brows knit. "I thought you and Tommy were going to catch that new *Harry Potter* movie tonight."

Sally crossed her arms over her chest and nodded toward the shower room. "We were until Frumpy McFartface over there cancelled on me!"

"I *said* I was sorry, okay?" came Tommy's voice from down the hall.

Pawly busied herself donning her hoodie and stuffing her wallet and cell phone into its pockets. "It's probably for the best, Sal. I have to finish cramming for finals and we all know I'll need his help."

Tommy emerged from the shower room and shuffled his way toward the building's entrance. "And don't you forget it, sis. Sally, I'll make it up to you, I promise. Call you tomorrow, okay?"

Pawly followed him, pulling the door shut behind her to drown out the deafening silence.

Chapter Twenty-Eight

SEA OF JAPAN. SAME DAY.

RITZI SHIVERED AFTER THE helicopter's side bay door slid open and locked into place. He pulled the hood of his jacket over his head as the chilly ocean air bit at his bare skin. The helicopter swooped around the bulk carrier's stern and came to a hover amidships. A zip line deployed from a rig outside the open side door and landed on the deck fifteen or so yards beneath them.

One by one troopers in combat fatigues and helmets fast-roped down until four of them stood in a rough semi-circle facing the forecastle, barely visible through the fog. The remaining trooper pointed to a spot beside the litter Lim lay strapped into. "Kneel here," he said while the flight nurse clipped his rigging to the litter opposite Ritzi. The trooper likewise secured Ritzi's gear to the litter before flashing a "thumbs up" to the flight nurse.

The nurse shuffled along on his knees toward the helicopter's open door. The trooper beside Ritzi shoved him in the same direction, making clear he needed to do likewise.

The four troopers on the boat deck had Ritzi and Lim free of the rope within seconds after touching down on the boat deck. After the final trooper executed his descent behind them, the helicopter turned and flew off out of sight to the ship's port side. The deck thrummed below Ritzi's feet as the thing roared past, making a beeline for the mainland before its fuel ran out.

Ritzi removed his helmet and looked out over the open ocean, tension draining from his shoulders at last. He hoped to find a berth soon. Exhaustion would surely claim him soon now that he and Lim were out of danger. Of capture by the Chinese, at least.

He recognized Blaznikov as he approached. Within a moment he was among them, hooting and back-slapping and carrying on with the troopers as they shucked their gear. Certainly, Blaznikov trusted these men. Certainly, Blaznikov had requested them personally escort Ritzi and Lim here following their escape from Hwanggumpyong Island.

The men hoisted Lim's litter onto their shoulders and made their way aft toward the superstructure. As he trailed along behind, Ritzi wondered whether any of these men—surely each a long-serving member of DPRK's Special Forces—*really* knew the sorts of things that went on aboard this ship. He had spotted sharks circling behind the ship upon their approach, far more than he would have expected to come chasing after mere galley scraps. About as many as a diesel-powered wood chipper might attract while "disposition-ing" one or more of DPRK's ailuranthropic research program test subjects, declared sub-optimal following their latest round of exper-iments. Just like Ritzi had seen on the video months before when he had first arrived.

Blaznikov drew up behind Ritzi and slapped him on the shoulder. "Welcome aboard. You will be on this ship for some while, yes. I hope you will find she suits you."

He nodded toward Lim. "A well-equipped sick bay would be a good start."

"There is one indeed," Blaznikov said as a pair of troopers ahead of them maneuvered the litter through a bulkhead door. "But we go to one of the staterooms now. You and her should be more comfortable there until you are both ready to work."

Ritzi cocked an eyebrow. "'Work?'"

"Why yes, *Panie Doktorze*, our new resident expert on *Amanita muscaria*," Blaznikov replied with a chuckle. "Who better to tend our pinning beds? So mushrooms produce the most potent shipment of Windfall ever delivered to the Americas, right aboard this ship. Buyers from Costa Rica and Colombia eagerly await our arrival in Panama City."

Ritzi wondered if Blaznikov's guests would be foolish enough to insist on trying some for themselves. "For you see, *Panie Doktorze*, one of the benefits of doing business aboard a mobile platform such as this," his host went on, "is we are free from scrutiny by the international community."

"Is that why you're doing those...those horrible things here now?" Ritzi replied, an edge in his voice.

"Party leaders keeping up appearances for their future 'clients', yes. We are on a world tour, showcasing ailuranthropic capabilities to Spetnaz, Islamic State, Aryan Nation. To kick off a new arms race, this one with parahuman soldiers. From which DPRK can profit."

"You're not even close to having anything to offer them," Ritzi said, waving his hands. "Sure, you could accentuate the ailuranthropes usefulness in psy-ops operations. But they're little more than berserkers right now, posing intrinsic risk to allies and enemies alike."

"That is how I believe young Lim here can be useful," Blaznikov replied with a twinkle in his eye. "You've already contemplated using her as a control to help you help your own family, yes?"

Ritzi gulped. "Well, I'd thought about it, sure, but I hadn't decided yet how to work it out with—"

"Lim's genetic stock ought to not go to waste. Nor should her fighting skills, which we plan to pattern our own ailuranthropes after."

Ritzi shot Blaznikov a sideways glance. "Even if those children she cares for weren't still missing, she will be laid up for weeks. And anyway, what makes you think she will want to?"

The elder man fixed Ritzi with a smarmy grin that would make the Cheshire Cat himself envious. "We have time, no? Plenty of time to get to know one another better. Yes."

RITZI SCRIBBLED ON THE yellow pad the steward had brought him, seeking to balance several pages' worth of chemical composition matrices. A single array made world-champion sudoku look like a child's word search by comparison. After months of calculations, he was closing in on answers, albeit theoretical, how best to maintain Alex's condition. And to ensure the twins would never suffer a similar fate. After weeks at sea, the ship would call at New York then make for Chicago. At least then he'd be able to deliver Nat and Annie the Cliff Notes version of his work to date.

Lim moaned and stirred.

He dropped his pencil and sprang to his feet, managing to slam the rickety table loudly against the cabin wall with his knee. Out of respect for the girl, he knew better than to cry out.

She sucked in her breath and clutched at her abdomen.

Though Ritzi had confidence in the quality of Nat and Annie's work, he knew she was still in pain and would be for some while. "Shush now, Young-Hee, lie still," he said and leaned over the nightstand beside her bunk. Atop it were several syringes filled with pain killers, laid out on a stainless-steel tray. He took one in hand while feeling around her arm for a suitable vein. Locating one, he injected her. Within seconds her fidgeting subsided. Orange and white fur from her shed clinging to his hand, Ritzi stroked the jet-black hair above her forehead. "You're safe here."

"Where is 'here'?" she asked, turning to face him.

"Aboard a merchant ship, about a half-day's sail out of Chŏngjin."

Lim's eyes went wide. "No!" She bolted upright and scooted on her butt toward the porthole window. "I have to find Soon-Bok and the others! They...they need me to..." Her eyes went blank.

Ritzi caught her after her chin slumped to her chest. He guided her down, nestling her head into the pillow before withdrawing his hand from the back of her neck.

A long, uneasy moment passed before she blinked and looked up at him. Lim's mouth opened and closed several times before she tried sitting up again. "Must find...must find the children."

"You're not going anywhere." Ritzi gently yet firmly pressed down on her forehead. "Not for a while, anyway."

"But you don't understand!" Lim cried out before she began to weep. Ritzi opened his mouth to say something, but remained silent. "The children and I were in Sinŭiju, delivering food to workmen rebuilding the railway bridge to Dandong," she managed between sobs. "We were trapped when the raging floodwaters washed out the section closest to shore. Then the one behind us."

He sat on the bed beside her and patted her shoulder. "Go on."

"We found a large rope. I asked the children to tie themselves together at the waist. Then I led them all to the edge of the bridge. And pushed them off."

Tears dripped from Lim's chin as she stared down at the cabin floor. "I changed into my tigrine form and jumped in after them. That's when...that's when I began to bleed."

Scraped around inside herself as if trying to scramble an egg, what appears to be two or three days ago...

Ritzi stuck his fist in his mouth, recalling Annie's words from the night before.

"I came to shortly before you found me. And blacked out again afterward. Now...here we are."

"You...you..." Ritzi swallowed and began again. "You don't remember anything else?"

Lim sighed and shook her head.

Ritzi leaned over and gave her shoulder a squeeze. For her sake he hoped she *wouldn't* remember, ever. Wouldn't remember Alex or Nat or Annie. Wouldn't remember the Chinese.

Wouldn't remember the baby.

"So glad to see this most important parcel you deliver me was not damaged in transit, *Panie Doktorze.*"

Ritzi turned toward the sound of Blaznikov's voice, booming from down the passageway outside the compartment. "She and I...we...well, we haven't talked about any sort of 'arrangement' yet, in case you're wondering," Ritzi replied, trying his best to keep an impassive face.

Blaznikov strode through the open hatch, hands to his hips. "And why not? Is she unsuitable?"

"Well, no," Ritzi replied before Blaznikov leaned up against the wall and lit a cigarette. "She's a different breed from you and me, after all."

The elder man took a long, slow drag and blew out the smoke. "You will work with us quite fine," he said, beaming at her. "We here are all Kindred, yes?"

"No! The children need me!"

"Those...*urchins?*"

"Yes, I need to—"

"No. No, you don't."

Blaznikov held his hands out in front of him and clapped them three times. A door opened across the passageway from their stateroom, followed by several pairs of footsteps.

Ritzi turned toward a loud gasp to find Soon-Bok standing in their cabin's doorway. In an instant the other boys and girls pushed their way past her, screaming and crying. Every bit as much as Lim.

Soon-Bok took charge, making sure the younger children didn't get too rough with Lim as they hugged and kissed and wept. Though Ritzi didn't know how or when Blaznikov had found the kids, he had no doubt the man had also alerted the Chinese to Lim's presence at the Red Cross compound in the first place. Oh must have told him, having spotted Ritzi fleeing their ruined lab site with Lim in his arms as Alex led him back to their camp.

Blaznikov flicked his ash into the half-full teacup Ritzi had left sitting atop the credenza. "A new home awaits all you children in New York City. And we would love to have you remain with us, Miss Lim. We will surely return to the Peninsula, seeking out your kind so I might offer to rehome them. Would that suit you?"

"Yes, it's what I've always wanted," she said in a hoarse voice after regaining her composure. She hugged the children close to her and murmured their names one by one. "For all of you, too."

"And we shall see to it you children are cared for between now and then. In fact, I think there might even be cake and ice cream and balloons in your futures, too."

He cast a glance Ritzi's way, eyes issuing both an acknowledgement and a challenge. His demeanor made clear he would not hesitate to remove any human "distractions" in the future if they ran counter to his aims, by whatever means necessary. No matter how close a relationship might be.

Ritzi crossed himself, resolving to accompany their captain to the bottom if this ship proved itself less than seaworthy. Because, at this point, his life was forfeit anyway.

Chapter Twenty-Nine

CHICAGO, ILLINOIS. TWO WEEKS LATER.

WHERE THE HELL IS he?

Pawly paced back and forth along the alley behind their building, waiting for Tommy. J.J. had called not an hour ago with news the Coast Guard's sea trials concluded a week early, thanks to a long stretch of fair weather. The boat crew had tied up for the evening and had tomorrow off, being it would be Sunday. And first thing Monday morning, the crew would pack up the descrambler and ship it out.

While she and Tommy might have wanted to do the heist tomorrow night, their mother and *Halmonim* had insisted they treat Mrs. Biggs to one final girls' night out tonight in lieu of a baby shower. She and Tommy would need to move and move *now* or their weeks' worth of planning—walking around on eggshells since their mother's unexpected early return from Korea—would have been for naught.

J.J. would be no help since he was on his way to the airport in San Francisco. The twins' window of opportunity to pull off the Coast Guard job was closing. Fast. And they needed to find a set of wheels they could borrow on short notice without arousing suspicion. All the computers and radios they had at their house were good for nothing if they couldn't transport them to the site.

She glanced down at her watch again. Tommy had left almost a half hour ago now, assuring her he'd be back soon with a vehicle. A low rumble drew Pawly's attention to where a white box van trundled up the alley toward her. An instant later Tommy smiled at her from the driver's seat of the St. Vincent de Paul Society delivery truck from St. Connie's. "Oh, you have *got* to be kidding me," she said, palm to her forehead.

Tommy narrowed his eyes. "My ego and I would appreciate your at least *pretending* to be grateful, sis."

"Does Sister Clarice even know you have this thing?"

"Of course, she does. I told her one of these weekends I'd run down and pick up those hand-me-down PC towers from St. Francis de Sales. Sister told me at school yesterday that Mr. Kitteridge would be there this afternoon getting ready for summer school. I called her after I left and told her I could use the truck now. And that you would be helping me."

"Oh, that's just great," she said. "Fabulous."

"C'mon, it's the perfect cover. Calumet Park Beach and the Coast Guard station are a mere half mile away."

Pawly made a face and rapped on the van's hood. "Let's just hope we won't need to make a quick getaway."

"Do *your* job and we won't need to," he said, crossing his arms. "Sister expects we'll load up the truck tonight and haul all the computers back to school tomorrow after noon Mass. So, we've got this ol' gal all night. With plenty of room in back we can set up shop."

"But even if we tell Mom we're taking our time and going for a pizza or something, she might think something's up if we don't check in right away."

Tommy shoved the gear selector into park and leaned out his window at her. "Which is why I also called to tell her we were going to go catch the movie at the Calumet Park Fieldhouse afterward. Went right to voicemail."

"Hey, *Halmonim* told us the cellular reception inside Horseshoe Casino was awful, right?" The sides of Pawly's mouth curled upward. "If she and Mom and Mrs. Biggs hit upon a lucky streak and stay for a few rounds at the buffet, we might have this thing wrapped up even before they leave Hammond. C'mon, let's go get our stuff," she said as she trotted around the front of the van to the passenger door. Before she buckled in, Tommy mashed the gas, causing the old truck to sputter and lumber forward.

Pawly pursed her lips. *Let's hope* our *luck holds, too.*

I AM FLYING.

Around me are only seagulls, their pudgy dark forms blotting out the city lights surrounding the harbor. It is a warm night and people are out.

But none of them see me. Because I am invisible.

Not really, but close enough. I am everywhere and nowhere, a focus without form. A whisper without weight. I land atop one of the lights beside the crowded walkway and push off, silent but strong.

Tommy's murring in my ears is the only sound I hear. His constant, calming reassurance tells me what part of me to move, when. My gait is as relaxed as if he and I were once again wandering through the woods on Pilot Island gathering raspberries. Every time the wind blows, regardless of the direction, it is at my back. Lifting me, supporting me, hurtling me forward toward my goal.

I overshoot the first time, but I don't mind. Tommy sees my moves even before I make them, six and seven and eight ahead. Even challenging a chess champion like Bobby Fisher would hardly be a fair game. I sail over top of the breakwall and push off against the harbor light. A moment later I tiptoe from one channel marker to the other, their bells chiming as I brush past, to which no one will give even a moment's notice.

Including the Coast Guardsmen aboard the cigarette boat ahead. They stand laughing and talking amongst themselves, ogling the ladies as they trot beneath the pier light behind with barely more than a candy bar wrapper's worth of fabric to cover them. I feel a twinge of jealousy—when will *I* command such attention from a troop of gorgeous, chiseled men?

Hey, hey! Eyes front. Pay attention.

I side eye to my left, toward where my boom mic sprouts forth from my earpiece. The red haze is there, skulking about just outside my peripheral vision. Like the wolves circling the campfire I'd read about in *White Fang*.

Tommy's right, though. I'll likely only get one shot at this, so I need to keep my focus. My heart leaps as he returns to his murmuring, making the red haze retreat. I float skyward once more.

When I touch down again, I'm aboard the Coast Guard's patrol craft moored behind the cigarette boat. I am still, then I move, then I am still, then I move again. If anyone could have seen me, I'd have looked like I was doing some kind of crazy robot dance. But I am about ten times faster than a normal human can move. No. Twenty times. So, none will see me, because I am invisible.

There's the descrambler, fastened to the console above the helm. Drug interdiction units developed it to seek out go-fast boats and semi-submersibles using active ECM and stealth technology to camouflage themselves during drug runs. Just like this cigarette boat here tried earlier today, proving the descrambler a resounding success. Apparently why J.J.'s client is determined to have it. Likely the Coast Guard keeping it would be bad for business.

I clench my thumb and index finger together over top of one of the hex-head bolts fastening the descrambler in place. After drawing my breath, I press and slide them away from each other as if snapping my fingers. The bolt whizzes around before launching itself into the air, landing in the water twenty yards astern with a *plip* only I can hear. Three more times, a gentle tug on the harness connector, and the thing is free.

Wicked. I didn't even need to break out my Leatherman tool from its pouch at my waist. Why the hell haven't we thought of this before? Waves of warm, delightful tingling wash up and down my lower abdomen and groin. I gasp and grip the descrambler, content to pause a moment until the sensations pass. Which they do, all too soon.

I peek over the console at the Coasties to find their eyes—minds, anatomy, whatever—focused elsewhere. Good. A moment of agonizing slowness allows me to stow the descrambler in my backpack with two seconds passing in normal time. Tommy's murring calls my cadence as I spring atop one of the lamp posts and flee inland. I am flying once more. And I am invisible. Still.

P AWLY'S EYES FLUTTERED OPEN, but she could see nothing except darkness. She fumbled about and felt cool metal at her side, a vinyl seat beneath her butt. The gray haze surrounding the street lamp at the mouth of the alleyway came into focus. Hundreds of bugs swarmed about in its light. She sighed and slouched back down in the seat.

We did *it. Holy shit.*

Pawly squinted at the van's dashboard, trying to make out the time on the radio's clock. Ten minutes past midnight. "Tommy!"

Her brother snorted and sat up in the driver's seat. "Huh, must've worn myself out, too...oh, shit, is *that* the time?" he said, jamming his hand into his pants pocket.

"Head down to 108th Street, I've got cash for the toll. We can hop on the Toll Road there and take it to the Skyway. Haul ass and we ought to make our curfew with time to spare."

The van's engine sputtered to life after Tommy keyed the ignition. "Good," he said and pointed down at the floor between them. "I spent the last of the cash I had on me on that pizza there."

Pawly blinked at him. "You *what*?" she said and tugged a tuft of fur free from her cheek. "No shed, no shoes, no service, you know!"

"I thought you'd be hungry when you woke up. So I called the pizza place and told them to look for the bills over there." Tommy pointed toward a dumpster near the mouth of the alley while Pawly leaned forward and picked up the box. "Then to leave the pizza and keep the change. I didn't get out of the truck until the guy's taillights disappeared around the corner."

"Well, I am friggin' *starving*." Pawly flipped open the box's lid and jammed nearly an entire slice into her mouth. "You drive now," she managed to mumble as she chewed. "I'll spot you after the Loop so you can have some too."

"All right then," Tommy said and put the truck in gear. "Besides, I think Aurelio's Pizza tastes better cold—*shit!*"

The van lurched to a halt, causing Pawly to drop her slice into her lap. "Hey! The hell're you doing?"

Tommy remained silent as he pointed out the windshield with one finger. The van's headlights silhouetted a lone fur-covered figure standing before them, palms flat against the edge of the hood.

"Now *I* will drive," came their mother's gravelly voice above the rumbling of the engine.

"Mom? But how did...where are...?"

The driver's door flew open. An instant later Tommy flew across the passenger compartment and slammed into Pawly, driving her head into the van's door pillar. She blinked away stars to find their mother seated behind the wheel.

After yanking the driver's door shut, Mom gunned the engine. "Whatever the hell *that* thing is," she said, stabbing one claw toward the backpack at Pawly's feet, "we're getting rid of it. Right now. Then I'm taking you both home and locking you in the basement until you're thirty."

Tommy sat up on the floor between the van's front seats and rubbed his head. "But Mom, J.J. said that if we—"

"J.J. is being played, Tommy! Along with you and Pawly, it would seem. Didn't you find it the least bit suspicious Blaznikov sabotaged our barge right after Myung-Duk last leaned on Sally?" She sighed and shook her head. "Here I thought your father and I had taught you how to *think*."

Their mother slowed as she took the corner. "I'm sure you haven't been, though, so let me break it down for you," she said as she got back on the gas and tore off down the empty street. "If you two were caught, our entire family would either be in jail or deported or both.

Because I know the Nohs would roll over on us all in a heartbeat. And deportation is to one's country of origin, not one's country of past residence. Do you know what that means? Well, do you? Answer me if you think you're that smart!"

"You...you'd go to Poland," Tommy said in a small voice.

"That's right," their mother replied, her whiskers twitching. "But *my* mother would go back to North Korea, a veritable death sentence! Bet you didn't think of that, did you?"

Pawly and Tommy looked at each other and hung their heads.

"Didn't think so. Besides, from what your Uncle Ritzi just told me this is just the sort of stunt Blaznikov would pull."

The twins both gasped. "Uncle Ritzi's *here*?"

"Yes, he is. Blaznikov has him on a tight leash or he'd've surely collared you himself. But he did confirm Blaznikov is in cahoots with the Noh family. He figures if our family were scattered, Blaznikov could round us all up one by one for whatever plans he...he..."

Their mother slumped over the steering wheel, her arms limp. "Mom, look out!" Pawly screamed before the van swerved and plowed into a utility pole, crumpling the bumper and spider-webbing the windshield. Steam shot out from the ruined radiator while she and Tommy picked themselves up off the floor.

"Mom! Are you okay?" Tommy said as he shook their mother's shoulder.

Pawly threw open the passenger door and sprinted over to the other side. "Tommy, the driver's door...it's stuck," she said as she tugged at the handle.

He sucked in his breath and growled. Fur sprouted across his forearm beneath the clumps left over from his previous shed. With an angry cry he slammed his hand into the door.

Pawly darted aside an instant before the door took flight. It slammed into the wall of a boarded-up tenement house across the street and clattered to the sidewalk. As her own fur returned, her stomach started doing cartwheels. Next thing she knew she knelt hunched over a sewer grate puking her guts out. Which, having nothing in her stomach once she'd given back the slice of cold pizza, hurt like hell.

"Can you stand?"

Pawly coughed and turned toward the voice to find a pair of furred feet. Her eyes darted to her Uncle Ritzi's face, glowering down at her.

"You two, dig deep and keep up," he said, gathering up their mother into his arms. "We've got to get you all back to my lab."

CHAPTER THIRTY

SOME WHILE LATER,

ALEX'S GROGGY MOANS FROM down the hall stirred the nagging doubts in Ritzi's mind. Just what the hell was he doing? Was he doing the right thing? And who ought to decide, anyway? These thoughts and their myriad brethren had been assailing him since the moment he had revealed himself to the twins.

"Excuse me." Sheila scooted her baby belly past Ritzi's chair on her way to their makeshift recovery room, fashioned from an old broom closet.

Ritzi paced the length of a postage stamp-sized remnant of open floor in his temporary lab space. It took up an entire wing of the building Blaznikov had purchased from Krzysztof Olszewski, the same place where Janie had first stowed Ritzi's equipment following his eviction from Loyola. He could do little else *but* pace, given Sheila's assurances that Alex was resting comfortably. And that all they could do now was wait.

A chime from his console told him his imaging application had completed its post-processing. He swooshed at the screen to the right side of his console and enlarged the image of the chromosome chain.

Ritzi squinted, noticing the base pair in Alex's genomes change shape slowly, subtly over the time-lapse images spread out across his screens surrounding them. Almost imperceivable, he noticed, easy for the untrained eye to miss. So much so that he too had missed it at first.

His fingers flew across his console's keyboard. The screens blanked out before the images of Pawly's DNA appeared piece by piece. Ritzi gasped before even the third screen had finished repainting. Because her chromosomes had morphed three times already.

"Did you ever find that box from your old place's kitchen?" called Sheila from the doorway. "You said there were some cookies and cocoa in it. Figured our girl here might perk up a bit with something in her stomach."

Ritzi turned to find Pawly shuffling along ahead of her. His niece flashed him a wan smile then laid her head aside Sheila's arm, looking as if she might nod off at any moment.

He stood and strode over to a countertop in the room opposite the hallway from him. "Oh, I saw those over..." Ritzi's voice trailed off while he rummaged around on a shelf. "...here." He pulled a tin of instant cocoa mix from the back of the shelf and popped the lid free. "But doubt you'll want any," he said, squinting inside while patting at the bottom of the tin with his open palm. Nothing came out.

"Not gonna try making no cocoa with a damn chisel," she said with a click of her tongue. "C'mon, baby girl, let's get you down the street to the 7-11."

"Watch her, okay?" Ritzi said to Sheila while Pawly stumbled down the hall ahead of her. "Multiple morphs inside of a day's time take a lot out of even me. By the way, is Tommy awake yet?"

"No, but his vitals were okay when I checked," she replied as she shuffled past. Despite being seven months pregnant, she was still a nurse, first and foremost. Ritzi was grateful for her dedication to his family, especially after his panicked call to Alex following his aborted hunt behind Calumet Park. Surely ruining their casino night, what with his report of Pawly skulking about near the park's neighboring Coast Guard station.

He went back to his console and copied his imagery over to a memory stick. When the twins were ready to go home, he'd make sure to send it along with them. Nat and Annie were still in China, Alex had told him, together with Dory on some sort of "need to know" endeavor. They would need this and more to continue the stabilization regimen he'd begun for Alex and the twins. But at least he seemed to be making headway, for the first time in more years than Ritzi could remember.

When the file transfer was complete, Ritzi stood up and ambled over to the window. On to the deserted street below, Sheila and Pawly emerged from his building's side entrance and set off down the sidewalk toward the 7-11. He stepped over beside the bed where Alex lay and brushed her blond bangs from her eyes with the back of his hand. "We'll get you home and comfortable as soon as we can, sister dear. Then come Monday morning we'll begin the next phase."

"Like hell you will."

Ritzi whirled around to where the voice had come from. A man dressed head to toe in black crouched before the door. "How...how did you get in here?"

The man drew back the balaclava covering his face to his throat. "That's for me to know. And for *you* not to."

Ritzi thought his heart might stop. "B-Barry? What are you...how did you—?"

"I blew off my post-mission debrief at Little Creek just to get back here from Korea all the sooner, you traitor. Vowing the whole way to break both of your arms if you had *dared* lay a finger on my kids. Or my wife."

Barry's smoldering right eye could have burned through Ritzi like a high-powered laser. "'Traitor?' I...I don't know what you're—"

"Save it. And just what would you call someone on Kim Jong Il's payroll, hm?" He gritted his teeth and grabbed Ritzi by his shoulders. "I told you what kind of douchebag Blaznikov is, didn't I? First narcotics and weapons trafficking. Now, as Dad's teams have confirmed, human experimentation. And you, Ritzi...you're fucking working for him? I...I don't even *know* you anymore."

Ritzi opened his mouth to say something when a moaning came from down the hall. In hardly more than a heartbeat's time, the two of them stood at Alex's bedside. "It's okay, babe," Barry said, reaching beneath his wife's neck as she lifted her head. "I'm here. We're gonna take you home now. It'll be all right."

Alex screwed her eyes shut. "No. Please Bear, no."

Ritzi placed his hand on Barry's shoulder. "I know that this is hard on you, but give me a moment to—"

"Touch me again and I'll rip off your arm." Barry gripped Ritzi's hand like a vise, squeezing with every other word for emphasis. "I don't care if she is your sister. She's my *wife*." He released Ritzi's hand and scooped up Alex into his arms. "I am taking her and our kids and going home. Right now."

A trace of movement out of the corner of Ritzi's eye drew his attention to the instrument tray beside Alex's bed. He glanced down in time to watch Alex's fingers clench tight around the syringe containing the morphogenetic serum he'd used to stabilize her. "No!" he cried before she lunged forward.

Straight toward Barry.

Ritzi's body moved before his brain could object. He drove his shoulder into Barry's and knocked him sideways. Alex's makeshift weapon penetrated Ritzi's face, immediately below his cheekbone. His gasp turned into a pained howl as the syringe emptied into his sinus cavity, flooding it with serum. His entire face felt like it was on fire.

Patting madly at his face, Ritzi screamed and fell to the floor. In his fleeting moments of lucidity, he grasped the syringe and withdrew the needle. Red fog swirled around the edges of his vision; a wave of terror washed over him. "Out! All of you, get—" was all he managed before the room disappeared.

Chapter Thirty-One

IN THROUGH YOUR NOSE, out through your mouth. Locate your center, no room for doubt.

Pawly sat with her hands folded on top of her lap, mouthing the mantra her mother and grandmother had taught her and her brother. The comforting coolness from the concrete bench through the seat of her jeans helped her focus on something other than the waves of nausea washing over her. Without thinking, Pawly rubbed her lips with her arm to try and wipe the sick taste from her mouth. She hesitated before realizing her shed would have sloughed off the makeup she'd put on the previous morning.

She laughed to spite herself. Worrying over such a trivial thing, not knowing whether anyone else had spotted her and Tommy fleeing the Coast Guard station earlier. Not knowing where her Uncle Ritzi had ditched her day pack with the descrambler in it. Not knowing what fate awaited J.J. if he didn't deliver the descrambler to his client on time. Not knowing what fate awaited any of them.

"Think you can keep this down?" Mrs. Biggs took a seat beside Pawly on the fountain dais. In her hands were a pair of Slurpees, one to a hand.

"Couldn't hurt to try, I guess," Pawly replied, taking the one offered to her. It was sure to taste better than the cold pizza had the second time around.

The elder woman chuckled as Pawly took a sip and gazed out over the streetside park. Aside from the occasional customer going in or out of the 7-11 across the square, they had the place to themselves. But by morning the place would be busy, screaming kids splashing away their Sunday beside the fountain while their older siblings hung out. Or, at least, so Sally had told her.

"Oh, and I got us a snack, too." The woman reached into the plastic bag around her wrist and pulled forth a package of cookies. After splitting open the cellophane, she plucked one out and handed it to Pawly. Oatmeal raisin wasn't Pawly's favorite, but it would be sweet and chewy and fill the space. "Two full morphs in less than twenty-four hours. Let your blood sugar get much lower, child, and you'll end up out cold like your brother. Now eat up. Doctor's orders."

"But you're not a doctor."

Mrs. Biggs shot her a look. "Nurse's orders then, Snarkerella. I dragged you out here to make sure you keep your keel in the water while your uncle tends your mom and brother. Eat, honey."

Pawly grimaced and took a bite. Coincidence couldn't account for her Uncle Ritzi's appearance right after her mother passed out behind the wheel of their van. It had been months since she had heard from him before tonight. And he had only encountered them now because he just happened to have been out hunting, taking a break from his hush-hush lab work in the old warehouse. Their uncle had explained earlier, on their way back to the lab, he had called their mother the previous afternoon to tip her off about the twins' heist. Pawly thought it strange then he would only show himself after their mother's collapse, though. What sway did Blaznikov hold over him, anyway? And what had driven Blaznikov to seek out her family in the first place?

"When you're done, you and I have to take a ride."

Pawly scrunched up her forehead. "'Take a ride?' A ride to where?"

"Your uncle said you all had ditched the descrambler in a dumpster somewhere near where 102nd St. turns into Avenue O," Mrs. Biggs said before biting into her cookie. "You need to show me so we can get the thing back to the Coast Guard before the cops come looking for it. It's still in your bright purple day pack, right?"

"No! Er, I mean...yes, but..." Pawly stammered as she sprang to her feet. "J.J. is counting on us!" *Counting on* me!

"Your uncle told me the Nohs are now and forever off limits to you and the rest of your family," the woman said with a wag of her finger. "Blaznikov has his hooks too deep into their organization to be able to trust any of—"

The sound of breaking glass from down the street cut Mrs. Biggs off. Pawly turned to find a lab bench hurtling through the air until it crashed into the roof of a parked car. With a gasp, she gazed up toward where the bench had come. Several large panes of broken glass dangled from the top of her uncle's floor-to-ceiling lab windows. One of the larger pieces let loose and tumbled to the deserted sidewalk, showering shards of broken glass in every direction as it landed.

"Mom! Tommy! Uncle Ritzi!" Pawly tossed her Slurpee aside and took off in a sprint down the street.

"No! Wait!" Mrs. Biggs called after her.

Half a block later Pawly felt something sticky and crumbly in her clenched fist. She shook it out and looked down, finding a few oat flakes and a raisin clinging to her open palm. Right beside a patch of gray fur.

Pawly looked back up to see the red haze oozing from her peripheral vision. Instantly she practiced her breathing exercises. The sting of a thousand needles consumed her head to toe as her pelt burst forth from every follicle in her skin. For the third time tonight.

She cursed and bit back another wave of nausea. Tommy was in no shape to help, and she didn't have time for this. She needed to focus, needed to maintain control over her transformation. Because right now, she had to fly. And, Pawly realized as pain washed over her face, she would need to do it fast. The alarm on the ruined car across the street from Uncle Ritzi's lab blared on; someone would soon notice.

Pawly grimaced as her tail sprouted forth from beneath her jeans, tugging her panties up around her bikini line. She breathed deep and drew in scents she couldn't recognize. But rather than allow them to disorient her, she willed them to help her keep focus. Help her keep the red fog from blinding her while she reached down and yanked her shoes and socks from her feet.

A familiar scent made her gasp. One that should have been in Virginia. One that should not have been anywhere near here. *Dad?*

She scanned the buildings around her, looking for window ledges, balconies, fire escapes. After glancing down to avoid tearing open her paw pads on shards of glass, Pawly leapt up to the awning above her and threw herself toward the building across the street. Back and forth she went, wall to wall once, twice, three times until she reached the balcony outside her uncle's office.

Her tugging at the door handle wiggled the remaining top half of the window pane free. By instinct, she drew her arms up over her face an instant before it shattered, pelting Pawly with little shards of glass. She shook like a dog out of water to keep the damn things from working their way into the skin beneath her fur. Then she yelled for her mom and dad.

Though Pawly was not yet an expert at scenting, she could tell her father's angry stink was fresh. He was surely here. Only now returning from Korea, no one expected him until after his scheduled debrief in Virginia concluded. Two *days* from now.

A pained moan from within the cloud of dust jarred Pawly back to the present moment. "Mom!" she screamed and reached around through the broken window to turn the knob inside. She bolted into the room and toward the direction she'd heard her mother's voice. On the other side of the room, beneath a file cabinet laying kittywampus atop an overturned desk, Pawly found her mother, her father kneeling alongside.

And a *yeti* standing between her and them.

Thick, shaggy, red-brown fur covered the thing from head to toe. The tufts atop its ears brushed the ceiling tile. Its legs and arms were as big around as tree trunks. Savage-looking canines jutted downward to well below its chin.

"Pawly! Stay back!"

The beast's ears drew up in alert at her father's warning. It turned and faced her, snarling and gnashing its teeth as it sized her up.

She did the same. Surely the thing's sheer mass would put it at a disadvantage, which was why Pawly almost wet herself when the thing closed the distance between them in one bound. Pawly jumped straight up and felt a handful of sharp claws whiz past the seat of her pants, each one as long as a mooring hook. She somersaulted in mid-air and pushed off the ceiling, then rolled through her sloppy landing to spring back up and face her opponent. The beast howled and whirled around, scanning the room with wild, angry eyes.

Behind them, her father hoisted her mother's unconscious form up onto his shoulders and wobbled to his feet.

Pawly locked eyes with the beast, desperate to keep the thing focused on her. She succeeded. Its feral gaze bored into her like an apex predator staring down its prey before delivering a killing strike.

The beast belted out a gurgling roar and charged, right before everything washed out red.

Chapter Thirty-Two

The first thing Ritzi remembered was the pain. It tore across his chest from right shoulder to left thigh. He roared in agony and slashed at the air around him, but his claws connected with nothing.

His surroundings emerged from the red void. Workbenches, gurneys, computer monitors. His nose twitched, the scents it perceived reminding him he was not alone. Slowly their forms took shape.

Alex, lying face down atop one of the gurneys with one arm slumped over the side.

Barry, standing beside her, waving some sort of edged instrument toward Ritzi.

And Pawly *was* here. His dim vision confirmed what his nose already knew. She was close. The sound of her panting resounded in his ears like the roar of a passing train. Hadn't she and Sheila gone to the corner store? Why were they back so soon?

THEM HURT. THEM DIE.

Wait. What?

THEM DIE! ALL THEM DIE!

Ritzi's body moved, though not of his own volition. He watched his arms and legs thrash about, trying to shred any and all nearby with his claws. Lines of fear and primal anger creased Pawly's face in response. Just like how his father had described Alex's the night their ship went down on the North Sea. Just the way Alex herself had described Pawly's face the first night the girl herself had raged.

Pawly flitted to and fro about the room, raking her claws across Ritzi's flesh with each pass. She was raging now indeed. And, Ritzi realized, so was he.

By sheer force of will he pushed aside his panic. Ritzi had never experienced the Rage firsthand. The Soviet sub commander had pistol-whipped him following Alex's first transformation, so he had missed seeing hers. But last fall he had witnessed Pawly raging with his own eyes. Alex had reported not long afterward that the heavy oaken door in their Virginia home's basement barely contained Tommy when his Rage debuted.

But Ritzi's Affliction had manifested in a different way. By the time his first transformation came around, Dory had brought him and his sister and his adoptive parents with him back to the States. Ritzi had come into his own late one night as he and his family sat around a campfire singing Polish children's songs together on Pilot Island, a plentiful supply of wild game all around with which to indulge his primal urges. Unlike Alex and Pawly, *his* transformation had not been the result of witnessing the assault of a loved one. So Ritzi had never raged before, had never felt like a hostage within his own body before. Though he certainly did now. And didn't much like it.

Ritzi grunted and embraced the pain. Pain was good. Pain was what he and his father had come to believe wrenched Alex and Pawly free from the bonds of their Rage following their first transformations. Soon he would follow suit and this nightmare would end.

Only it didn't.

Oh, hell.

Barry vaulted over Alex and lunged at Ritzi, landing a strike aside his head. He yowled and swatted at Barry with a massive paw. His brother-in-law ducked and came up at him again, connecting his fist with the bottom of Ritzi's jaw. He growled and jammed his claws between an overturned lab bench and the floor. With a grunt, he sent the bench careening toward his opponent.

Barry sidestepped the airborne bench, revealing Sheila Biggs as she shuffled to Alex's side.

Dear God, no! Sheila!

His heart shattered to pieces after the bench mowed her down. While Sheila lay screaming, clutching at her abdomen, Ritzi went on slashing and snarling at Pawly, powerless to stop his body from responding to its feral urges. Surely, he would kill them all. If they didn't somehow manage to kill him first.

Our Father, who art in Heaven, hallowed be thy name...

Barry yelled something to Pawly, though her narrowed eyes remained fixed on Ritzi. Her father tried again to get her attention—but for the twitching tufts atop her ears she appeared to ignore him.

She sidestepped back and forth in front of Ritzi in a semicircle, baring her fangs, as if sizing him up before launching a new offensive. One his body had no intention of permitting her to follow through on.

Claws out far enough to make his fingers hurt, Ritzi leapt across the room at Pawly with a two-handed slashing strike

She dodged aside.

He planted one heel and let his momentum carry him around into a roundhouse kick, impacting her side with full force.

Pawly screeched and flew across the room into the wall opposite them. Shaking her head, she reached up with both hands and hauled herself upright by the autoclave's gas line, snapping it in two. With a roar she lashed out at the loud hissing, shredding the autoclave's control panel. An arc ignited the escaping gas. The lab shook as though seized by an earthquake as a plume of flame erupted forth from the broken line.

FORGET THEM!

Ritzi growled and looked to his right and left. His body and mind coordinated efforts to seek out the source of the message, every bit as compelling as his rage but counter to it.

FLEE. FLEE NOW.

Goosebumps formed beneath his fur. Ignoring his mind once more, Ritzi's body turned toward the full-height windows forming the wall of his lab. Or, more correctly, where they used to be. The force of the explosion had left jagged shards sprouting up from the floor between him and the street four stories below.

FLEE! NOW!

"Yes, flee now," Ritzi tried to respond. It came out in a hoarse-sounding grumble that made his throat tingle.

Off to his left, Pawly snarled and leapt atop a workbench. She threw herself at him, razor-sharp talons sprouting from her fingers and toes slashing at the air madly.

Ritzi drew his hands to his chest and lunged at her, his own claws bursting forth from his fingertips.

Barry screamed and fell to the floor with both hands clutched around his middle.

Pawly barrel-rolled beneath his arms and launched herself head first into his rib cage.

Pain swept over Ritzi's chest and abdomen before he doubled over.

His niece sailed over top of one of the benches and disappeared while he stumbled through the glass shards at the window's edge.

Then came the sick feeling of weightlessness. The faces of Ritzi's loved ones flashed before his eyes before darkness consumed him.

Chapter Thirty-Three

Some while later.

Awareness' return found Pawly in a wooded glen, fangs deep into a dead rabbit's neck. After scarfing down enough feed to keep her rage at bay, she drew her sleeve across her mouth and took to the canopy. From treetop to treetop she bounded until she came to a street, following it until she recognized the intersection of 95th and Ewing, nearly a mile past the Skyway from where she needed to be.

She cursed and leapt toward a neighboring building. Galloping rooftop to rooftop, she made her way south toward 101st Street. There she'd swing west toward her uncle's lab, situated in an old warehouse past where the street dead-ended into the Calumet River.

Pawly focused on her route, knowing it would take her past where she and Tommy had ditched her backpack the night before. Uncle Ritzi's suggestion—a dumpster full of scrap plastic in a dimly lit alleyway behind a nearby polyforming plant. No one would likely toss in any new material on top of her pack until Monday morning at the earliest, and, being only half-full, no roll-off truck would be coming to cart it off any time soon. And any would-be dumpster divers looking for food or usable wood or scrap metal were sure to steer clear.

Or so Pawly kept telling herself over and over, desperate to keep the horrible images from the previous night from overwhelming her. Her father was most certainly dead, her uncle was missing, and she had last seen her mother unconscious. Pawly had no way of knowing what had happened since she'd fled the lab consumed by her rage.

Purple blended with pink in the eastern sky to her left. Dawn would soon break. She didn't want to take the chance of daylight making it easier for a passing police chopper to spot her bright purple day pack while passing overhead. Because they were all well and truly screwed as it was.

A strong and familiar scent broke her concentration minutes from her destination. She glanced up and gasped, seeing Tommy beside her, whiskers blown back alongside his muzzle, his pace matching hers perfectly.

"Over there!" he yelled, pointing to a van parked on the deserted street beneath them. Her grandfather's strong, peaty musk wafted up from below as the van's side door slid open. "Get in," he said as the two of them touched down.

"But, Grandpa D, I—"

"Zip it. Lie down on the floor beneath the seats, both of you. I'll drive."

Pawly gulped and did as she was told. Tommy slid in beside her as their grandfather slammed the sliding door shut.

A moment later Grandpa D sat down in the driver's seat and keyed the ignition. "We figured you'd come looking for your pack in due time," he said as he goosed the van's engine and sped away from the curb. "But your operation is already compromised. I rented this van from O'Hare after I touched down so I could scope out the area unnoticed before picking Tommy up." He scanned the road in front of them from side to side. "This place is crawling with undercover cops. I'm sure they're just waiting to pounce on whoever shows up at that dumpster."

Pawly gasped. "How...how would anyone have known about—"

"Oh, for fuck's sake, sis!" Tommy rolled on his side and poked her in the chest. "Clearly the Nohs betrayed us. *J.J.* betrayed us."

Pain stabbed at the pit of Pawly's stomach. She rolled onto her back and stared blankly at the bottom of the bench seat above her head. *No. No, he wouldn't have. He couldn't have. Could he? No, it must've been Myung-Duk. Maybe Blaznikov put him up to...*

The roaring of the van's engine dispelled her dark thoughts.

Tommy slid toward her as Grandpa D powered around a curve, pinning her up against the seat support.

Their grandfather swore loudly and slammed his cell phone down atop the van's center console. "Change in plan, kids. Stay down and hang on!"

THE VAN VEERED LEFT then right then left again several times with Pawly and Tommy flat on their bellies below the back seats. Both kids kept their arms outstretched to keep from bouncing around into one another. After too long a time, the van rolled to a stop.

Grandpa D poked the lock button and the passenger door opened. "Where's Alex?" he said as someone climbed in the passenger seat and pulled the door shut behind them.

"Fourth floor," *Halmonim* replied. "She was in an ambulance already when I arrived. Ducked out the back door while I was speaking to the paramedics. They were called away to help Sheila, so I went looking for Alex. Spotted her when she landed and dashed inside."

Grandpa D gunned the engine and sped around a corner. Pawly could tell from the echoes they were in some sort of alleyway. He stopped the van and poked a button above his head to open the sliding door. "Time to go to work, you two."

"Take this," *Halmonim* said after Pawly and Tommy scrambled out of the van. She held out what looked like an Epipen in front of her. "Carfentanyl will calm her down, but only if you get close enough to inject her."

"We don't have much time," Grandpa D added. "Sedate your mother and get her back down here. We can't risk any of you being seen. The fire department is clearing out now. After their final sweep they'll turn this whole place over to the police and none of us will be able to get near it."

Before anyone could say anything, Tommy plucked the Epipen from *Halmonim*'s hand and bounded off.

Pawly cursed him under her breath and followed. They bounded up the side of the building, landing on the fourth-floor ledge beside where ceiling-high windows had once stood. She hugged herself to ward off her sudden chill and stepped across the threshold. Shards of glass crunched beneath her feet, surely leftovers from last night's explosion. She dabbed at the corners of her eyes with her thumb then jabbed it in Tommy's direction.

Tommy replied with a wave of his hand to the left.

Pawly nodded her head to the right. In silence they worked their way around the perimeter, searching and sniffing.

"Anything?" Tommy whispered as they approached the back of the room.

"No," Pawly replied as she stepped over to a brass panel lying on the floor beside the elevator doors. Wires sprouted out of the thing in all directions. She stuck one of her toe claws under it and flipped it over, revealing the elevator call button.

"Hey, shouldn't there be an emergency door back here some-where?"

Pawly looked up to find Tommy standing in front of a side-by-side refrigerator. Marks on the floor suggested someone had slid it there from across the room. "Mom must've pushed that thing in front of it," she said, crossing her arms. "To keep everyone out. Or at least keep them from getting in here without announcing their arrival. But why would she—"

"Look out!" Tommy yelled before the laboratory door across from them flew open. He plowed into her, bowling them both over before a gray-and-blue streak flashed by. Pawly wrestled her-self free of Tommy's grasp to find her mother tossing rubble into the air all around where she crouched next to the wall. A lump formed in Pawly's throat.

"Get down!" Tommy grabbed Pawly's shoulder and yanked her to the floor right before a flask shattered against the wall where her face had been a moment before. Their mother's claws and enhanced strength sent things flying off in every direction. Sharp and pointy things, at that.

"Where? Where is it?"

Their mother rose to her full height and cast her wild gaze to and fro about the room, fingers pulling at the ruff of fur covering her neck. Her ear tufts twitched as she sniffed at the air. She focused on a particular pile of rubble across the lab from them and sprang, landing with a crash before she resumed her frantic digging. "It's gotta be here somewhere," she said, her voice nearly a growl. "It's gotta be!"

Pawly stood and approached from behind with slow and careful steps. "What, Mom? What are you looking for? If you're looking for the descrambler, it's not—"

She snarled and whirled around, claws on both hands at the ready. "Oh, it's you," she said, sheathing them. "I...I..." Before she finished, their mother bounded over in front of the twins and wrapped her arms around them. "I love you both very much," she said, rubbing her muzzle aside Pawly's and then Tommy's. "No matter what happens, don't ever forget that."

Pawly pushed herself away. "I love you too, Mom, but what is it? What are you looking for?"

"The video tape. From the security system. I can't...I can't let anyone else see..." Her mother's voice trailed off as she locked eyes with Pawly. The change in her scent was near instantaneous—from sweet and sickly fear to crisp anger to pungent rage. Feral rage, sharp enough to set Pawly's own nose to twitching.

The elder woman leapt with a roar and landed near the cubbyhole behind Pawly. The wall cabinets took the brunt of her fury, glass smashing and various colors of chemicals mixing together with a sinister hiss.

"Mom, stop!" Tommy cried before getting his growl on.

Following his guttural commands, Pawly leapt from wall to wall as if acting out a fight scene from *Crouching Tiger*. Within seconds, she was on the floor next to their mother. After getting right in her face, Pawly pumped her diaphragm to belt out the most menacing roar she could manage.

Her mother's feral animal instinct accepted Pawly's challenge. None too soon, she noted, as the toxic soup their mother had sloshed all over the shelves smoked and smoldered. Pawly bunny-hopped backward and waved her claws in front of her mother, who took the bait. She winced whenever their claws connected, wondering whether her mother was *trying* to declaw Pawly or something.

But then her mother let out a high-pitched squeal and stood up straight on her tiptoes. She roared as she swatted at her back, unable to crane her head far enough to see what had struck her. Pawly knew right away when Tommy leapt up to the ceiling and pushed off toward the nearest corner. Pawly's breath caught in her chest as he rolled his landing, coming to rest only inches from the broken windows. Beyond lay a forty-foot drop to the sidewalk below.

Their mother let out a yowl and a whimper before collapsing to the floor. The pen stuck out of her back like the tranquilizer darts Pawly had seen park rangers use on Animal Planet to take down big game for veterinary treatment. She shuddered. Was she glimpsing Tommy's future also? Her own?

Pawly trembled as she stepped over to her mother's prone form and knelt down beside her head. She wedged her index and middle finger in between her mother's jaw and neck and positioned her ear over her mother's mouth. Just like Mr. Drueker had shown her. "Pulse and breathing seem okay," she said as Tommy scrambled over opposite her and took a knee.

He grunted and slid one hand into the small of their mother's back and the other beneath her neck. "Good. Let's get her down to *Halmonim* so she can check her out and get her home." With a grunt he squatted low and lifted their mother up to his knees. He paused for a moment to take a breath, then grunted again while he got to his feet.

Pawly's gaze wandered over toward one of the few lab benches still intact, the rest having been smashed into kindling or charred beyond recognition.

"You coming?" Tommy said from where he stood beside the ledge.

"I will. In a moment. I want to try to see if I can find that tape thingy Mom was all frantic about."

"You'd better make it quick, sis." He nodded toward the blocked fire door beside the disabled elevator. "Those won't keep the police out for long."

Pawly met his gaze and nodded. "I will."

With their mother held tight in his arms, Tommy stepped off the ledge and disappeared.

Pawly sighed and retraced through the smoke-stained hallways the route she and Mrs. Biggs had taken hours before. After a moment she came to what she thought had been Uncle Ritzi's office, though found it hard to tell at first. Anything not reduced to charred rubble already had enough soot and dust covering it to be almost unrecognizable. But with some poking and prodding and coughing, she was able to make out the camera system's control panel and cassette deck. Or, at least, what was left of them. Whatever tape might have been inside was slag by now, too. Pawly stepped around the corner and toward the ledge. She jerked to a stop in front of a man-sized puddle of sticky black goo.

Her knees gave way and she crumpled to the floor. Tears blurred the world all around her. Every breath she drew in came out a scream, mourning as her life continued to come crashing down around her ears. One big, jagged piece at a time.

Oh, Daddy...

Her pain and anger spent, Pawly knelt there some while as tears streamed down the sides of her face. Murmured voices came from behind the fire door. Banging noises against the back of the refrigerator her mother had pushed up against it soon followed. Pawly stood and sniffed, wiping her eyes with the back of her hand. She stepped over to where the ceiling-high windows had been and turned her face toward the stiff Lake Michigan breeze.

Then she jumped.

PAWLY STEPPED OUT OF the bathroom, the draft around the motel room door setting the bare skin on her legs and arms to tingling. *Halmonim* leaned over to where Pawly's mother lay atop the bed's stained comforter and kissed her forehead. "Any change?"

Halmonim shook her head. "No. None."

Pawly shuffled over to the other bed. She pulled back the covers and grimaced at the grimy sheets, unsure whether sitting on them or the comforter would be less gross. Settling on the chair beside the room's dirt-streaked window, Pawly looked down at her mother and bit her lip.

Mom's eyes had fluttered open on the way across town to this dump of a place, which Grandpa D had chosen because he knew the front desk took cash and asked no questions. How he knew that was a question for another time.

She leaned her head up against the wall. Hopefully they'd be gone by the time the place's usual pay-by-the-hour clientele began trickling in. Surely the walls between rooms here were thin enough to leave little to the imagination as to what was happening on the other side.

From the time her mother had come to, she had been unresponsive. She lay staring straight ahead, her body limp, having had to be carried in by her Grandpa D while *Halmonim* stood watch.

After waiting on some passers-by, Pawly had joined them in the room. Tommy had done likewise, ducking into the room across the hall he would share with Grandpa D.

Three knocks came at the door, followed by two more. Halmonim stepped over to the door and peered through the peephole before opening it.

Grandpa D stepped through with a pair of McDonald's bags in each hand. Tommy followed right behind, in human form once again following his own shed. Her brother's new clothes, straight off the racks from Walmart, were a travesty, ill-fitting and laughably mismatched. Any other time she would have given him shit for it. But not now. Not today.

Tommy set a drink carrier filled with cups down on the small table in the corner. With his other hand, he tossed Pawly a gray plastic bag from Walmart.

She caught it and dumped it out on the bed, wincing at the pair of blue jeans with floral-patterned embroidery all over their back pockets and the tee shirt printed with Taylor Swift's latest album jacket. At least her new bra and panties were the right size. Though she always found new clothing uncomfortably itchy if she wore it before its first trip through the washing machine.

"Couple of sausage biscuits in here if you want them," Grandpa D said as he handed Pawly one of the bags. "Tommy's got a couple coffees and a couple cups of hot chocolate. Everyone, take what you want. I drank mine already."

Halmonim pulled a hash brown from one of the bags and took a bite. "Did you try Top? Any word about Sheila? About her baby?" she asked as she chewed.

"No," Grandpa D replied after a long pause. "She is conscious, but refuses all visitors. Even...even her husband. Doctors will not even tell *him* anything."

Aside from *Halmonim* sharing with Grandpa D and Tommy that she had no further news about her mom's condition, no one said much for the remainder of their meal. Pawly finished her greaseball sandwiches and turned toward the window, sipping at her hot chocolate while the few people who had slept through the night wandered toward the office to check out. The sun crested the roof of the hotel, a long, horrible *now* stretching forward despite just another day beginning for the world around them. As if mocking her refusal to think of anything but the moment when her father had...when he...

"What...what's going to happen to us now?"

Grandpa D sighed and leaned the back of his rickety chair against the wall. "Life on the run is no life at all, *Tomasz*. Keeping you from hunting during any length of incarceration might have well been a death sentence for the pair of you. But your Uncle Ritzi saw to it your systems should be stable for the immediate future at least."

Pawly swallowed her lips and stared down at the floor, tears blurring her view of the threadbare carpet around her feet.

"Better for you two to turn yourselves in to the police. Then we can deal with whatever comes of this fool's errand you were on together. So that we can all..." Grandpa D's voice trailed off. He stood there for a long moment, his lower lip quivering.

Pawly had just lost her father. Grandpa D had just lost his son.

He cleared his throat and opened the motel room door. "So...so we can all get on with our lives. Barry...he would want that."

Tommy nodded and stepped past him without a word.

"Try to get some rest now, everyone, while I make some phone calls. This evening will be tough for all of us," Grandpa D said, closing the door behind him.

CHAPTER THIRTY-FOUR

DAYS LATER.

R ITZI BLINKED HIS EYES, then threw an arm over his face to ward off the stinging sunlight. He groaned as his muscles burned, fatigued even by that minimal effort. Good thing he was already lying down. On what felt like some sort of bed, no less.

For several minutes he lay there and focused on his breathing. Twinges of mental anguish assaulted his mind as he tried to piece together what had happened before he blacked out. He and Sheila Biggs had been caring for Tommy and Alex before Barry showed up. They had argued, Barry branding him a traitor for consorting with Blaznikov and the North Koreans. Ritzi remembered a sharp pain beside his nose before he blacked out, but couldn't remember anything after that. Had someone punched him? *Stabbed* him?

Using the pillow's texture against the bare skin on his cheek and neck, Ritzi confirmed what the muted scents he perceived had led him to believe. He was back in human form.

After a moment, Ritzi chanced a peek beneath his arm at the rest of his body. Though naked and uncovered, he didn't notice any uncomfortable hot-and-cold sensations like he often did right after a shed.

His body lodged a dozen simultaneous complaints as he rolled onto his side to take in his surroundings. Ritzi lay on a thin mattress set on top of a steel frame, just like the one he glimpsed above his head. An easy chair upholstered in shabby brown vinyl sat next to an end table with a lamp across the room. On the wall beside him sat a small wooden desk with a straight-backed chair pushed in underneath.

A low thrumming registered while he squinted up at the small porthole windows, one each above the desk and easy chair. With a grunt, Ritzi heaved his legs off his bunk and planted his soles on the floor. It was cool, as though made of metal.

He wobbled over to the porthole window and beheld the massive steel uprights of a railroad lift bridge straddling a canal lock. Arresting booms, bascule spans and radio towers stuck up on either side like a ridge of quills along an angry porcupine's back. Canadian maple leaf flags flew smartly from every pole in sight.

A pounding on the wall drew Ritzi's attention to a bulkhead door. "The clothes on the top bunk should fit you, *Panie Doktorze*," came a man's voice in Polish from the other side, one Ritzi did not recognize. "Help yourself to a bottle of water from the lower right desk drawer. I will go tell Blaznikov that you have woken."

"Where in the world are...?"

The man scurried off down the passageway without saying any more. Afterward, the low thrumming returned, to which Ritzi attributed the ship's engines churning away several decks below his feet. He stood on his tiptoes to look down as far as he could toward the ship's stern. A white and red flag flapped in the wind bearing the Polish crowned eagle emblem. His tongue examined his parched lips while he stepped over to the drawer and took out a water bottle. After twisting the top off, Ritzi guzzled down its contents all in one go. He smacked his parched lips together as he stepped over to the top bunk and examined the clothes set out for him. After trying three times to pull up a pair of overly long briefs with gaping holes in all the wrong places, he realized they had given him an A-shirt. Ritzi cursed and yanked the thing over his head. At least he hadn't started with the boxers.

Another knock at the door came as he finished tucking the baby blue button-up shirt down the waist of his navy-colored trousers. "You are decent, yes?" came Blaznikov's booming voice.

Ritzi bit his lip and zipped his fly. "I am now."

Blaznikov entered the compartment with no further invitation. He pushed the door closed with the bottle of *starka* in his hand—Polmos Szczecin 30 Year, specifically.

"With our captain's compliments." He sat the bottle beside the table lamp and produced a pair of shot glasses from the pocket of his suit jacket. "Please, join me," he said with a wave toward the easy chair.

"Where are you taking—?"

"We have much time, *Panie Doktorze*. I will explain many things if you are amenable," he said as he pulled out the desk chair and dragged it across the floor to the end table. "And we ought not deny the captain his courtesy. Would be rude, no?"

Ritzi snorted. Apparently shanghaiing him was *within* the bounds of proper etiquette.

"Our new clients are quite taken with young Lim, yes. It is good. But as for you, well..." Blaznikov plunked down on the wooden chair and picked up the bottle. With an audible pop, he pulled off the glass-topped cork and poured a generous shot for each of them. "Under circumstances I expected family resistance. But not...quite like *that*. Nor such a strong reaction from you." He pushed a glass across the table toward Ritzi as he raised his to his mouth.

"Wh-what happened?" Ritzi said, eyes wide. "Is my family okay? Oh, dear God, if I hurt them, I don't know if I could ever—"

Blaznikov shushed him by tapping at Ritzi's lips with his index finger. "Hear me out, I ask you. But we visit ill upon us if we speak of such things before we drink. *Budzma!*" he said before tilting his head back and downing the glass' contents in one gulp.

Ritzi sighed and did likewise, thankful the earlier water had helped rehydrate his parched lips. It did little to keep the high proof stuff from burning his throat all the way to his stomach, though he found the tingly warmth a comfort and a torment both at the same time. A reminder of the family this boat carried him further from with each passing minute.

"Among my clan, we take first one quick," Blaznikov said as he refilled their glasses. "Savor next one while we talk."

With a nod, Ritzi took a sip while Blaznikov set down his glass and stood. He stepped over to the porthole window and crossed his arms. "You have looked outside?"

"Yes, though I don't know where we are." Ritzi had been through the Soo Locks several times before as a deckhand aboard Bobby Katczynski's *Pride of Polonia* during summer breaks in his undergrad years. But none of these locations looked familiar.

Blaznikov nodded toward the bulkhead. "Montreal is just ahead. We passed through St. Lambert's lock minutes ago."

His eyes went wide. "You mean like the St. Lawrence Seaway? Where the hell are you taking me?" Ritzi held up his hands and shook them. "No, wait, never mind. It's not important. Just put me off at Montreal or Quebec City and I'll find my way back to Chicago. Somehow." Though Ritzi had neither his driver's license nor passport on him, at that moment he didn't much care. His family *needed* him. He would swim the channel in the dark and swipe the cell phone from the first person he encountered, if it came to that. *Where there's a will...*

The elder man shook his head. "Among our kind we have an ancient saying: 'harm not the Children of Affliction.' You are a risk to yourself and others if I permit you to—"

"Risk? What risk?" Ritzi hopped to his feet and dashed across the compartment toward Blaznikov. "Has anything happened to my family? I have to know!"

The man wrapped his arm around Ritzi's shoulder and led him back to the chair. "No one gets on or off this ship until we arrive in Rotterdam. By then we have an agreement how to help your family further. And the rest of our kind as well."

"Fuck you," Ritzi said and batted Blaznikov's arm away. He stomped past the easy chair and thrust open the bulkhead door. It slammed hard up against the wall, making his ears ring as the sound of the impact reverberated back and forth along the passageway.

"Very well, then," Blaznikov said in a loud voice from behind.

Ritzi's pace quickened as he strode off toward the ladderway. He chanced a glance back over his shoulder to find Blaznikov poking at something mounted on the wall beyond the compartment door. When he brought the mouthpiece of a handset to his face, Ritzi broke into a run.

"Now," Blaznikov's voice boomed across the ship through speakers embedded into the overhead.

The response was instantaneous. A compartment door ahead of Ritzi flew open. Men dressed in black combat fatigues rushed into the passageway, cutting off his route topside. Ritzi drew to a halt and turned to find the same scene playing out behind him. One by one they each drew a black metal tube from a loop on their belts which looked like some sort of skinny flashlight. One by one they flicked their wrists and the tube telescoped out ahead of them. One by one the tubes crackled to life, a blue arc dancing about each tip.

"Go!" one of the men signaled before the rest rushed forward.

"No, don't! Please!" Ritzi cried as their repeated electric strikes set his nervous system ablaze.

A FOUL SMELL ROUSED him, though it was some time before Ritzi realized his eyes were open. He lifted his head from the floor and rubbed at his temples to ease their throbbing. The thrumming noise he had heard before was louder now. He must be in the belly of the ship. Below deck, someplace.

Panic flooded his mind. He had served his time, pulled his hitch. Had given Blaznikov all that he had asked for and more, allowing him to figure out how best to stave off the self-destructive effects of his family's Affliction. He had started a course of treatment for Alex and Pawly and Tommy, but each would need follow-up and a lot of it. Ritzi despaired of being able to treat them further, being able to see them ever again. For all he knew, he was halfway across the Atlantic by now.

Something fluffy and stringy covered the floor all around, though Ritzi couldn't make out what it was. He flailed around in it to try to get his bearings, allowing him to get a good whiff of the stuff. He recognized his own scent and another—something else he couldn't quite place.

A screeching sound from behind revealed a small hole a few feet above Ritzi's head. The dim light coming in allowed him to recognize the fur littering the floor all around him. The same color as his pelt but much longer. And a whole lot more of it than he had ever dropped during a normal shed. But his nose told him the fur was his. All of it.

"My apologies, *Panie Doktorze*," Blaznikov's voice echoed throughout Ritzi's confines. "We felt circumstances required us...r eaccommodate you."

Ritzi got to his feet and stumbled over to the wall. Light peeked through a trio of seams which appeared to border a door. With his face pressed up against the door's peep window, Ritzi could see Blaznikov rolling what appeared to be a video monitor on a cart toward him. "I never like to watch the movie alone. We watch together, yes? Sorry, no popcorn."

A wave of anger washed over Ritzi. He pounded on the door and gnashed his teeth. Blaznikov ignored him and went about fiddling with the channel dials on an ancient television set connected to a bulky VCR decorated with fake wood grain. His anger spent, Ritzi slumped to the floor and hugged his knees.

"Is playing now. You ought to come see."

Ritzi huffed and laid his cheek atop his forearms.

"Your sister, that is. Along with your niece and—"

Ritzi's thrashing drowned out the elder man's voice. Once on his feet, he pressed his face against the peep window. There on the monitor he recognized the security camera footage from his laboratory. Pawly leapt to and fro across the screen while Barry tried to hold Alex back from her. The girl slashed at some rusty-furred monstrosity stooped over with its head nearly to the floor. But when it looked up toward the camera, Ritzi saw his own eyes staring back at him.

"What...what the hell is—?"

Blaznikov flashed Ritzi a smarmy smile. "*You*, of course." He waved his hand toward the television to underscore to Ritzi what he did not want to believe. "Watch what happens next."

Ritzi couldn't not. In fact, he didn't even so much as blink the entire time Pawly fought the...*thing* that he had ostensibly become. He watched, mouth agape, as his doppelganger punched through walls and flipped over oaken workbenches like they were scraps of paper. Including one that slammed into Sheila Biggs as she shuffled toward Alex's unmoving form.

He remembered none of it.

Pawly had managed to stay one step ahead of his attacks until the moment she tore open the gas line. But then Alex, somehow, summoned the strength to rush Ritzi despite Barry's attempt to restrain her. She was in human form, though from the lines on her face she appeared consumed by her Rage nonetheless. He side-stepped her to the right outside of the camera's field of view behind a cabinet used for reagent storage.

Pawly followed, Barry and Alex right behind.

A moment later Ritzi reappeared in the frame, stepping away from the camera toward what remained of the shattered glass wall.

Pawly emerged from behind the cabinet, back to the camera, and leapt at him with claws fully deployed.

Hazy memories from the fight came into crystal-clear focus as he watched.

Barry stepped between them as Pawly charged.

Ritzi swatted Barry aside with one massive paw just as Pawly delivered a vicious two-handed slash. He bunny-hopped backward an instant before she landed her strike. Her momentum carried her arms around in a circle, her claws raking across Barry's middle before driving her head into Ritzi's solar plexus. The force of her charge must have knocked him off balance; a moment later he tumbled out the broken window and disappeared.

Barry's eyes went wide as his hands grasped at his abdomen. Blood oozed from between his fingers as he shouted to Pawly and dropped to one knee. He attempted to stand but fell forward instead, arms flailing. His entrails reached the floor before him, covered by Barry's own body after he landed atop them an instant later.

Ritzi blew out his breath with a squeaky cry, having held it while the entire horrific scene had played out before his eyes. "Barry, no!" he managed to choke out before collapsing to his knees. The metal floor reverberated beneath him as he vented his fury with his fists. He screamed, he snarled, he spat, he swore. Cursing himself for allowing Blaznikov to lead him and his whole family down this deadly path. "Barry! Oh, no, Barry…"

Anger spent, Ritzi hugged his knees to his chest and wept.

"'Harm not the Children of Affliction,'" came Blaznikov's voice from the peep window above Ritzi's head. "As before I told you."

Ritzi looked up and wiped away the snot and saliva dribbling from his chin with the back of his wrist.

"This is *our* law, *Panie Doktorze*," the elder man went on. "Which too many of us have violated throughout history. I shall not. So I could not leave you there."

Ritzi rolled over onto his bum and leaned his head against the wall of his cell. Blaznikov gazed down at him through the peep window with neither scorn nor contempt in his eyes. Strangely, Ritzi found in them…empathy.

"I meant what I said. I need your help. All our kind needs your help. You would be no use to anyone shot. Or in prison. Or someone's laboratory animal. So, I had Noh's people track you down. And bring you here."

He glanced around at the walls of the cargo hold. "Where is 'here', exactly?"

"Lim and I finished New York business. Sent her ahead aboard another of Chong Pol's boats to Rotterdam." Blaznikov waved his arm around their cabin. "I had just arrived in town, afternoon before the explosion at your lab—"

Ritzi gasped. "Explosion?"

"You saw your niece on the video tear open the gas line, no?" he replied matter-of-factly. "I was calling on the Nohs when it happened. Together we sought you out afterward and secured you aboard this ship. When the Nohs left, I ordered us to sea."

Ritzi flinched and grabbed his side, a ghost reflex to the taser batons Blaznikov's men had used on him in the passageway. A flood of memories came back; Noh's men had used similar instruments to subdue him in the park near his laboratory. Made sense that he would have fled there to lick his wounds after falling to the street.

"I also cannot permit what happened to dull your brilliant mind with self-loathing. Or allow you to remain in the public view, forever under suspicion. Research shall resume after we meet Lim in Rotterdam. The other ship will return for your remaining equipment. Then its crew will burn what remains of that warehouse to the ground. Yes."

Darkness enveloped Ritzi once more after the peep window clanked shut. "But I cannot risk you returning to your family. Grieve, you must, for your sister's husband. Your nephew and niece's father. Start by indulging your Rage. With fresh kill."

Another metallic screech came from the other side of his cell, near to the floor. He blinked and rubbed at his eyes, trying to will them to adjust to the low light. But he didn't need any to see the red haze creeping into the edges of his vision. Right after he got a snootful of the delicious scent of a pair of rabbits. Their fear was palpable. Delectable.

They hadn't even taken two hops beyond their confines before Ritzi's canine teeth morphed into fangs once more. He pounced and sank them into the neck of one rabbit, its melodious screams overwhelming his ravaged soul with feral joy.

Chapter Thirty-Five

Chicago, Illinois. Later that summer.

"I said. Who. Is. Hungry?"

Pawly sighed and tugged her earbuds out one at a time. Out of the corner of her eye, she could see Tommy doing the same as their mother sat down a tray on the table between them. She peered past her across the atrium toward the courthouse's tiny cafeteria. A small smile crept across Pawly's face. Whatever she'd brought them would surely be better than juvee food.

Mom set a plastic cup filled with what looked like fresh-squeezed lemonade down in front of Pawly and fumbled at a sandwich wrapper. "This is the beach club," she announced after locating turkey and sprouts hiding between two halves of an oversized croissant. "The other one's a ham sammy."

Tommy reached across the table and pulled the ham sandwich toward him. He took a sip from the other lemonade Mom had brought and dug in.

Pawly poked at the shriveled-up sprouts and set the sandwich back down. Maybe *not* better than juvee food, after all.

Their mother drew her palm to her forehead. "Yes, dear, you're quite right. How could I forget the mayo? I'll be right back."

Pawly sighed and watched their mother go. Her fussing was every bit as much a coping mechanism as the sullen resignation she and Tommy employed. Because everyone knew the twins' lives would be forever different once Mr. Biggs emerged from the judge's chambers.

But no one knew for certain just *how* their lives would change. After Mom returned, Pawly globbed mayonnaise atop the dried-out turkey slice and took a bite. She glanced over to see Tommy staring off into space, mechanically chewing a mouthful of his sandwich.

Though Pawly found the courthouse's cafeteria food underwhelming, being here was a far better thing than being at the detention center. Over the past six weeks, each had completed their summer school classes and high school graduation requirements; cut off from family and friends, they had had little else to do. The ankle bracelets they wore now still precluded them from taking any trips to Pilot Island to hunt as they had longed to do. For now, they would have to make do chasing rabbits from their hutch around the backyard at home as quietly as they could manage.

Her stomach churned even now, thinking about the horrible choices facing them if the judge handed down either her or Tommy a prison sentence. Becoming fugitives or CIA lab rats—Pawly wasn't sure which alternative was more heinous. Because rather than permit anyone to lock away her fellow Kindred, or to experiment on them, their mother had said she would as soon kill them both.

Kill her own *children*.

And the worst was J.J. had managed to weasel out of any responsibility. Investigators found his car two days after the explosion, abandoned on a Des Plaines side street not half a mile from O'Hare, so he had likely fled. The gorgeous conniving bastard had played her like a harp. And here she had believed he understood. Believed he cared. Believed he...

No, stupid! Not now, not ever. Bad idea to begin with.

J.J. had used the twins' abilities to try and raise his standing in his family's organization. Clearly, he had bet on their *not* going to prison, being they were both minors. One of the few things Pawly supposed she and Tommy were grateful for, and for good reason. The police had found them out, so J.J. must have rolled over on them. Playing them all, as he'd been played. Just as the twins' mother had predicted.

But jail or no, the Navy had rescinded their full-ride NROTC scholarships to Northwestern as soon as they got word of their arrest. "Conduct unbecoming" and all that. Neither she nor Tommy had any idea of what they were going to do with their lives now, though Pawly was open to whatever outcomes kept them on *this* side of the bars.

Then there was the thing with Mrs. Biggs. Right after she'd woken up in the hospital, the woman had filed a restraining order against Pawly and her entire family. Her own husband, too. Word was Mrs. Biggs had had her baby, injured *in utero* somehow. Whether she'd had a boy or a girl, neither Pawly nor anyone else in her family knew.

Pawly wiped her mouth with the back of her hand, not noticing the dollop of mayo stuck to her lip. It dropped into her lap with a *plud*. In the summertime, she liked wearing skirts from time to time, but never seemed able to keep them neat and tidy. She had enough odds stacked against her. She didn't want to appear before the court looking like a slob on top of everything else. *Exhibit A, your honor.*

She reached across the table for the napkin dispenser then carefully dabbed at the offending glob in her lap so as to not work it in between her skirt pleats. When Pawly looked up to find a trash can for the slimed napkins, she noticed Tommy staring across the atrium behind her. She turned in time to see their mother throwing her arms around a man coming up the steps.

"Grandpa D!"

Tommy was already on his feet by the time Pawly slid out of her chair. She snatched her clutch from the table top and followed. Their mother had just let their grandfather breathe again when she and Tommy approached.

"I'm sorry I'm late," he said as he drew the twins together into a hug. "I'd have taken a taxi if I'd known the CTA was single tracking on the Blue Line. Something about a signal problem, or so I heard."

"That's okay, Dad. Are you hungry?" their mother asked their grandfather as she led him toward their table. "We're eating already but can get you a sandwich or something before court reconvenes."

"No, thanks. I hoofed it over here from Franklin and scarfed down a red hot from a cart along Wacker Boulevard."

"Oh. Well, let me at least get you a coffee then."

"Mom," Pawly said, waving one hand between her mother and grandfather. "Look." She nodded toward Mr. Biggs approaching, his uniform cover cradled in the crook of one arm.

The gray-haired man accompanying Mr. Biggs stretched out one hand toward her grandfather. "I wish we could have renewed our acquaintance under better circumstances, Kat."

"Thanks, Moe. I appreciate your help all the same." Grandpa D shook the man's hand before doing likewise with Mr. Biggs. Or, more correctly for the moment, *Lieutenant* Biggs. "So, Topper, how did it go?"

"Frankly, sir, I'm at a loss to explain why Noh Sung Jin agreed to give a deposition on the twins' behalf," he replied, tugging at the hem of his white uniform dress coat. "But I think Mr. Mochowicz here knows more than he's telling."

"Like any attorney worth his salt ought to. And why the Noh family pays me so well," the other man said with a shrug. "Though, I assure you, Sung Jin is incensed and embarrassed at both of his sons' cowardly and dishonorable behavior."

Her grandfather snorted. "No further questions, you old coot. Just make sure the Coasties don't ask any more either."

"Then we're agreed," the man said and plopped his fedora onto his head. "I'll leave your man Biggs here to brief you on the details. I have a pressing engagement at City Hall." He gave them all a nonchalant wave and set off across the atrium toward the foyer steps. Her grandfather watched him go, the look on his face suggesting Mr. Mochowicz's "pressing engagement" would involve putting the squeeze on *somebody*.

Mr. Biggs glanced up at the clock fixed to the atrium wall above their table. "Your hearing will resume at the top of the hour. The DA concedes he's got a weak case and has agreed to drop the charges. Though the descrambler was found in Pawly's backpack, no one *saw* either of you actually take the thing." The corners of his mouth turned up and he winked at them both. "Nor can anyone offer any plausible explanation how you could have in the first place. Agree to the DA's terms and the judge will likely order your ankle bracelets removed today before you leave."

Cheers and whoops rose up from all around Pawly. Tension drained from her so fast she thought her knees might buckle. "Pilot Island, here we come!" their grandfather said with a twinkle in his eye.

"Enjoy it," Mr. Biggs said with a small smile. "Because you'll need to be back here come the end of the month."

Pawly's eyebrows shot up. "Back here for what?"

"Do we have community service or something?" Tommy added.

Mr. Biggs shook his head. "If you define 'community' as 'country,' then yes. You're scheduled for the next class of recruits starting basic training at Great Lakes."

The twins turned and stared at each other, their jaws hanging open.

"We're...we're going in the Navy? Like, active duty?" Pawly asked at length.

Mr. Biggs nodded. "Take it from me. You didn't want to be a butter bar ensign anyway. I think you'll both be a better use to the Fleet as enlisted."

Pawly's head swam. She and Tommy had wanted to follow in their father's footsteps into the Navy full-time, but Mom had wanted them both to go to college. They had compromised on NROTC, though Pawly realized while sitting in the klink she and Tommy had blown that bridge all to hell.

"I still have my reservations," Mom said and dabbed at her eye with her thumb and forefinger. "But once you're in, that bastard Blaznikov won't dare come near either of you."

Mr. Biggs clasped Mom's shoulders. "We've been through this already, Alex. It was either that or lock them up until they turn eighteen come September. The alphabet agencies don't have the budget to spend on surveillance. Because as far as DHS is concerned, these two are both still a threat to national security."

"And I think all of you are," came a woman's familiar voice from behind him.

Mr. Biggs gasped. "Sheila?"

"I won't be long; I have a train to catch. My parents are watching my daughter."

His lips drew to a thin line. "*Our* daughter."

"You might be her father, but I can assure you she'll *never* call you 'Daddy.'"

Their mother stepped toward Mrs. Biggs. "Sheila, Top didn't mean to—"

"Stay where you are, Alex. My attorney is on the balcony watching us. Any of you so much as come near me and he'll bring the cops running." Mrs. Biggs nodded toward Pawly and Tommy. "Wouldn't want a fuss over a restraining order with those two around, now, would you?"

"Why are you here, then?"

Mrs. Biggs thrust her arm into her husband's chest. "To give you these, *dear*. My attorney was in court today and called me when he saw you. He offered to serve them for me. But I told him that since I was downtown already, I'd much rather do it myself."

He slid open the envelope flap and peered inside. "This...this is a divorce filing. I...I would have thought we could, you know, talk first—"

"There's nothing *to* talk about," Mrs. Biggs said, fixing Pawly and Tommy with a searing glare. "Despite their having tried to kill me and our daughter both, you help them, even now. You've made it clear these...*things* are more important to you than us."

"Sheila, please," Pawly's mother said, holding out both hands. "Come to our house and we can all talk about this. Call your folks and I'll be glad to give them directions. We'd all love to meet your baby girl."

One corner of Mrs. Biggs mouth turned up. "Not a chance. Because *all* of you should be behind bars. Whether in jail or in a zoo makes no difference to me. Which is why *I* made the anonymous call tipping off Chicago PD just where they could find the Coast Guard's missing device."

Pawly bit back the urge to puke.

"Tell me, Alex, do your kids know? That you used to rip the faces off of shop owners behind on their 'insurance' payments while their families watched in horror? Pimped out to the Noh family's patriarch as a stone-cold killer by your own mother?"

Mom drew back, as if Mrs. Biggs had slapped her.

"Yeah, that's right. Maybe your kids ought to call you 'Alley Oop' or 'Alley Kat' or whatever the hell you used to go by. Oh, I know, take on 'Raven' and 'Beast Boy' here and you can make it a family affair! Suppose your brother rat-fucked their DNA as much as your father rat-fucked yours, hm? Maybe they're as predisposed to killing as you are."

Their mother took Pawly and Tommy by the wrist and led them away toward the courtroom. "You will come with me now. Both of you," she said in broken Korean. Pawly only ever recalled her mother speaking in *Halmonim*'s native language during training. And whenever she was *really* pissed. "Let us go. So Top and Sheila may have privacy."

Grandpa D patted Mr. Biggs on the shoulder and followed.

When they reached the courthouse doors, Mom wrapped an arm around the twins' shoulders and drew them close. "Our people...our allies have made tough choices to ensure our survival. Now you two ...you two must learn to do likewise."

Chapter Thirty-Six

Szczecin, Poland. The following Autumn.

THE DEER'S HEART QUIVERED in Ritzi's hand as he raised it to his mouth and took a bite. He chewed and swallowed, the familiar, comforting, loathsome sensation of sated bloodlust radiating from his mouth through his whole body.

"Here," Ritzi said, handing the bulk of the organ to Lim. "This should help."

She clenched her teeth and drew her claws down the length of the tree beside him. Curls of bark fluttered to the ground while she pressed her forehead up against its trunk. "No...I cannot. The urge is...I...."

"Sate it," Ritzi said and held up the heart beside her cheek. "Eat."

Her eyes flashed with feral desire an instant before she lunged.

Ritzi pulled his hand away and she caught the heart in mid-air between her teeth. Two snaps of her jaw and it was gone.

Lim leaned her head back against the tree and blew out her breath. A cloud billowed forth into the night air from her mouth, resembling the steam rising from the deer's fresh carcass beside them. She drew in more air and exhaled again, less forceful and quieter this time. After a moment, her breathing had nearly returned to normal.

Ritzi draped his arm around her shoulders. "See? Isn't that a much easier way to stem your rage?"

She looked up at him and smiled. "Yes. It is. I feel so much...calmer now. Contented."

"And that's not all." He cupped his ear and turned his head in the direction of a chiming bell. "Hear that? Bet that's the first time tonight you've heard it."

"Why...why, yes."

"That's because that church is two miles away from here. It has tolled at the top of the hour every hour since we disembarked, but your human ears had yet to discern it."

For the first time since they had met, Lim's dark eyes shone with wonder and anticipation like the child which, in many ways, Ritzi believed she still was. Her tongue flapped back and forth out of her mouth, as if only now realizing her other senses were similarly heightened as well.

He poked the side of his nose with one finger. "My sense of smell doesn't work as well as it once did. Breathe deep in through your nose and tell me what scents you can register."

Lim hugged herself and did as asked. Her eyes flew open and she gasped before stumbling forward into Ritzi. "They're...they're here."

He grabbed her by the shoulders and held her out at arm's length. The scents of other passers-by on the walking path across the forest preserve from them had been wafting through the trees all evening. "Who? Who is here?"

She looked at the ground and drew her hands to her abdomen. "The man and woman you said did surgery on me. On...on that night. And..." She wrinkled her nose and looked back at Ritzi. "More of our kind, too."

He set his jaw. It was time. "Are you sure?"

Lim nodded and shivered.

"From where? Which way?" Ritzi asked and darted his eyes to and fro about the forest surrounding them. She said nothing and pointed to her left. He cocked his head that way to listen.

"The twins and I will approach Papa's house on foot so you guys can drive around the block," came the voice of Ritzi's brother. "We'll keep watch behind that big tree in the neighbor's yard and wave you in if we see he's at home."

A woman groaned in reply. "None of us met the neighbors our last time here, Nat. What if they spot you all skulking about in their yard and call the police?"

Alex!

"Don't worry, Mom. I contacted them all via email last week, so they're in on the surprise. And they're sure to recognize our uniforms. Grandpa N had to have told them well before now that Sis and I are both in the Navy."

Good thinking, Tommy. I'm sure he's just as proud of you both as your own father would have been.

"I just hope I don't have to wait long so I can change out of my uniform. My legs have been freezing since I stepped off the train wearing this stupid skirt!"

Pawly hadn't changed a bit. Ritzi couldn't help but chuckle. With one hand, he drew Lim's chin up until their eyes met. "Will you be...okay here, for a little while?"

She bit her lip. "Yes."

"Good. I won't be long." Mostly because he didn't dare. The church bell had chimed seven o' clock a moment ago; Blaznikov wasn't due to be back at the ship for hours yet. However, he didn't want to risk the older man discovering he and Lim were both missing. The crew would be doing changeover with the bus full of DPRK operatives posing as welders and riveters from the shipyards. Ritzi hoped the bustle would provide adequate cover for them both.

Lim's reaction suggested she had already figured out he had cooked up this whole "training session" ruse to put him in proximity to his father's house. His bribing one of Blaznikov's computer techs into quietly helping him had yielded his family's travel plans weeks ago, which Ritzi had elected not to share with anyone once he found out his ship would call at Szczecin just ahead of their visit.

"Eat while I'm gone," Ritzi said, waving toward the deer's carcass. "I recommend the rib meat, especially."

Lim nodded.

With a pat to her cheek, Ritzi sprang atop the tree limb above his head and dashed off toward the house. Four bounds later, he made it to the old gnarly oak opposite the chain link fence from his father's garden. He knelt down to get a better look at the furrows dug where black radishes would surely have been mere days ago. Brought in already to make them all *kanapki*.

Ritzi reached around behind into the pouch fixed to his web belt. His fingers clenched around the satellite phone he'd been hiding, having reported it missing weeks before. He wasn't sure if Blaznikov had believed his story about it slipping out of his hands and falling overboard while the ship was underway, but the elder man hadn't pressed the issue since. He popped open the back of the unit and rummaged about in his pouch until he located the battery. With his thumb, Ritzi pressed the piece of tape back down over top of its terminals. Then he popped it back into the phone and waited—though, by a stroke of good luck, not for long.

He drew his hand up to shield his eyes from the glare of a car's headlights as it turned up the driveway. It stopped beside the patio door and killed its lights an instant before Ritzi glimpsed his father's surprised face through the kitchen window. He came out of the house screaming with delight, and crushed Pawly and Tommy in a bear hug. They wrapped their arms around his neck and waist until Alex pried them off.

Eomeonim stepped out of the car to await her turn while Tommy straightened his neckerchief and Pawly leaned forward to tug at the hem of her uniform skirt. Papa and *Eomeonim* managed to share a passionate kiss as Nat hustled over to the other side of the car and opened the door for his wife.

Annie emerged from the car with a serene smile, clutching a bundle of white cloth to her breast. Everyone grew quiet when she pulled back the blanket to reveal a beautiful baby with a full head of black hair. A baby, which Nat had confided to Ritzi even before his wedding, would be impossible for Annie to ever bear. "She came home with us from Korea," Annie said in a soft, reverent voice. "Everyone, meet Nastusia."

"Which means 'stronger than death,'" Nat said as he gathered up everyone's coats from the car's back seat. "'Stuie' for short."

Annie managed to hand the baby off to Ritzi's father before the gathering devolved into happy chaos. They all rejoiced for Nat and Annie and their baby, but also for Pawly and Tommy's first sea duty. The twins were, in fact, on their way to Redzikowo for the stand-up of a new land-based Aegis missile installation. They lumped everyone's luggage inside while Alex stacked four Styrofoam containers from the sedan's passenger compartment atop its roof.

Eomeonim held the door open as Ritzi's nephew and niece carried their family member's bags inside. Papa gave Annie's baby back to her as Ritzi sprang across the yard and landed atop the tiny coach house at the end of the driveway. On his belly he shimmied up to the edge and peered over to find Alex cradling the foam containers to her chest.

Despite less-than-ideal olfactories, Ritzi made out the wonderful scent of venison stew. His stomach gurgled from equal parts hunger and homesickness.

But Ritzi recognized another scent, too. A Kindred scent. Though he recognized those of Alex and Pawly and Tommy, there was a fourth one. A new one.

He shook his head to clear it. This was the moment Ritzi had been waiting months for. No foreign scent was going to spook him into missing this opportunity. Ritzi reached into his pouch and drew out the satellite phone. He would need mere seconds to hand the phone to Alex, implore her to turn it on upon her return to the States, and bound off into the night.

A guttural snarl came from the tree line behind him. Ritzi whirled around to glimpse Lim burst forth and push off against a gnarly oak with both feet.

She flew toward Nat and Annie, both standing with their backs to them, both oblivious to the danger which Lim embodied. Fangs bared. Claws out. A murderous stare fixed to her orange-and-white striped visage.

Ritzi dug in his toe claws and launched himself from his perch. His foreclaws extended without his even thinking, causing him to drop the cellular phone somewhere over the backyard. He screwed his eyes shut as his stomach folded over on itself, knowing he would be too late to stop Lim.

Blaznikov's angry pheromones wafted over Ritzi before the elder man bumped past him at speed. He face-planted into the dirt, looking up in time to glimpse Blaznikov body checking Lim into the backyard fence. Their combined momentum carried them both over the top of the fence and out of sight. Loud rustling came from the other side as they shredded away at the backyard hedge that had broken their fall, each trying to get free before the other.

A door's slamming drew Ritzi's attention back toward the house. He looked up to find the patio deserted. Instead, he found Alex's face pressed to the window, scanning back and forth across the backyard looking for whatever had prompted her to herd her family inside. She met his gaze. Her eyes went wide. She mouthed his name.

"Forgive me, Alex," he whispered in reply before springing off toward the tree line.

Two hours later.

RITZI SAW STARS AFTER his head slammed up against the bulkhead. His legs went limp, but he didn't fall. Because he couldn't. Blaznikov held his neck firmly in his grasp.

"Do I even *want* to know what that was all about? Hm?"

The elder man tossed Ritzi aside like a rag doll. He flew across the compartment and plowed into the footboard of Lim's metal bunk frame.

She snarled and gnashed her teeth, muttering anew like she had as he and Blaznikov had wrestled her into her restraints. "*Jingeum jug, jingeum jug!*"

Kill it now, kill it now.

"Not only did you risk exposing us, you could have gotten *more* of your family members killed. Should have ordered you sedated as soon as we sighted Świnoujście. Your short-sightedness astounds, *Panie Doktorze*."

Ritzi picked himself up from the floor and cradled his throbbing face. His right eye was already swelling shut, turning his view of Blaznikov's face into a gray blur. Footsteps approached in the passageway outside the open cabin door.

"Is everything all right in here?" came the captain's voice in Korean.

"Yes. Everything is. Is the crew renewal and resupply complete?"

"Indeed. We wrapped just before you arrived, in fact."

"Good, Commander Suk, very good. Take us to sea at once. Tell our pilot we'll drop him at Świnoujście, then set course for New York. We won't be returning."

Blaznikov crossed his arms across his chest and fixed Ritzi with a piercing stare. "Not like Commander Mawro here has any such family to come back to." He stepped over beside Lim's bed side and knelt down. "Isn't that right, Hana, my dear?" he said, smoothing her hair away from her face with one claw.

She cast a vacant look up at him, her mind still consumed by feral rage.

"Aye, Captain," Suk replied before he saluted and left.

After silence returned to the passageway outside their cabin door, Blaznikov drew himself up to his full height and sauntered across the cabin toward Ritzi. "Because you see, *Panie Doktorze*," he said and clasped both of Ritzi's shoulders with an iron grip, "Hana and I *are* your family now."

AFTERWORD

This book and the rest of the FOREST EXILES SAGA, each featuring the modern-day remnant of an ancient clan of werecats, are the books I wanted to read but couldn't *find*. The paranormal sci-fi thrillers which I had in my heart to write. Thank you, dear reader, for letting this one into yours.

Share your thoughts, please—and help others who might enjoy the book to discover it—with a review on Amazon.

Link:

http://www.amazon.com/review/create-review?&asin=B0C51XDK9R

QR code:

Or please post one at the site of whichever vendor you purchased this book from. Reviews on Goodreads also are both greatly helpful and greatly appreciated. Thank you.

ACKNOWLEDGEMENTS

This novel was over twenty years in the making. Neither it nor my other books would have been possible but for my previously having written fanfiction for anime, manga and anthro fandoms. Several of the friends I made along the way number among my longest and staunchest supporters. Thank you to Ken Wolfe, Mike Morrey, Daniel Snyder, and Laura Lee for their providing a sounding board as I detailed my series outline. They also, along with Angela Carina Spears and Deanna Vaughn, encouraged me throughout the drafting process. Thank you all.

A number of people also helped during the book's editing phase. Deserving special mention are the members of Allied Authors of Wisconsin, most notably David Michael Williams and Christopher Whitmore. Thank you. Others I'm grateful to include beta readers Jodi Herlick, Frances Pauli, Elizabeth Roderick, and "Filigree". Thank you, and again to Ken, Mike, and Dan for their help here, too. Special thanks to Kereah Keller of Kereah Keller Editorial for her copyediting work.

I also want to recognize those who have helped me develop and execute plans to get this book and the others in the FOREST EX-ILES SAGA series in front of the very people most likely to enjoy them. People like *you*, dear reader. Jess Owen, R. A. Meenan, Matt Doyle, Chris Brucker, Stephen "Scuba" Coghlan, "Wolfie," and

"APC" along with Ken, David, Christopher, Carina, and Filigree once again—thank you, one and all, for helping me see my vision through.

Lastly, and most importantly, I want to thank the One who makes all things possible:

> *For God so loved the world,*
> *that he gave his only Son,*
> *that whoever believes in*
> *him should not perish but*
> *have eternal life.*

(John 3:16 ESV)

About the Author

Boyhood interests in trains and electronics fostered Mark's career as an electrical engineer, designing and commissioning signal and communications systems for railroads and rail transit agencies across the United States. Authoring industry trade magazine articles, coupled with long-time participation in anime, manga and anthropomorphic fandoms, led him to write paranormal sci-fi thrillers featuring the modern-day remnant of an ancient clan of werecats. Growing up in Michigan, never far from one of the Great Lakes, Mark and his wife today make their home in Wisconsin with their son and a dog who naps beside him as he writes.

Mark is a member of Allied Authors of Wisconsin, one of the state's oldest writing collectives, and the Furry Writers' Guild, dedicated to promoting quality anthropomorphic fiction and its creators.

Visit Mark's web site...

Author Mark J. Engels (mark-engels.com)

...and subscribe to his mailing list to receive details on release dates, special promotions, and in-person appearances.

You may also connect with him via these platforms:

amazon.com/stores/Mark-J.-Engels/author/B074Q51T9R

https://twitter.com/mj_engels

facebook.com/mark.engels.39

linkedin.com/in/mjengels/

goodreads.com/author/show/17095069.Mark_J_Engels